Dharma

Dharma

A Rekha Rao Mystery

Vee Kumari

Great Life Press

2020

Print ISBN: 978-1-938394-42-3
Ebook ISBN: 978-1-938394-43-0
Library of Congress Control Number: 2020904890

published by
Great Life Press
Rye, New Hampshire 03870
www.greatlifepress.com

Please visit the author's website at:
veekumari.com

This book is a work of fiction except for the minimal information given on the discovery of microliths in India. The author has attempted to do justice to its setting in southern CA, Pasadena and Eagle Rock in particular. Any references to events and people are fictitious and products of the author's imagination, and any resemblance to actual events, places or people, living or dead, is coincidental.

To my extraordinary mother who stood taller than her generation and instilled in me a love for words.

To my father who defied traditions and taught my sister and I to set the bar higher and higher.

"The Sanskrit word *Dharma* has no direct translation into English. Among other things, it can be thought of as righteousness in thought, word, and action. It comes from the root *Dhr*, which means to uphold, sustain, or uplift."

—Shankara Bharadwaj Khandavalli and Krishna Maheshwari, http://www.hindupedia.com/en/Dharma

~ Chapter 1 ~

Saturday, March 25, 2017

It was a lazy Saturday morning in March that I'd earmarked for indulgences. Like sleeping in, enjoying a book or daydreaming over sips of warm chai. The choice was out of my hands, with one phone call.

The caller was Peter Striker, co-director of the J.P. Mallory Institute of Archaeology, fondly referred to as JPM. He conveyed to me that the Pasadena Police Department needed my help to identify a statue found on the body of a murder victim. The victim was Joseph Faust, Professor of Archaeology, my mentor, and father figure.

Later that morning I was directed to a cramped evidence room at the Pasadena Police Department, where a heavy statue decorated with droplets and irregular patches of blood lay on a metal table on top of a plastic sheet. The sight and smell of it made my stomach churn as I worked hard to contain my grief.

A tall, attractive man walked in and closed the door, shutting out loud whistles and howls from the squad room. With twinkling coffee-colored eyes, he said, "Pardon my buddies, they like making fun of me. I am Al Newton, Senior Homicide Detective. You must be Professor Rekha Rao. Pleasure to

1

meet you." His matter-of-fact voice blended authority, confidence, and curiosity.

We shook hands and he sat across from me, the width of a battered oak table separating us. I continued to study the statue. I was there to do a job, and I needed to focus, something that had always come to me readily in the past, but now required conscious effort. I kept my eyes on the statue, mesmerized by the beauty and the horror of it. As I studied it, I felt a tremor start at the tip of my toes and course through my entire body. "Where did you find it?"

"The perp beat Faust's head to a pulp with it and left it on his back. We could use your help to figure out the whys. Why the idol? Why leave it on his back?" He leaned closer to me, frowning. "Sorry, Professor. Do you need more time?"

My hand flew to my hair, tucking errant strands behind my ear. This man was already getting my shackles up. I forced myself to sit still, find the ground beneath my feet, as my therapist had recommended. I didn't want him to jeopardize the progress I'd made healing my post-traumatic stress disorder (PTSD). "I'm fine." I said.

"I'm told that Striker and Faust were the co-directors of the Institute. Are you also an archaeologist?" He leaned his chair back on its hind legs.

"No, I'm a professor of Art History at Oxy, I mean Occidental College." I kept to myself that I was half-time, non-tenure track, and earned half the salary I had at UCI, the University of California, Irvine. "The JPM is affiliated with Oxy. I can't believe Faust is dead." I pointed to the statue. "This just made it real."

Newton said, "We can give you gloves if you'd like to hold it."

I shook my head and swallowed the nausea that tickled

my throat. So, he was not only attractive, but thoughtful.

He coughed. I would become familiar with this cough soon enough. "I bet you know her, don't you?" He gave a half-smile.

I took in the features of the idol. Approximately nine inches long, of equal width, and a couple of inches thick, it was carved from black stone and looked heavy. The figure seemed familiar, yet unfamiliar. It was a bare-chested female sporting round, full breasts, a necklace, ear ornaments, bangles, and armlets. She had four arms, three of which held a sword, a trident, and a mace. The fourth arm seemed to hold the tail of an animal resembling a buffalo, held down beneath her right foot, as she pierced the creature's neck with the trident. She exuded strength and radiance that could move even an atheist.

Yes, I knew her from the *Amar Chitra Katha* graphic novels my brother and I had devoured a million times growing up. She was the Hindu Goddess Durga, in the incarnation of *Mahishasura Mardini*, the killer of the buffalo demon, but not in her typical contemporary depiction. In images familiar to me, she had anywhere from six to twelve arms, and rode a lion, and the buffalo demon had a human head that emerged from his severed neck.

"Well?" Newton asked. His shirt was open at the throat, exposing a small patch of dark hair. His hands were now on the table, fingers loosely intertwined, his wrists adorned by powder blue shirtsleeves with silver cuff links. A well-dressed cop. I stole a look to find his eyes, slightly narrowed, still on my face, as though he wasn't quite sure what to make of me. Oh, go ahead, judge me, I said in my head.

"Detective, this is a manifestation of Durga, the most powerful female deity in the Hindu pantheon, in an incarnation called Mahishasura Mardini, but her presentation is somewhat atypical. I need to do some research—"

"—Just give us what you have now." A hint of impatience played in his voice which had gone up an octave, compromising his authority.

"Mahishasura Mardini means the one who killed Mahishasura, who was a half-human, half-buffalo demon who wreaked havoc on earth, heaven, and hell, as the story goes. This incarnation of Durga was created to punish Mahishasura, to end the devastation he inflicted on the world. Here—" I pointed at the idol. "You can see her piercing the demon's neck with a trident." Seeing his eyes widen, I realized that this might be too high a dose of Hindu mythology for a man who likely knew little about Hinduism.

Newton sat back ramrod straight and looked down at something he'd drawn on a notepad. Another annoying habit he'd repeat many times during our meetings. His auburn crewcut displayed streaks of gray that added a measure of dignity. I guessed he was in his early forties, by the wrinkles on his forehead and at the corners of his eyes. "Thank you, Professor Rao, we're lucky to have you here to identify her. We had no idea."

He got up and came around to stand behind my chair, making me feel uncomfortable. It's PTSD, I assured myself and took a deep breath. He said, "I don't see any demon here. It looks like an animal she has trapped."

I wondered if he had any understanding of other cultures. "That is one of the atypical features I noticed. Usually, the demon has a human head that emerges out of a buffalo's neck. Here he's just a buffalo. The other missing feature is the lion that's traditionally depicted as her vehicle."

"But you are sure of the identity of the object?" He sat

down in the chair next to me, bringing with him a mild whiff of something lemony.

"Yes, I've no doubt at all. Where did it come from?" I kept my eyes trained on the idol, to hide the attraction my confused heart had begun to feel for him.

"The current hypothesis is that the killer brought it with him. There's also a rumor that it was unearthed at Faust's excavation in Jwalapuram, a town in Andhra Pradesh in India. We're waiting for confirmation." He paused and coughed. "Do you have any initial impressions about the placement of the idol on the victim? Could it be some ritual?"

I stared at him, thinking about the word victim. I'd hated the word and had looked it up after Dad's murder three years ago. I'd learned that the prefix *vict* comes from Latin and means to conquer. The victor is the conqueror, and the victim, the conquered. As if it were a battle of equals, when one wielded a weapon, and the other was defenseless.

"The simplest explanation I can offer is that the killer was familiar with the mythological story of the Durga and was telling us that Faust was a demon who deserved to be eliminated for obliterating the killer's personal world." My eyes fell on the idol again, and, the sight of it brought a crushing sense of finality to the loss of my mentor. I blinked.

Newton said, "That seems far-fetched, Professor Rao. He was a well-known archaeologist." This made me pause and look up, to see a wide smile that puckered up the corners of his eyes. For the first time, he seemed less detective-like.

I focused my eyes on his. "I knew Faust very well and can assure you he was not only world-renowned for his discoveries but also an outstanding human being. I can't think of anyone who might even have disliked him. And who knew enough of the story to leave the idol on his back." I smiled for the first time, with a deepening sense that we came from different walks of life. He, a cop who used pattern recognition to track down criminals, and I, an academic who searched for new truths, even if I had lost my tenure at UCI.

He leaned forward on his elbows and locked his hands together. "The meaning of the idol is the main reason we called you in. There's also another reason. You are an Indian American professor of art history, and we hope we can stand by your interpretation of the idol as authentic. We don't want the local Indian community to descend on us because we misidentified one of their gods." He smiled again and pointed toward the squad room. "Why don't you come to my office? I've some photos for you."

I crossed a squad room that was tightly packed with cubicles along the periphery, weaving my way through an obstacle course of tables and chairs at the center where officers were taking statements and reviewing logbooks. There was a hush as several pairs of eyes checked me out.

The room I entered, Al's office, was immaculate and the glass-topped desk held a metal tray with several manila folders, each closed with a rubber band. Along one side of the desktop, under the glass, my eyes caught slips of papers with handwritten verses, at least one of which I recognized. "She walks in beauty . . ." I had memorized that passage from Lord Byron for a recitation competition in high school and practiced it endlessly in front of Ma and Dad until they were satisfied with my rendition. I was amused at this homicide detective's penchant for something I loved, Romantic poetry. So, he's human.

Framed certificates adorned one wall of the office. My plaques and certificates for teaching excellence had found their way into the bottom drawer of my filing cabinet. I didn't think it was necessary to prove my teaching ability to the entire world. I knew it, and my students knew it. But I could guess that dealing with criminals was a different cup of tea than teaching students. Maybe Norton needed sustenance from his accolades on a regular basis to pursue the bad guys.

He returned, put down two photographs, and offered me a magnifying glass. One photo was an eight-by-ten blow-up of the Durga lying on Faust's back, and the other, a legal-size print of a montage of the crime scene. Everything was scaled down in the montage, with the body right smack in the center. Faust lay prostrate half in and half out of an artificial pond of rocks, his arms outstretched as though affixed to a crucifix sans nails. He wore gray pants, black shoes, and a pale purple dress shirt that was torn and bloody. The back of his head was unrecognizable, hair matted and scalp peeled off in places. My stomach felt queasy, and I stood up. "May I use the restroom?"

Newton got up in a hurry and directed me to the far side of the hallway. "Take your time."

Inside the restroom, I splashed cold water on my face, leaned on the wall, and took some deep, slow breaths. This was Dad's murder all over again. The killer had beaten him up so badly that no one was allowed to see his face except my uncle who had to identify the body.

Back in the office, I sat down and looked at the photos again. I was grateful none of them showed Faust's face.

"You knew him well, didn't you? Sorry." Al said, his voice soft, with a hint of genuine kindness.

"Thanks. What more can you tell me?"

"This is what we know so far. Your professor and his colleagues partied at Roy's in Pasadena from approximately nine in the evening till well after midnight. Faust had planned to spend the night with Bob and Angela Davidson, his buddies in Pasadena, before taking off to Santa Cruz on a lecture tour. I gathered he was avoiding a drive back home to Culver City. This is what we think happened. Faust made it to the driveway of the Davidsons' house and got out of his car. The killer approached, delivered several blows to his head with the Durga, proceeded to drag his body into the Japanese garden, and dropped the idol on his back." It was an unemotional, clinical statement.

I took out my notebook and wrote down the details, then looked at the montage again. The artificial pond at the edge of a quasi-Japanese garden contained a Buddha statue and several oriental lanterns. The body partially stretched across it gave the impression that with his last breath, Faust had sought a place of safety. A bloody trail of drops, smudges, and pools created a staggered broken line from the body to the front porch, stopping short by a few feet. A black car with its front passenger door ajar stood in the driveway. An unopened briefcase, a conference bag with its contents scattered, and a pair of glasses with cracked lenses lay on the driveway near the car.

I looked at the five-by-seven close-up of the Durga on Faust's back and noticed two narrow rectangles of blue and yellow stripes on a white background on the bloody shirt, above and below the idol. "There's something strange here, Detective. Can you tell me what these stripes are? Was that his tie?"

"Yeah, we noticed that too. His tie got turned around to the back, most likely during the struggle. No big deal, happens all the time." He was dismissive.

"One more question. The amount of blood on the idol seems small if it was the murder weapon. How so?"

Newton thought for a moment. "You're a quick study, Professor. I'm not sure why you need these details to work on the meaning of the idol, but I can tell you it was wrapped in plastic that took most of the blood."

And fingerprints too, I thought. I pulled my unbuttoned jacket closer to my chest. "May I keep these photos?"

"Well, I can give you the close-up of the idol, but not the photo of the murder scene." He paused and looked at me as he picked up the smaller photo, put it into a manila envelope, and handed it to me.

"Thank you." I attempted a smile that never fully emerged. "Who found the body?"

"Bob Davidson, the homeowner, a retired professor and Faust's colleague from the Institute."

"When was Faust killed, if I may ask?"

The official steeliness was back. "All I can tell you at this time is that Bob Davidson called the police at about seven in the morning. He said he went to bed at eleven the previous evening and discovered the body when he woke up, and promptly called 911. So take your pick. We're awaiting the autopsy."

I couldn't shake off his attitude, but if he expected me to wither and cower, he'd got the wrong person. I had prior training from the cops I dealt with in Irvine.

Newton tapped the table with his pen. "What was your relationship with Faust?"

"He was my mentor when we were both at UCI. He moved to Oxy four years ago. When I started there this January, I'd hoped to benefit from his continued guidance." I spoke with detachment, more in control, not wanting him to witness my emotions.

He sat back and twirled his pen. "So, at this time, your

best guess is that the killer wanted to destroy a man who caused him harm."

"The Goddess was punishing the demon, avenging him for the damage he had done. At least, that's what millions of Hindus believe. And as I said, I do need to look into other interpretations of the story, if any." I was tired and wanted to get out of there.

"When can you give us your confirmation? We don't want to dive into a rabbit hole that might detour us from the real motive and the real killer."

"Give me until Monday afternoon." I got up and turned to leave, but asked, "Is there anything more you can tell me? Did you get any fingerprints from the idol or the plastic?"

The pen clanked as it fell on the glass desktop. He raised his eyebrows. "Look, Professor Rao. Or is it Ms. Rao? You ask interesting questions. Are you trained in criminal investigation? Or do you read murder mysteries?" His voice had lost all pretense of camaraderie.

"It's Rekha, Detective. And yes, I do have a penchant for mysteries." Like yours for Lord Byron, I almost added. Despite his rudeness, there was a charisma about this man. I wiped off the smile that came to my face, thinking he'd missed out on being the next Clint Eastwood, with Hollywood in proximity.

He turned to me, eyes like magnets. "Professor Rao, crimes in real life are not like what you read in books or see on TV. So please, stick to your job and let us do ours. Also, I'm sure you know this, but I have to ask you to keep all the details confidential. We can't risk leaks until we narrow down our persons of interest." He added as he leaned back in his chair, "No offense."

I stood up. "None taken, Detective." As I turned to leave

the room, he stood up, folded his arms across his chest, and said in a crisp voice, "Thank you for helping us."

* * *

I got to my car, my heart still racing from the exchange. I took a second to calm down.

I turned my phone back on and discovered I had received two texts. One was from Ma reminding me about the special dinner next Saturday, translated as *meet the suitor*. I chose not to call her back. A murder and my family were too much to handle at the same time on my limited store of adrenaline. The second, from my brother Sanjay, was a caution. "Sorry, Ma pried it out of me that you're working with the cops again." A bunch of wild emojis followed this. I regretted leaving him a voicemail earlier, letting him know where I was going. I was excited that this time, the police called me for help, a role reversal that I knew my brother would applaud. He was the only one I could share life's events with and not fear criticism.

I drove west to Oxy. I needed to look through my office papers for contact information for one Mr. Reddy. Who would want to kill Faust, and in such a brutal way? My mind drifted back to a past when Faust was alive, his absolute humility a contrast to his world-renowned archaeological discoveries. I'd seen him the day before in his office. As the recipient of this year's Balzan Prize in archaeology, he had been preparing his acceptance speech for that evening's annual meeting of the Society for American Archaeology, a speech that would come several hours before his murder. I'd walked in unannounced, and he, tall, slightly stooped, his thick-framed spectacles hanging from his neck, had welcomed me with the usual crooked smile that lifted one corner of his mouth. He was so like Dad.

More memories floated up from the depths of my brain. Three years ago, my dad, a respected physician, a kind man, was bludgeoned to death in his clinic. The Irvine police had arrested and convicted Eduardo Lopez, a Latino janitor who had found the body. His name was etched in my memory. I was convinced that Lopez, an unassuming, soft-spoken man in his fifties, was no killer. My father had befriended him and had promised to set up a scholarship for his daughter if she finished high school. Convinced that the cops had the wrong man, I worked myself into a frenzy to unearth new information. I talked to Lopez's relatives and friends, and the doctors and staff at my dad's clinic, and pored over Dad's appointment books. With the new evidence I gathered, I relentlessly pressured the Irvine police to reopen the case. Detective Templeton was polite in the beginning, annoyed after a while, and downright nasty later when he refused to hear me out any more. The gossip that spread through the grapevine alienated my family from their friends in the local Indian community. I failed to get tenure at UC Irvine, since the time I should have invested in publishing papers was spent on a fruitless search for the real killer of my father.

I was determined to keep the promise I'd made to myself when I closed the book on Dad's case. I would have nothing more to do with the police from then on. Now that I had unwillingly entered their territory, I'd do just what Striker asked of me, no more. And even that, only for a man who had become my father figure.

* * *

I parked and walked over to my office in the Weingart Center for the Liberal Arts on Bird Road. Being a Saturday, the campus was quiet, the way I liked it, although I was truly fond of and dedicated to my students. Someone called out, "Hey, Professor Rao, here on a Saturday?" I waved, smiled, and walked on.

I wanted to confirm the idol was from Faust's excavation in India. About six years ago, when I was in New Delhi for a year to do research for my doctoral thesis, I had met Raghunath Reddy, at the National Museum of India. He and his wife Bimla had put me up in their apartment in a room that used to be their daughter's. She had gotten married and moved to Saudi Arabia. The additional income was very welcome since Reddy was a staff member at the Museum and earned a modest salary. I remembered the short, dark man who wore pants and a long shirt or *kurta*, and a shawl, and adorned his forehead with a perfectly round sandalwood dot after his morning *puja*. He would tease me, "Rekha-ji, if you do not open your mouth, you can be a perfect Indian woman. The minute you talk, you give yourself away with your American accent."

The website for the National Museum was no help. There were no names or contact links. I rummaged through a box of papers I'd shipped back from New Delhi and hit gold. There was my old frayed address book. I found Reddy's email address and telephone number at the Museum and hoped he was still there. I called, but the number was no longer in use. I scanned the photo of the idol, and sent it attached to an email, and asked him if he could confirm that it was the statue found in Jwalapuram during Faust's excavation. I asked if there was anything else related to the find he could tell me. It was already 1 pm. Because of the twelve-hour time difference, the earliest I would get a response would be this evening. That is if he remembered me.

* * *

Back home, I started to tidy up the house, a chore I did on Saturdays. I loved my house in Eagle Rock, a small two-plus-one, built in the seventies, the interior replete with multicolored shag carpet and walls painted in matching colors. The house had a narrow galley kitchen at a time when buyers were asking for open kitchens, but with two counters on each side in green melamine, a sink on one side, and a stove on the other, it served me well.

I made a cup of chai and sat down to look at two newspapers I'd picked up from campus. The special edition of *Pasadena Star-News* had a column devoted to Joseph Faust, "a son of Pasadena," who had grown up and attended schools in town. It gave minimal information about the murder and talked about the conference where Faust received this year's Balzan Prize. The other paper was *The Occidental Weekly*. I knew it was published both online and as a hard copy on Wednesdays, but this was a special Saturday edition. Thanks to a diligent investigative reporter, Neil Anderson, it gave the same information about the murder, but more details and photos of Faust's recent participation in the excavation in Jwalapuram that led to the discovery of microlithic technology dating back 30,000 years. I recognized the reporter, a brilliant student in my sophomore Indian Art History class.

I sorted my mail and found the usual monthly letter from Eduardo Lopez, the man who was serving life without parole for Dad's murder. It was brief, crudely penned, and said, "Professor Rao, I hope you are believing in me. I did not kill your dear father. Please help me. Thanking you, Eduardo Lopez." I'd met with Lopez almost weekly since he was incarcerated, trying to find ways to exonerate him, keeping his hopes up. At the end of two years, I had failed miserably, and, I'd stopped seeing him after my move to Eagle Rock. It was then that he started to write monthly, pleading for help. The letters came regularly, but over time the contents had dwindled in length and detail as if Lopez felt all hope had been exhausted, and he himself had given up. I placed the letter back in its envelope and put it away in a drawer with the previous ones. Sorry, Eduardo. Sorry, Dad. I failed you both when you needed me the most.

I shook off the gloom and called Ma. After some initial chit-chat on how we both were doing, she asked, "Are you taking care of yourself, Rekha? Taking Ambien and doing therapy?"

The year before I moved to Eagle Rock, I was diagnosed with PTSD, brought on by Dad's sudden and violent death three years ago. That my ex-boyfriend had beaten me up, did not help. I had become apathetic, lost weight, and had persistent nightmares. Any object that Dad used, like his old umbrella, or *chappals*, brought on unexpected bouts of grief. I was on medication and regularly saw a therapist, but neither had helped. My decision to move away from home was a battle I'd fought with myself and won.

On the one hand, my family stabilized and grounded me, but on the other, I desperately needed to make my own decisions, even if they led me to mistakes. Since joining Oxy, I'd found a new therapist who took me off most of the drugs and trained me on CBT, Cognitive Behavior Therapy. It was starting to pay off.

"Yes, Ma, I'm doing well. Stop worrying."

"You sound OK. Eagle Rock and the move seem to suit you. Maybe we were the problem." She sounded upset. I was sure she missed me and would have liked me to live closer to home. But would she admit it, oh no.

"No, Ma, no. I'm thirty-two, I should learn to live on my own. And you're all there any time I need you."

"What is Sanjay telling me? Are you back working with the police? I don't think it's a good idea. After everything that happened."

I said, "Faust's colleague at the institute asked me to help the police with an idol found at the crime site. They don't know anything about Hindu idols. I'm educating them. That's all, I promise." I tried to hide my growing irritation.

"OK, I hope that's all it is. Don't forget the Saturday dinner." She hung up. It sounded like she hadn't bought my explanation.

I missed Dad, who had been my haven, with Ma firmly upholding traditions, duties, and high standards of academic performance, which she believed would lead to happiness. Defined as a professional Indian husband, two children and wealth. Dad was the one who took me and Sanjay for ice cream, taught us how to play tennis and chess and bought us little gifts for no reason. He also taught us the basics of Hindu philosophy, without making it a heavy burden on our teenage shoulders. "*Dharma* is the boundary for *Arth*, our material life, and *Kama*, our sensory, emotional and aesthetic fulfillment. Practicing Arth and Kama with dharma as the boundary will lead us to *Moksha*, salvation from cycles of rebirth." I had asked, with palpable anxiety, "But, how do I find the boundary so I wouldn't go off the path?" He'd laughed, "By trial and error, and with consideration to the consequences of all your actions. Following the path with conviction is all you can do. But don't expect it to always lead to a pot of gold."

I refocused on my task. On the one hand, I needed to do the research to confirm my speculations about the idol. On the other, I was on fire, fueled by thoughts of who, how and why. I was facing a fork in the road. One path would restrict me to do my job and leave the sleuthing to Newton. The other would allow me to follow my heart and try to find the killer. I knew I had to take the former.

With some light lunch in my stomach, I was ready to explore the story of the Mahishasura Mardini. I opened my laptop, created a file under Durga, and jotted down the question Newton wanted me to answer: Why was the idol left on Faust's body? I put down the logical explanation I'd offered him that the killer wanted to let the world know that Faust was a demon who deserved to be killed, like Mahishasura. What would make Faust a demon to someone? His colleagues seemed to value and respect him. His students adored him. But my rational mind warned me that the man I respected like my father and had placed on a high pedestal, was also human, with his share of foibles. I reminded myself that I must leave the thoughts of why and who to the suave cop, Newton. Instead, I switched my focus to confirm the possibility that the idol's value made it a target for theft.

I Googled "Chasing Aphrodite," a website created by the writers of the book of the same title, to track and report illegal acquisitions. It posted photos of several stolen artifacts, including a Kushan sculpture of a Seated Buddha that had to be returned to India. I had no doubt that the idol found by the police was another Aphrodite making her way through illegal channels to a museum or to an antique collector who'd show her off as a conversation piece at cocktail parties. But how did she end up on the back of a murdered archaeologist? And what was her connection to the murder?

My laptop announced an incoming email. I was delighted to see it was from Reddy.

Dear Rekha-ji,

What a delight getting your email. I retired right after the Jwalapuram excavation but still keep my work email address. I am devastated by Professor Faust's murder. He was my guru, my teacher, and a great man.

Thank you for the photo. I have no doubt the photo is the image of the very idol we unearthed from the excavation in Jwalapuram. It was an intact Mahishasura Mardini, but not in the typical configuration. She had only four arms, and the Mahishasura was mostly in the buffalo form, not with the human head as he is typically depicted. And, mind you, no lion.

It was quite a stir, I tell you. The morning after She was unearthed, I went to box Her up along with a few other broken idols for transport to the National Museum in New Delhi, and the idol was gone. That was when the rumors started that the Americans—pardon my expression, they meant Professors Faust and Davidson—had stolen the Durga with my help. Nonsense. The Kurnool District police were called in to search our hotel rooms and bags. The professors were cleared, but because I was in charge of cataloging, I am still on their radar. They did not have an ounce of evidence to charge me. My Indian colleague from the museum, Dileep Patel, and I cross-checked all the finds with a list that we entered into the computer. The Durga was there when we did the lockup for the night. Gone the next morning. The lock was forced open. As you can imagine, illegal antiquities have a huge market now through online auctions and websites.

This is in confidence. I suspect my colleague Patel may have had a hand in the theft. We both had applied for a sabbatical with Professor Faust, and when I was selected, he started acting strange. But I have no proof.

Dear Rekha-ji, do stay in touch. I will surely send you any information or even a gossip that I hear at my end. And I hope you can help find the killer.

Respectfully,
    Raghunath Reddy. M.S. (Archaeology).

I thanked him and mentioned that I'd be grateful for any information he got because I knew that Newton would not apprise me of any new developments.

I went out to get groceries and pick up dry-cleaning, mindless routines that calmed me. I worked on my CBT exercises, encouraged by the advances I was making. I ate lunch at the Oinkster, my favorite place. I started compiling my notes on what I had to do, not in any particular order, just the order in which they came to mind. I wanted to invest the entire next day in researching the Durga.

In bed, my mind played tricks on me, switching on and off images of the tall, strong, handsome man I had met that morning. My lizard brain alerted me I might be falling for him, but my executive brain laughed it off.

~ Chapter 2 ~

Sunday, March 26, 2017

I sat and stared at the Mahishasura Mardini for inspiration. I'd settled into my comfortable cushioned armchair in the living room, with my books and laptop on a side table, the close-up photo of the Durga on an end table, where it leaned on the wall, below the framed photo of Dad.

There was a knock. I opened the door and my brother walked in. The first thing he saw was the photo. "Isn't, isn't that the goddess who killed the demon? The—Mahi—Mahisha—"

"Hey bro, you're supposed to call before you come."

"Some busybody turned her phone off."

I looked at my cell and the red silencer stared back at me.

Sanjay took after our father in every aspect of his physiognomy, and whenever I saw him I felt Dad's presence. He was four years younger and several inches taller than me. He had our father's south Indian complexion and his large brown eyes, but in place of Dad's straight black hair that gathered flecks of gray with age, pitch-black hair stood up from his scalp like springs. His oval, pointed face came from Ma.

I ignored his question, punched him in the belly, and held him by the shoulders at arm's length. "Looks like you are working out. Is there a girl on campus?" Sanjay had stayed on at UCI to do a Master's in bioengineering. He loved Indian food but didn't know how to cook it. So he did the next best thing and found an apartment only minutes from Ma's home-cooked meals.

"Oh, stop it, Didi. Give me a break. I went to see a professor at USC, the University of Southern California, who knew Dad, a pre-med advisor." He broke out of my hold and said, "Ma said to talk to him and see if my Master's would help me get into med school." I loved it when he called me *Didi*, meaning sister in Hindi. In the presence of his friends, he'd resort to Sis.

I said, "Wow, following in Dad's footsteps. You'll soon be the pride and joy of the family." My parents didn't hassle me about my decision to specialize in Indian art history since they—especially Dad—believed their children should find and follow their own vocations. Thankfully, they were immune to the societal values of prestige and wealth that my uncle and aunt espoused.

"So, what's with the photo? That's the idol the police wanted you to identify?"

"Yeah, it's the Mahishasura Mardini, killer of the buffalo demon, an incarnation of Durga. Remember the Amar Chitra Katha books we used to read?" The series of Indian cartoon books we collected over the years gave us our first lessons in Indian history, religion, and mythology. I wished I had them at hand to give Newton a visual story of the incarnation, but they were in storage in Ma's condo, waiting for the next generation of children yet to be born.

"The police had no idea what the idol was?"

"No, why should they? They aren't Indians. Or scholars." I chuckled. "Even you couldn't come up with the name. Some Indian you are."

"Where did they find it?"

"The idol was left on Faust's back." I hesitated to give him more details, but couldn't hold back. "I only saw the photos, thank God. Even then, it was horrible to see him lying outstretched on the ground, the back of his head a mash of blood and hair. Thankfully, I didn't see his face. Still, I think I'll carry that image to my grave."

Sanjay was quiet for a moment. "So, if you told the cops the idol was a form of Durga, what more did they want?"

"They want to know if there's any religious or other significance to the idol left on the body. As if everything Indians do has a religious basis. Do you know what I think? The real question is why someone would choose an idol of Durga as a murder weapon in the first place. People don't carry around idols just in case they get the idea to kill someone."

"I get your sarcasm. Promise me that's all you will do, right, Didi? Help them with the meaning of the idol?"

I said, "How about some chai to get you back home?" I walked into the kitchen and he followed me.

Sanjay had been the typical younger brother when we were growing up. Thrusting frogs in my face, pulling dead insects from behind my ears and hiding under a sheet in my closet like a ghost. Always a sweetheart, my bond with him got stronger after Dad's passing, with Sanjay defending me in my absence when I'd become the target of family chatter, letting me in on prospective suitors my family had found for me, and threatening to set me up with some of his professors.

He snapped his fingers in front of me to break my thoughts. "What's going on, Didi? How are you holding up? I know how fond you were of Faust. To have him murdered, especially after Dad's—after Dad died. Are you OK?" His voice was soft, almost apologetic.

I poured milk and water into a saucepan and set it to heat. "I don't know. It's all happened so fast, I haven't sorted it out yet." I watched the watery milk gather bubbles.

"Tell me you will not poke your nose into this murder. You know the heartbreak it caused you—all of us—when you chased after Dad's killer for two years. You want to go through all that again?"

He had a way of turning into the older brother I'd never had. "I'll tell you what I told Ma. Striker from JPM asked me to help the police with the idol, and that's all I'm doing. For Faust's sake."

Sanjay stared at me. "You sound defensive."

I desperately wanted to share with him my building desire to do more than just research the idol for the police. I so wanted my baby brother's approval to go ahead, get involved, find the killer because the police would mess up as they did with Dad's murder. I craved his agreement that it was the righteous path to follow, that it was my dharma.

But I knew what his answer would be. So I added, "Tell me about my marriage prospects. Who have they lined up for me this time?" I ground up two cardamom pods with a mortar and pestle and added them to the milk, then rummaged around in my kitchen shelf to find the chocolate-covered raisins I'd hidden from myself.

"A son of one of Uncle Naveen's classmates from India. I believe he came to the US to go to law school. He's a successful defense lawyer is all I know. No one would tell me anything more because they're afraid I'd warn you off." Sanjay made a face.

"Gee, a lawyer dude is all I need now." I turned the flame down, added two heaping teaspoons of tea leaves to the watery milk, stirred it, and turned off the stove. Silence pervaded the kitchen as we waited for the tea to steep. I strained the wheat-colored chai into my favorite mug, black with a rising sun, and handed it to my brother. I poured mine into my second favorite, a brown mug with wispy green leaves.

We walked into the living room. I pulled up the yellowing plastic blinds and opened the windows. It promised to be a cool day. I sat on the sofa, sipped and watched Sanjay savor the chai and raisins. I felt so like a big sister.

He said, "Heavenly. You make it almost as good as Ma." We both laughed. "You're coming, aren't you? Dinner on Saturday?"

"Yeah, like I need one more reminder." I knocked on my head with my knuckles. "Ma called me and Aunty Leela left a message to bring Indian clothes to wear." I imitated her accent, "And please for once, sweetie, be on time, Okay?"

Sanjay roared.

"I won't disappoint Ma. Besides, I've decided to check out this arranged marriage business. You know what a poor judge of men I am." I giggled.

"Seriously? You got to be kidding me."

I said, "Seriously."

His face clouded. "Didi, has Matt bugged you since you moved?"

Matt Porter was my first serious boyfriend at UCI, a pre-med poised to get into one of the top med schools. My family tolerated him, hoping he was a passing fancy, but Sanjay took an instant dislike to him that never changed. Against my family's advice, I kept seeing him, only to discover a control freak under the intellectual garb. The night he back-handed me, gave me a bloody eye, and almost strangled me, I dumped him. I reported the incident to the Irvine police, who questioned him, but let him off with a warning. They asked me to get a restraining order against him.

"No, thank God. I haven't given my phone number to anyone other than our family, with strict instructions not to give it out. Why?" I felt a chill, more by the raked-up memories of Matt than by the breeze wafting in, but I got up and closed the windows.

Sanjay said, "I ran into the pest today. Told me he's collaborating with a professor at USC, hoping to get a tenure-track position. Asked about you. I didn't tell him anything."

"Hopefully, he's finished with me." I stroked my right cheekbone where his punch had landed three years ago. "I sure am finished with him." I reminded myself to reinstate the restraining order against him, an omission after my move from Irvine.

"You set your burglar alarm at night, don't you? You ought to get a dog, Didi. Can you rely on your neighbor to help in an emergency?"

"Aren't you full of wisdom today? Thanks for looking out for me, bro. No dog for now. My neighbor is over eighty. First, you get a girlfriend."

"I'm declaring bachelorhood. What do they call a celibate who studies the holy books? Yeah, a *Brahmachari*. One in our family would be good, don't you think?"

"Ignore Aunty and Uncle. You know Ma means well, Sanjay. Grin and bear and then do what you must."

I had wondered for some time now if Sanjay was gay. He wasn't turning up with one girlfriend after another on his arm, and I was certain girls would fall for him. However, I didn't want to probe. I believed he'd tell me in his own time. I hoped he realized that I'd support him no matter what.

I turned to the photo on the table. "Hey, you want to help me with the idol?"

I got back to my armchair and pulled out another chair for Sanjay before he could protest.

"It's common knowledge that the Mahishasura Mardini depicted the sixth incarnation of Durga who was created from parts of the trinity: Shiva the destroyer, Vishnu the preserver, and Brahma the creator." I showed him the images I'd found, dozens of them on one page with more pages to follow. "There's no dearth of these, but no consistency in the number of arms, the weapons held, the forms of the lion and the demon, you name it. Looks like the Durga devotees went rampant with their creativity."

Sanjay leaned over to look, and said, "All these have more than four arms. But look, her lowest arms are always working on killing the demon, as you'd expect." He frowned. "What do you make of the discrepancies?"

"I hope to find out," I said as I dragged out a box of books and papers I'd collected for my doctoral thesis on the Ajanta caves, rock-cut Buddhist monuments in the Aurangabad district of Maharashtra in India. The caves were built in two phases, the first group starting around 200 BCE, the second around 400–650 CE. They contained the largest body of surviving ancient Indian wall paintings. My work had focused on the period 475–477 CE, when a woman closely related to the emperor was believed to have sponsored and influenced the work. "Look, all my books are on the Buddhist caves. They won't include any Hindu deities."

"How about this?" Sanjay had dumped out all the contents of the box and pulled out *Ellora, Concept, and Styles* by Carmel Berkson, published in 1992 in India. I'd used it for comparative evaluation of the artistic styles displayed in both sets of caves.

"You might have just hit the target. Pure luck," I made

a face. The Ellora caves, also located in Aurangabad, were influenced by Buddhism, Hinduism, and Jainism, and were likely to provide an early example of the Durga incarnation. I thumbed through the index and found three wall reliefs dated 600–700 CE in Caves 14, 17, and 21 that showed four-armed versions that held weapons, but none of them precisely matched the murder weapon.

Sanjay stood up and walked over to Dad's photo on the wall. "I miss him, Didi, don't you? He had so much patience for us. Remember his bad jokes? Here's one. What did the newspaper say to the magazine?"

"Dude, you got issues," I said. We laughed, relieved to move beyond grief and reassemble our shared memories of the person we'd lost. "I miss him too, Sanju. When he was alive, I could always ask him which way to go with any decision, and he'd make me define my choices and leave me to it. I made mistakes, but Dad never said I told you so."

"I'll never forget how he'd squeeze our faces with one hand, and say, how's my best daughter? My best son?"

I thought of Faust, who'd also burst out with laughter at the silliest of jokes. Birds of a feather who never met.

"Listen, Sanju, you focus on your classes and grades, and don't worry about your sister," I said in a voice as firm and gentle as Dad's.

He spun around, shouting, "Eena, meena, deeka—" our childhood game, based on a popular Hindi movie song. As he grabbed my ponytail, I went for his loosened tie, and we circled each other, growling. I said, "Done." Sanjay's tie had turned around during the game and now hung down his back. I playfully tugged at the ends and he pretended to choke.

"Thanks, I don't remember laughing like that in a long while." I pulled out the rubber band hanging from my head by a single hair and put my hair back into a ponytail. I thought of Faust's tie that was turned around in the photo. Did it signify a noose? Why a noose for a man who was brutally beaten to death? Was that another message the killer left?

"I better go," Sanjay said.

I opened the door, and we walked out into the cool porch and down the steps to the driveway. I decided to tell him. I wanted him on my side. "Promise me you won't tell Ma. I'm thinking of looking for Faust's killer. I don't want to leave it to the cops. And don't try to change my mind."

He stared at me, belief and disbelief taking turns on his face. "Why would you do that? Are you craz—I'm sorry, Didi, I remember the day you lost your tenure. You said you were humiliated. You shut yourself up for days, wouldn't even talk to your girlfriends. Are you now going to jeopardize your new job?"

"Listen to me, Sanju. If Dad were alive, I'm certain he'd tell me that given a choice, one must always follow the path of dharma, but follow it for its own sake, with no expectation of a reward. The mistake I made last time was to expect too much. Also, in pursuit of one dharma, I'd neglected all others."

"Promise me something, Didi." Sanjay came close to me and looked me in the eye. "This time, let me help you, please. I promise I wouldn't do it at the expense of my grades. And I wouldn't let the cat out of the bag."

I nodded, and relief flooded his face. I extended my right hand, and he put his on mine, our childhood way of locking in a promise.

I hugged him tight and then watched as he drove away. There goes my best buddy. If only I could hold on to him always.

* * *

Back inside the house, I found new energy.

I searched online for images of four-armed Mahishasura Mardini again and came across an article: "Durga Worship in the Upper Mahanadi Valley." I downloaded it. It described several four-armed figures that were attributed to anywhere from 500 CE to 700 CE. Of these, one description came close to the murder weapon: the demon was a buffalo, the goddess used the trident to pierce its neck, and her lower left arm held the tail of the creature. This was dated 500 CE, but there was no photo. The article suggested, although it did not explicitly state, that over the years, the number of arms increased to over twenty, but with some broad overlaps, with no explanation for this metamorphosis.

For confirmation, I needed images. Googling, I came upon Wikimedia Commons that led me to a wall relief almost identical to the murder weapon in Cave 1 of the cave temples in Badami, a town in the northern part of the state of Karnataka, India. This one, in sandstone, had four arms, one of which was impaling a buffalo with a trident. There was no lion, and, it was dated 600–700 CE. Incorporating both sets of data, I concluded that the idol was ancient, and with a wide range in date from 500 to 700 CE, it would be worth hundreds of thousands, if not millions, to collectors.

I moved on to find documented stories about the goddess and the demon that might inform me why the idol was used as a weapon and left on Faust's body. Again, Google led me to the oft-told story of Mahishasura, a demon with the head of a buffalo who wreaked havoc in heaven, hell and on earth. He was a staunch worshipper of Lord Brahma. After years of penance, Brahma granted him a wish that he would not be killed by man or animal, but only by a woman. Mahisha continued his devastations, and, when individual Gods could not defeat him, Brahma, Vishnu, and Shiva combined their powers to create Durga. Incarnated as Mahishasura Mardini, she waged war against Mahisha, beheaded him with her trident, and cut off the human head that emerged from the buffalo body.

What did the story tell me about the murder? On the surface, it meant that Faust's "evil" acts were punished by someone who held a grudge against him. The problem was that I couldn't imagine my mentor committing evil acts. Against whom? His colleagues, competitors, or students? Bob Davidson? I suspected he'd be the top "person of interest" in Newton's eye because Faust was staying at Davidson's house.

Searching Oxy's library catalog online, I found another book, *The Divine and Demoniac: Mahisha's Heroic Struggle With Durga*, also written by Carmel Berkson. It promised to be a good resource. So I walked over to the Mary Norton Clapp Library on Campus Road. It provided a good stretch for my lazy legs.

I looked for Carmel Berkson's book using OASys, the digital database, and luckily, it was on the shelf. Grabbing it, I sat down and leafed through it. The book, 318 pages in small print, covered details of the mythological story of the incarnation. There were chapters on Mahisha's birth, his labors, demonic transformation, encounters with the Goddess, followed by the battle leading to his death. The contents were too voluminous to digest in one sitting, so I turned to the last chapter titled, "Life Stages of the Hero: Depictions in Stone" that referred to twenty-eight photographic plates and categorized them. Plate 19, ascribed to 400-500 CE, best resembled the idol I had seen at the police station. The Durga was the prominent figure, and the buffalo small, at her feet. She held his tail in one hand and pierced him with a trident held in another hand. I adjusted my earlier speculation that the idol could date from 400 to 700 CE.

How did the earlier and later depictions relate to this period? Before 300-500 CE, both Durga and Mahisha were carved as a single piece in a symbiotic relationship. She held the buffalo close to her, suggestive of motherly protection of an infant or closeness to a lover. The Goddess held a weapon but did not use it, telling us that the battle hadn't started yet. In the subsequent depictions, a human head emerged from the cut neck of Mahisha, who slowly grew in size to be almost as big as the Goddess.

To use the idol as a murder weapon based on the story, the killer had to be knowledgeable about the details of Durga's life stages I'd just read. A Durgaphile. Would Faust's colleague Davidson fit the bill? I had no idea what his area of expertise was. To my mind, the possibility of an expert on Mahishasura Mardini being the killer was an unlikely scenario. However, the information led me to consider a rejected lover, or Faust's son, as suspects.

Alternatively, the Durga could have been a weapon of opportunity. If so, how did it happen to be there? Again, Davidson was the most obvious choice, being the only other Oxy archaeologist at the excavation, and who also happened to be at the site of the crime, on the night Faust was killed. Another possibility was that Faust himself stole the Durga, was caught with it by Davidson, who then killed him. I'd leave Newton to formulate that theory.

My brain fried, I looked down at four pages of my notebook filled with scribbles, ramblings, half sentences, crude drawings, and question marks. I needed to put this together in some cohesive fashion for my meeting with Newton tomorrow. I also had to prep a lecture for the afternoon.

I checked out the book and went home. As I entered my living room, the first thing I saw was the photo of the Durga on the table. Like Sanjay, my eyes went to it, but this time, they landed on Faust's tie turned around to his back. Why did the killer do that? Or, was I reading too much into it?

I fell asleep after a long time, with the aid of an Ambien.

* * *

I woke up with a start and sat up in bed.

The surrounding air reverberated with Dad's voice, pure and clear. "You didn't fail, Rekha. You took the right path as far as you could. Remember, walking the path of dharma, the righteous course of action, is its own reward. Don't hesitate to take it again."

For the first time in three years, I found it possible to forgive myself. I hadn't failed Dad or Eduardo. I'd made the mistake of following the path of dharma for the reward of finding the killer. I'd also trusted the cops to follow up on the new leads I'd dug up. I'd been flagellating myself for their ineptness.

I had no doubt that the cops would fail again. Newton would screw up, despite his badge, cop persona, and smugness.

My dharma was beckoning me to find Faust's killer.

~ Chapter 3 ~

Monday, March 27, 2017

There were two phone messages on the machine when I got to my office.

One was from Newton, left early in the morning. "Professor Rao, this is Al Newton. We need to talk to you about your student, Bill McGraw. Can you stop by the station at your earliest?" My heart skipped a beat. I wanted to see him again.

The second one was from Bill McGraw left late the night before. He stuttered, "Professor Rao, I just got back. I have to report to the police station tomorrow. I need to see you before that. May I stop by at noon? This is a nightmare. I need your help. Please."

Bill was a sophomore in my Introduction to Indian Art History class and my advisee since January. Oxy had a well-oiled system for student advising, with each faculty member assigned three to five students. We were encouraged to meet with them once a semester to check on their academic progress, career goals, and social integration, and to be proactive in figuring out if they were heading for poor performance. Although I held an adjunct position, my Chair had encouraged me to become an advisor, since, in her words, my reputation for helping troubled students at UCI had preceded me to Oxy. I'd plunged into it, pleased that I was given the opportunity to use my natural talents.

I'd had two meetings with Bill since the beginning of the spring semester. A modest young man with no fake airs, he came from a family that could not afford Oxy without a scholarship. He lost his parents in a car accident and adored the great-aunt who had taken him in. He came to my office hours with well-thought-out questions and seemed to take pleasure in learning. Not a student I expected to get into trouble with the law.

Newton's message seemed urgent. It'd help to know what he had on my student before I met with Bill. I decided to go over to the PPD.

* * *

Newton's office door stood ajar, and I found him deep in thought, gazing at a whiteboard densely packed with photos, maps, and newspaper cuttings, linked together with arrows and lines. The murder board. I must have moved into his peripheral vision, because without turning his head he said, "Professor Rao. Thank you for coming."

He walked over to his chair and sat down, pointing to the chair across from him. "How's your research on the statue coming?"

"I'm about halfway through, I need a couple of hours to put my notes together. I should have something for you by later today. I understand you want to talk to me about Bill McGraw?"

Newton's eyes examined my face. "You seem to be coping better than the last time I saw you." He smiled, and added, "We have a new development. We found out from the Dean's office that Bill McGraw is your advisee." He looked at me with raised eyebrows that seemed to taunt me. I shook the feeling off.

"Yes, since January. So it's only been a couple of months, but I've met with him twice to discuss his coursework and check on his progress. He's also in my Indian Art History class and uses my office hours regularly. A diligent young man who's doing well. What happened?"

"Here's the scoop from Roy's, the restaurant in Pasadena where Faust held his celebratory dinner following the award ceremony. The bartender stated that the professor was the last to arrive, and as he made his way to the private dining room, a young man from a nearby table approached him. The waiter didn't hear what transpired except that Faust told the young man in a firm voice not to bother him anymore. That same waiter later served the Faust party and reported that the professor was frazzled by the encounter and commented to a friend at the table that students didn't know where to draw the line these days. Today, the waiter identified the young man as your diligent student Bill, from a photo we got from the Dean's office. Bill was there with a friend, both wearing Oxy caps." He paused, and added, "As you know, Faust died soon after he left the restaurant and arrived at Davidson's home. We think someone followed him from Roy's. Could it be Bill?"

"Well, this is all news to me. I'm sure he just meant to congratulate his professor. He's coming to see me at noon. I'd certainly talk to him about it. Who was the other student?"

Newton consulted his book. "Neil Anderson, an entitled young man, according to the waiter. He introduced himself as a reporter for the Oxy Weekly."

The zealous student who had written the lengthy and

informative report on Faust's excavation. Neil, like Bill, was a sophomore in my class. Where Bill was bright, Neil was brilliant. He had the potential to be the next Faust. "Neil Anderson is also in my class, but I don't know him well."

"We found out that Bill was an intern with Faust, and that Faust terminated his internship abruptly the day before the murder. No one seems to know why. We thought you would." He smiled, and did his chair trick, balancing it on its back legs.

This was the first I'd heard about the incident. "No, I don't. He stopped by Friday afternoon to discuss his assignment for next week since he was going out of town to visit his sick aunt—great-aunt. I knew of his internship, in fact I was the one who encouraged him to apply for it. But I'm sure Professor Faust had a good reason to terminate it." I felt my jaw tighten, sensing a stress attack coming on.

Newton spread his hands. "He might have held a grudge against his professor for ending the internship. Might have felt humiliated, the way the professor dismissed him in the restaurant."

I shouldn't have, but I couldn't stop words bursting out of me. "You must be kidding me. To hold a grudge because his internship was terminated? There are other ways to deal with it." Each sentence took on more venom than the previous one.

Newton didn't seem to register the anguish in my voice. "How come he didn't report it to you? You're supposed to be his advisor, right?"

I calmed myself down, drawing circles in my left palm with my right index finger.

"Detective, all I can assume is that Bill's internship was terminated after he stopped by at my office around 2 pm on Friday. He might have wanted to wait until after he got back from his trip to talk to me. Not much could be done about it on a Friday afternoon. Did you guys contact him? What did he say?" I wanted to talk to him before the police did. I knew from my knowledge about cops that they could put words in a person's mouth and were allowed to lie to extricate information. Bill, a trusting and naïve young man, would be putty in their hands.

Newton said, "We were unable to get hold of him. We called his godparents, the Gielguds in San Marino, listed as his emergency contacts. They gave us the telephone number for the great-aunt he's visiting. We called. Nobody was home. Left a message."

I stayed calm. "If you think he had something to do with the murder, that's crazy. He's one of my most hardworking students—earned a full scholarship to Oxy that I'm sure he wouldn't blow. He thinks the world of archaeology and his professor. And that's why he wanted to intern with Faust. Look—I haven't talked to Bill since he left. From what I've heard so far, the most egregious thing he did was to approach Faust in a public place. Let me talk to him, and if I learn anything new, I'll be sure to—"

"—Urge him to tell the truth, will you?"

I forced a smile. "What else, Detective? I would never suggest to anyone, let alone my student, to lie, since I wouldn't do it."

The good cop side of Newton emerged. "Of course, we're not accusing him of anything, Professor Rao. But one more question while we have you here. How well did you know Faust? We understand that he was your mentor at UCI. Did he collect Indian idols?"

An unusual testiness crept into my voice. "Are you suggesting that Faust stole the Durga? I'm sorry, but these are far-fetched theories, Detective. You don't know anything about these people, yet you condemn them so readily. Joseph Faust was a man of integrity and honesty. And Bill McGraw is a responsible student." I got up, proud of myself for remaining professional after my earlier outburst.

Newton's cheeks reddened and he stroked his chin, looking for a five o'clock shadow that wasn't there. "I can understand your concern for your student and professor. You want to protect them."

"Well, that depends. I want to protect them because I know them as human beings who are incapable of theft or murder. You're accusing them without an ounce of proof."

Newton leaned forward, grabbed a manila folder and started to look through the documents in it. He mumbled something as I left. It could have been a garbled apology or thanks.

* * *

I drove back to campus, thinking of ways to keep my cool with Newton.

I had a lot on my hands. A meeting with Bill at noon, a lecture at 2 pm, and organizing the data for Newton. I was determined to finish with him today. Whether it was his veiled impudence or my troubling attraction for the man in spite of it, I needed to get him out of my life. I tried to daydream about the suitor I would meet Saturday, but with no images in my head, it was a futile exercise.

I turned my computer on and created a print-out of my slides to review them for typos, mismatched arrows, and unclear labels. My lecture that afternoon happened to be on the art and architecture of the Gupta period in Indian history that spanned 320 to 550 CE and overlapped with the earliest presumed age of the idol. This was my favorite lecture every year, to impress on students the glory of the golden age of Indian art. I'd picked out images of the splendid murals that decorated the interiors of the Ajanta caves and examples of Buddhist *stupas*, mound-like structures containing relics of monks or nuns and used as places of meditation. I transferred the PowerPoint presentation to a flash drive and found my lecture notes, but before I could review them, there was a faint knock on the door. I said, "Come in."

Bill entered, his head covered by a flat-brim black Oxy cap decorated all over with multitudes of the letter O in white. The young man walked toward my desk and slouched into the chair across from me. He pulled the cap down over his face. Impeccably dressed in shirtsleeves, Dockers, and a pair of loafers in place of his usual t-shirt, jeans, and tennis shoes, Bill could have been on his way to church except for the hat. I gave him a few seconds until he pushed the cap back, letting strands of curly brown hair tumble onto his forehead, and leaned forward breathing fast.

"Professor Rao, you have to help me. I'm supposed to meet with the homicide detective at the Pasadena Police Department later this afternoon. I told him I had to see you first." He swallowed. "I have nothing to hide. I didn't kill Professor Faust." Bill's words came out like a drum roll. He sank back into the chair and let his arms fall to his sides. "Sorry, I stutter when I'm agitated. I think the police suspect me."

"Calm down, Bill. Take a few deep breaths. Let's talk about it." I took out my notebook and opened a new page. During the interviews I'd conducted with my dad's colleagues, the staff, and Eduardo's family, I'd developed the habit of keeping brief written records of what people said. I had a feeling this young man was about to spill the reason why Faust ended his internship.

Bill took his cap off and ruffled his hair. "I'm worried. I know they'll ask a bunch of questions. What did you do after you left the restaurant? Follow Faust's car? Did you kill him? Professor Rao, have you seen those interrogation rooms in TV shows?" His voice croaked. "Drab, with no windows. No, take it back, there's one window so they can see in, but you can't see them. How's that for fair treatment? They give you a paper cup of water to trap your DNA and keep pounding away at you. The same questions over and over again, hoping to catch you changing your answer." He took a deep breath. "I've seen plenty of *Law and Order.*" There was a touch of sarcasm in his voice.

"Listen, you know real life is not like what you see on TV. I talked to Newton, the senior homicide detective at the station. He's just looking for information. Why don't you start by telling me everything that happened after you met with me Friday afternoon?"

"Well, I stopped by Faust's office to find out if he had an assignment for me for next week. The lady at the front office—I had never seen her before, she said she was a temp—told me to go in and wait for him." Bill sat back and loosened his collar. "I saw his book collections on the bookshelf, and, automatically went there and started looking through them. I thought he'd be pleased to see my interest in his books. You know how much I love archaeology."

"You're sure that's all you did, look through his books? You didn't get into the papers on his desk? There can be confidential information there about recruits, promotion packets, and more. If you were anywhere near his desk, Faust would have reason to think you were snooping."

Bill buried his head in his hands for a few seconds and then looked up. "No, Professor Rao, I would never do anything like that. I swear I was at the bookshelf."

"Did you mess with his books? Put them out of order?"

"That was the funny thing. I was trying to take out a book from the inner row of the middle shelf, I think—closest to the left end. But the book wouldn't lift, like it was anchored to the shelf. You know how books sometimes stick to the bookshelf if they're left there for a long time? It felt like that, but I didn't want to force it. Besides, Professor Faust was at the door staring at me like I was a thief."

"What did he say?"

"He said—I mean shouted—'What the hell are you doing?' I knew he was angry, but he calmed down quickly, apologized, and said he didn't have time to see me and to come back Monday. I left, and when I was at my aunt's place, I got an email from his assistant that said he had to discontinue my internship because of his workload. I called her and was told that he thought I was snooping."

Bill's statement bewildered me. Faust was known for his patience and fairness with students and for encouraging their interest in archaeology. I had never seen him lose his temper. Was Bill lying? Was it about the book he tried to pull up? A rare volume, maybe? I knew Bill far less than my mentor, and if I were to suspect one of the two of poor judgment, it'd be Bill. But I felt the young man was telling the truth.

"Well, I suggest you tell the police exactly what you told me. Look, you can repeat the truth any number of times, and it never changes. It's when people lie that they get caught because they can't remember what they said each time. That's one thing you see on TV that does happen in real life."

"The truth. That I can do, Professor. I know what I did

and didn't do. And what I didn't do, is kill Professor Faust. I'm still worried. My aunt—she's really my great-aunt—knows they're questioning me. She's over eighty, with a weak heart." A rumbling came from Bill's tummy. He blushed. "Sorry, didn't eat breakfast."

I still hadn't heard what happened at Roy's. "Let's meet at Emmons in ten minutes. We can use one of their counseling rooms and get something to eat from the café. OK? Out you go."

* * *

At Emmons, I found Bill hanging around at the entrance. We ordered lunch at the counter. I volunteered to pay for his, which he accepted, and we walked into a small conference room with a table and four chairs. On the walls hung photos of the college and one of the current dean. The room had no windows and regrettably resembled an interrogation room.

As soon as I closed the door, Bill opened his hamburger wrapper. I watched as he shoved the food into his wide-open mouth like he hadn't eaten for days. I sat down and waited a few minutes to allow him to swallow his first bite.

"So tell me, what exactly happened at Roy's? We have barely fifteen minutes." I bit into my grilled eggplant on multigrain bread.

"I was at Roy's with Neil Anderson. He's in your class with me. He's very brainy and kind of quiet. He's an investigative reporter for the Oxy Weekly."

"I heard you tried to talk to Professor Faust." I needed to move this along.

Bill smiled and avoided my eyes. "Yeah, I know. Neil dared me to apologize to him, and without thinking, I took him up on that. I interrupted Faust as he was entering the private dining room. He brushed me off saying he had no time for me or something like that. I never felt so humiliated in my life. I'm sorry, I realize now I shouldn't have done that. It was his special night, and I intruded."

"What were you planning to do about the internship after you got back from your aunt's?"

"I was going to set up an appointment with him today to find out what I could do to get reinstated. But please don't think I'd kill him for that." The stutter was back. "Whoever gets fired from an internship? My interest in archaeology took a dip."

"How did you guys find out where Faust was hosting his dinner?"

Bill rubbed his eyes. "Pure chance. Neil happened to overhear him talking to a colleague, a British dude, in the lobby of the Langham in Pasadena, the conference venue. It was no secret."

I was beginning to think Bill was either downright naïve or the world's craftiest man. "How well do you know Neil?"

Bill stretched his back. "We're roommates. My godparents, the Gielguds, own a small condo on Eagle Rock Boulevard. They rented it to me and I found Neil to share the cost. I do the upkeep and they give me a break in the rent. And Neil is super clean, easy to live with. He mostly keeps to his books. Goes home every weekend to check in on his mom and sister."

"What did you guys do after you interrupted Faust?"

"We ate fast and split. We came in Neil's car. Mine was low on gas. After he dropped me off, he took off for Altadena. To his mother's."

"Did you see him drive off, Bill?"

Bill scratched his head. "Come to think of it, no. I heard

noises from the garage like he was looking for something. We store a lot of our stuff there."

"What was he looking for? When did Neil leave?"

"Looking for the gas can we keep in the garage. After a few minutes, he sent me a text to say he put some in my tank, enough for me to get to a gas station. Then I heard him drive off. It took about fifteen minutes."

"And then what?"

"I must have slept until my alarm woke me up at seven in the morning. Why are you asking me this, Professor Rao? You think I killed Professor Faust?" He looked at me with wide-open eyes.

"No, of course not. I believe you, Bill." I looked at my phone. I needed a few minutes to shift my frame of mind to teaching. Bill went for the rest of his Coke.

I got up. I felt compassion for this young man caught in an inexplicable situation in his professor's office, and now might be a suspect in his murder. "Look, Bill, there's nothing to worry about. Just tell the police what you told me. The truth, OK?"

He stood up, nodded, his shoulders hunched over. He twisted his cap around in his hands.

I added, "And ditch that cap."

I wasn't unduly worried about Bill's interview with the police. It was inevitable that they would question him about the disturbance at Roy's, but hopefully, they'd eliminate him as a suspect. They should know that he could have found another internship or registered a complaint with the Dean. Killing Faust was a punishment that didn't fit the crime.

"Thanks, Professor Rao."

"Let me know how it goes, OK?"

Bill's face brightened. "Neil is writing a report on your

role in the investigation of the murder for the Oxy Weekly. For Wednesday's copy, to follow up on the first report in last Saturday's special edition. Showed me the galleys. A nice one with your photo from the office. We're all proud."

I was aghast. The last thing I wanted was for the world to be aware I was vinvolved in the case, although I knew the news would leak in time. I made a mental note to check with the administration whether Neil should have obtained my consent. If my crazy ex-boyfriend knew anyone at Oxy, there was a chance he might see tomorrow's issue and realize that I worked here. If he hadn't figured it out already.

I said goodbye and headed toward the lecture hall.

The real reason for Faust to end Bill's internship still eluded me. That, and Faust's behavior at Roy's, were uncharacteristic of the sensible and compassionate man I'd known. Looking through the bookshelf seemed like a lame excuse for something else that Faust suspected, or feared Bill was about to do or had already done. Was my mentor hiding something in the bookshelf? I hoped to God it wasn't another idol. From the allusions Newton had made, I knew the police already suspected Faust in the theft of the Durga. Another artifact of any kind concealed in his office would seal the deal. I itched to get into his office and search the bookshelf. But I realized that so soon after his death, the office was likely restricted by yellow tape.

Why did Faust let Bill off lightly with a dismissal from the internship, instead of calling in the big guns? If he'd reported it, he'd have to give the Dean a legitimate reason. Reprimanding a student for looking through his bookshelf wouldn't cut it. I was now more than convinced there was something in the bookshelf that Faust kept private, something that might be linked to his murder. I needed to find it.

* * *

My lecture done, having elicited much animation among my students, I returned to my office and put together a PowerPoint slide show for Newton. I wanted to dazzle him with my research prowess. An hour later, I drove over to the PPD, determined that this would be my last dalliance with Newton.

I found him in his office, standing, looking out the window. He turned to me with narrowed eyes, and said, "Professor Rao. You have information for us." This man made a habit of speaking in statements when a question was warranted. He moved to his armchair and pointed me to a chair across from him.

His desk was cluttered today, with manila folders all over, some open, others closed with rubber bands. A yellow notepad lay open, folded to a page already half-filled with notes. I put my laptop on his desk and pulled up the photos of the idol I'd dated during my literature review. This prompted him to get up and come over to stand behind me. I ignored my heart.

I took Newton in reverse order through examples of twelve-, ten-, eight- and six-armed Durgas, and ended with the one from the Badami cave, the four-armed goddess, sans lion, holding the tail of the buffalo and piercing its neck with a trident. "My research suggests that the idol you found comes closest to this one. It could have originated in the range of 400 to 700 CE. I checked websites and found very few four-armed versions, and most of those are wall reliefs. Museums and collectors would pay any amount of money to acquire it."

"Great. There's your motive for the theft. Why the increase in the number of arms?"

"There's nothing in the references I checked. I'd guess

that the devotees who created the artworks ascribed greater and greater power to the Goddess by increasing the number of her arms, and the weapons she held."

Newton was quiet for a moment. "So, you've confirmed for us that this idol is ancient and valuable. We'd guessed that, but your research substantiates it. Now for the reason why she was left on the victim's back." He sounded unimpressed with my research.

"One second, Detective."

"The name is Al."

I ignored it. "I don't believe theft was the primary motive. If Faust was killed for the priceless idol, why would the thief leave it behind?"

He considered my question. "Happens all the time. Thieves often leave stolen goods behind when caught in the act. Someone must have walked into the scene. That's why the idol was left behind."

I hadn't thought of this. "A third person on the scene. Who could that be? The middleman or the buyer himself?"

"Don't know yet. Looking into it." His voice was sharp and curt. "Can you tell me how this incarnation of the goddess came about?"

I summarized the story about why Durga was created to kill a destructive Mahishasura, how the two battled, and, how Durga triumphed. "Interestingly, before the battle began, the demon asked for the hand of the Goddess in marriage. She refused."

Newton listened to me with his mouth slightly open. "Fascinating. So the killer could have been a rejected lover. But you don't expect me to believe that the killer knew the story and brought the idol for that reason? That's too academic, Professor Rao. C'mon."

"The name is Rekha. In our murder scenario, Faust represents Mahishasura, and the Durga incarnation, the unknown killer. Whoever the latter is, he or she had a grudge against Faust and wanted to kill him to preserve peace in their personal world. The brutal killing suggests it was a matter close to the killer's heart. However, I do agree with you it's too far-fetched to think that a suspect brought the idol because of a story associated with it."

This brought a huge grin on his face that warmed me. "I'm so glad we're both on the same wavelength here. Any more speculations?"

I smiled back. He seemed more like an Al now than a Newton. "I'd like to suggest that the idol was a weapon of opportunity. It happened to be there, and the killer used it to exact revenge. In fact, I'd suggest the killer had no connection to the Durga, did not bring it, did not value it, and discarded it on Faust's back to get rid of it. I bet he was confident he didn't leave any fingerprints on the plastic or the idol itself."

Al squinted and stared at the image of the Durga from the Badami cave. "Possible. Revenge is a common motive for murders. Why was Faust seen as a demon? By whom?"

"I'm sure those close to Faust are among your persons of interest. His son, wife, and possibly a lover of the wife. My top choice is a colleague who might have held a lifelong grudge that finally reached a boiling point. Namely, Davidson." I hoped he'd confirm it.

Al's eyes got bigger. "Where did you learn to talk like a detective, Rekha?"

Here was the dazzle I craved, but it was too late and too little. I was beginning to think I was drawn to this man because I enjoyed self-flagellation.

"Theft and revenge. Double motives, that's our conclusion

as well. You should have been a cop, Rekha." He'd picked up the small difference in the way the *R* in my name was pronounced, without rolling it. He rubbed his hands together and stopped since I didn't join in his delight.

I pressed on. "Do you think Davidson was involved in the theft or the murder? Maybe both? Or, were there two different perpetrators?" I knew he wouldn't answer me.

He said, "Can't tell you. We've hardly begun the investigation."

"Well, then let me suggest something. What if Davidson had arranged for the theft of the idol and came outside to meet the buyer? Faust caught him with it and had to be eliminated. Not wanting to be considered the idol thief, Davidson left the Durga on the body. That eliminates a third person on the scene."

He hesitated for a split second. "Did you know if there was any bad blood between the two?"

"No, I hardly know Davidson, but I've heard they were old friends." Since I held the unshakable belief that my mentor would not steal, I was sure now that Davidson was the most likely thief and killer, whether Newton agreed with me or not. Faust had introduced Davidson to me some time ago as his best friend from their college days. I could imagine the betrayal he must have felt when he faced Davidson holding up the Durga, ready to kill. I blinked. I felt an intense desire to meet Bob Davidson again and discover his grudge against Faust. The overkill, as cops called it, meant the motive was more than the discovery of the theft.

Al said, "What if Faust was the one who stole the Durga? He took it out of the car and Davidson caught him with it. They fought and Davidson killed him to save his own life."

I held my anger. "So, you consider Faust as the idol thief.

Don't you think you should include the integrity of a man in your equation to find the culprit? I do, since I believe that a man of high moral caliber, like him, does not commit theft, all of a sudden. As for Davidson, judge him yourself."

"Ah, your faith in human beings. It's touching, Rekha, but we've witnessed horrendous crimes committed by your so-called good people. Sorry to disillusion you."

I felt myself shrinking and held back the rude retort that came to my lips. I got up to leave. Al motioned me to sit down. "Before you go, I have one more question for you. To close the loop. How well do you know Ginny, the wife? Can she have a connection to the idol?"

Now I had to laugh. I closed my laptop with more force than was needed, making him jump.

"Sorry, Professor, I didn't mean any disrespect. You know we've got to eliminate everyone connected to the victim."

He started scribbling on the notepad.

I felt like a schoolgirl in the principal's office. He didn't thank me for establishing that the Durga was a rare depiction worthy of theft.

"I plan to talk to the family and colleagues. They may reveal information to me that they wouldn't share with a cop."

He got up, walked over, and pointed his finger at my face. "Wait a minute. You are not on our payroll. We have cops trained to do investigations better than you. So do us a favor and leave the detective work to us. Meddling with killers can land you in real danger. Don't tell me later I didn't warn you." His words rattled in my ears.

Forget it, cop man, I said to myself, and smiled at him. I'm going to do it, anyway. I gathered up my belongings and noticed a photo of a young woman in a corner of the desktop under the glass. Lush brown hair tossed to one side, exquisite eyes and a vivacious smile. Was that his wife? Girlfriend?

A commotion rose in the squad room and Al said, "Excuse me. I think someone is here to see me."

Chairs creaked and a pair of high heels went click-click on the old wood floor. I heard a high-pitched woman's voice say, "I am Antonia Gielgud. I was told to report to the station. Who's in charge here?"

I recognized that name, Bill's godmother. Could she have any connection to the murder? I left the station, determined to create an opportunity to talk to the Gielguds.

~ Chapter 4 ~

Thursday, March 30, 2017
Eagle Rock, Los Angeles, CA

Delivering my lecture, making up tests, and working on my proposal for an Indian Art History major at Oxy had kept me occupied and sane the last two days. I received an email from Bill McGraw that his police interview had gone well. I thanked God for that.

I hadn't heard of any progress on the case since my last visit to the PPD. I called Patricia, the administrative assistant at JPM. She was my covert liaison with the Institute.

Patricia sniffled over the phone.

"Hi, Professor Rao. So nice to hear from you. I was wondering how you were coping."

"Hanging in there, Patricia. And, please call me Rekha, I'm not for formalities. Is Professor Striker in?"

"Never mind, Detective Newton is here, and he wants to stop by and see you. Do you have a few minutes?"

I had to say yes. Why had Newton come over here?

Patricia had not hung up. She said, "Girl, that's one handsome dude. That Al Newton. You ought to ask him out." I shushed her, amazed at her spunk, and put the phone down.

An automatic reflex took hold of my hands, and they moved swiftly, rearranging objects on an otherwise uncluttered desktop. I turned back to my computer, pulled up my slides for the next lecture, and looked busy.

There was a knock, a sort of Morse code. Al entered, to my "Come in," and stood rooted just inside the office door as though he had entered an alien kingdom. I was impressed with how fit he looked, with a flat belly.

"Please sit down," I said, after clearing my throat. "What brings you to our hallowed halls?"

He smiled at me. My hands felt clammy.

"I wanted to update you on your student, Professor Rao. I already briefed Striker, but I wanted to talk to you also, as a courtesy."

"OK, so what more have you found out about Bill?"

"Last evening at around 6 pm, we arrested Bill McGraw for the murder of Professor Faust."

I jumped up from my chair. "What? What do you mean? How can you do this? What evidence do you have?" It was one shout after another. Once I finished, I wished I hadn't done it.

"Rekha, I know you are protective of your student. And so you should be, but hear me out. We have a witness who placed Bill's car at Davidson's house around the time of the murder. He identified Bill from his photo as the driver. We've impounded the car and are looking for trace evidence."

"This is unbelievable. How long are you going to hold him? Have you informed his aunt?" I paced back and forth behind the desk, arms folded across my chest, hair coming loose from my ponytail.

"He's in the LA Men's Jail. I'm sure you're familiar with the procedures. If we find evidence, we'll formally charge and arraign him. We've assigned him a Public Defender.

If there's no physical evidence, and if the neighbor cannot ID him in a line-up, we'll let him go."

"And still watch his every move, I'm sure," I mumbled under my breath.

"That's our job," he said emphatically. "Sorry. We have standards just like you academics."

"If that's all, thank you, Detective. Do you mind?" I got up and opened the door. "I need to stretch my legs." As I stepped out, he followed me. He seemed to be in no hurry and stood just behind me.

"You're dedicated to everything you do, Rekha." He sounded genuinely complimentary.

It could have been downright romantic except I had just yelled at him. I took a short path that brought me to Bird Road, Al at my side, keeping pace.

"Why does the fact that I'm dedicated surprise you, Detective? I'm as much of a perfectionist as you are."

He chuckled, "You sure are. That's something we have in common."

I walked fast to get back into my office, hoping Al would take a different direction and go find his car or something. But he stayed with me. At the corner of Bird and Gilman, I couldn't contain my anger any longer. I turned to him. "Cops, you're all the same. Accusing and jailing innocent people without sufficient evidence. I was wrong to think that the Pasadena Police would have more efficiency and decency than the cops at Irvine." I was up close to his face by now and couldn't hide my grief and hopelessness. About Eduardo Lopez, Dad's murder, and now Bill, arrested for Faust's murder. Tears welled up and flowed down my cheeks.

Al stepped back a little, his eyes narrowed in a question. "What're you saying? What does this arrest have to do with

. . . Irvine? I'm sorry, Rekha, did I offend you in some way?"

I halted my walk, feeling a little foolish for getting emotional. I took a couple of breaths and lowered my voice. I could see students walking along the road, but I blocked them out. "My father was murdered three years ago. Bludgeoned to death, like Faust. The Irvine police convicted a janitor because they were inept at finding the real killer. I pleaded with them to reopen the case when I found new evidence that clearly would have exonerated him. But would they, like the professionals they're supposed to be? No. I wasted my time, destroyed my academic future, and an innocent man is spending his life in prison. And now it's happening again."

I turned the corner on to Gilman Road. Newton came after me and grabbed my arm. "Rekha, I didn't know anything about your dad's murder or your previous experience with the Irvine Police. We in Pasadena play by the rules, no exceptions. We arrested Bill because we found circumstantial evidence against him. The best you can do now is to get him a good defense lawyer."

He let go of my arm and waited for a response.

I did nothing.

"I can promise you we'll treat him well. And once this case is wrapped up, with your permission, I can look into your dad's murder. I promise you that much."

I turned right from Gilman onto a path that would take me back to my office, but, in my wretched mind, I found the grace to face him. He sounded genuine, kind, and wouldn't promise anything that he couldn't deliver. I offered him my outstretched hand. "Thank you, Al. Good night."

He stood there like an amnesiac who didn't know which way was home. My lizard brain told me to run back and hug him. But my executive brain reminded me that I didn't know if he was another Templeton, or maybe even another Matt Porter. I might be looking for love in all the wrong places.

I unlocked my office door, closed it behind me and stood leaning on it, battling my conflicted anger and attraction.

From the door, I noticed the message light on my desk phone. I turned it on. There were three messages. The first one was from Neil Anderson, "They arrested Bill. He asked me to talk to you." His voice sounded plaintive and I could feel his fear. The next one was from my Chair, asking me to find out the details of Bill McGraw's arrest and report back to her. And the third was an unfamiliar shaky female voice that said, "Ms. Rao, I'm Bill's great-aunt, Nancy . . . his roommate Neil called me. . . . Please tell me what's going on. And, please help my nephew, he's not a murderer."

I fell into my chair, exasperated. "What the bloody hell . . ."

I knew the police worked fast to nail suspects, the detectives to save their jobs and the lieutenants, for serving it up to the Captain, the media, and the public. But still, what additional evidence did they find within such a short time to arrest Bill? I was still working on his dismissal from the internship and Faust's uncharacteristic behavior at the restaurant. I desperately needed to talk to both of them, but only Bill was alive, and he was in jail.

I emailed Neil, "Please meet me in my office tomorrow morning at eight."

* * *

Back at home, I couldn't sleep.

The police suspected Faust of theft and had jailed Bill, a young man who didn't have even a misdemeanor on his record. I felt the pull of my dharma to help them and did what was habitual for me in moments of uncertainty. I talked to Dad.

I sat cross-legged on the carpet on the floor in front of his photo, my palms together and eyes closed. I used dharma to justify my pursuit of Faust's killer. Did I have his blessings? Will I fail again? Will PTSD hold me captive? What was I to do with my feelings for an older white cop? Then I heard him, "Remember Rekha, there are no guarantees in life. You fail only when you do nothing when your heart compels you to do it." Dad's voice seemed to emerge from within me, as though it was my inner voice, convincing and strong. I promised him that once I found Faust's killer, I would work to free Eduardo Lopez.

I also made a promise to myself that I'd take care of all aspects of my dharma this time. I'd attend to my job, my family. Like Dorothy's yellow brick road, I saw my path in front of me, lit by torches. But, unlike Dorothy, I had no companions on this journey, and, unlike the road that led her to the Wizard of Oz, I didn't know what awaited me at the end. But one thing was certain, I must take it with conviction, without any ultimate reward as my objective.

I powered up my laptop and opened the list of suspects I had almost half-heartedly created earlier, not sure if I'd even use it. It had Davidson at the top, and then, in no particular order, Faust's wife Ginny Faust, son Kevin Faust, and Reddy's colleague Patel. The last one was way beyond my reach and I deleted it, knowing that Patel might have stolen the Durga, but wouldn't travel to the U.S. to kill Faust and leave the idol behind. It was a commonsense list, in part borrowed from police philosophy that close friends and family were the first to be ruled out. Davidson was on the top because the murder occurred in his neck of the woods. I recalled the possibility that Al had raised—the idea of an unknown third person who could have been at the scene, brought the Durga and used it to kill Faust. I'd heard the term "Unsub" used on my favorite crime show, *Criminal Minds,* to refer to an unknown subject or suspect. I added an Unsub at the bottom of my list.

My first task would be to talk to those on my shortlist. I was already familiar with the process, having done it three years ago to find new evidence related to my Dad's murder.

I couldn't wait to wake up the next morning.

~ Chapter 5 ~

Friday, March 31, 2017
Eagle Rock, Los Angeles, CA

I found Neil Anderson on the floor next to my office with a cup of coffee in his hand, a paper bag and his backpack resting beside him. As soon as he saw me, he got up, and as I opened the door, put a half-eaten donut back into the paper bag. "Good morning, Professor Rao."

I unlocked the door, put my satchel on the desk, and took out my notebook and pen. My office wasn't much larger than Al's at the PPD, but I'd given it my personal touch. On the wall, I'd placed a painting of the elephant-headed Hindu God, Ganesha, and on my desk, a *Bhagavad Gita*, and the latest family photo that included Dad. A small Indian rug kept my feet cozy.

"So, what happened, Neil?" I saw his eyes fixated on my notebook. "I'm just jotting things down before I forget." I made it sound casual.

Neil perked up. "It was yesterday, a few hours after Bill went to the station to make his statement. He came back and told me it had all gone well. Then they came over, turned the place upside down, and arrested Bill. They took his car. Later he called, to ask me to let you and his aunt know. It was a shock." He offered me the bag which I presumed contained more goodies.

I shook my head.

He put his hand in the bag, took out a donut piece, and put it in his mouth. Neil looked well dressed as always, in a striped, long-sleeved shirt and black jeans that showed off his pale brown complexion, dark brown eyes, and auburn hair. An Antonio Banderas look. Spanish or Native American blood must run in his veins, I thought.

He continued. "Bill told me he was arrested because a neighbor saw his car in the alley next to the murder scene. The neighbor was certain that he saw Bill inside the car in the driver's seat. That cannot be true. Bill didn't use his car. His car was low on gas."

"So, how did he get to Roy's?"

Neil's jaw was working quietly, but he looked worried. "I gave him a ride to the conference and to Roy's, the restaurant you know, and we came back together. He'd left his car at our house. Bill's a cool dude, Professor Rao. He was so in awe of Professor Faust, he'd never have harmed him. Besides, I wasn't sure if his car would even make it to the gas station. So before I took off home around midnight, I put just enough in his tank so he could get to the gas station. From a quarter can of gas I keep for emergencies,"

"That was very kind of you, Neil. Then what happened?"

He coughed, his face red, and swallowed some coffee. "I'm sure they're looking for physical evidence. Bloodstains, fingerprints, DNA, anything to nail him. Once they find it, they'll hold on to him until they prove he had the motive, means and opportunity to commit the crime. Bill now has an uphill battle to prove his innocence." He stopped and looked at me as though he had spoken too much.

Neil's verbosity surprised me. In class, he never spoke. I wondered if he had been in any skirmish with the police in the past. "I wouldn't put it as you did, but the police have one-track minds, once they find physical evidence. But let's hope there wasn't anything to find."

Neil said, "I'm also under suspicion now and had to give my statement. They took my blood and fingerprints. They will talk to my mom about what time I got home that night. It was just after midnight."

"What happened at Roy's?"

"Well, the conference ended, and it was a huge letdown for us. We wanted to follow the celebrities for a drink . . ." Neil stopped and stared at me.

"Where you go in the evening is not my concern. But what prompted you to get Bill in trouble? Didn't you say he's a friend?"

Neil's voice was now barely audible. He took another swallow. "I'm not sure why I did it. I guess I saw Professor Faust about to enter the private dining room and thought it was a good opportunity for Bill to apologize and get his internship back. I didn't think Bill would follow through. I'm sorry I prodded him." He looked down at the bag in his hand. When he looked up, I could swear I noticed a shine in his eyes. "Will the Dean reprimand me for that?"

"Talk to your advisor. Where did you guys go from the restaurant?"

"After the 'incident'," Neil made air quotes, "we finished our meal and left in a hurry. I dropped Bill off, put gas in his car and went home to Altadena. I do that on the weekends if I can. To help my mother and little sis, Melissa." He hesitated. "Mother must have heard me come in a little after midnight. In the morning, I had breakfast with her and Melissa. But

I guess a mother's words are not good enough."

I realized his father was probably not in the picture. What a kind young man, to go home from college on weekends to help his family while others were partying. In my book, it amounted to something, "Don't put yourself in the box yet, Neil. Do what your advisor suggests. Get back to your studies."

He crumpled up the empty paper bag and started to aim it for the trash can in the corner, stopped, walked over and dropped it in.

"Bill must have told you his internship was terminated. Did he tell you why?" I got up, opened the mini-fridge in the corner and took out a bottle of water. "Would you like some?"

"No, thanks. Bill emailed me the same day from his aunt's place. He'd heard about it from Professor Faust's assistant. He said all he did was look through the bookshelf. He was going to set up a time to talk to the professor. He thinks his grade report might include the dismissal and might work against him. He did nothing wrong. I feel sorry for him."

"Why didn't you apply for an internship with Professor Faust?"

"I thought I didn't need one since I'm planning to apply for a student membership on his next dig. He reserves two spots for seniors and selects them based on a thesis proposal early in the junior year. I've been working on it and hoped Professor Faust would read it before it was due." The left corner of his mouth went up in a partial smile. "Straight and narrow never worked for me."

"So, did Professor Faust read it? It's unusual for a sophomore to submit a junior thesis proposal before it's called for." How arrogantly confident. I rubbed my forehead where a headache was building up.

Neil gave a small laugh. "No. He wouldn't read it. I asked him several times in several ways, but he said to wait until it was due. I found that very discouraging."

"Well, Neil, he did the right thing. We, the faculty, cannot show favoritism to students. That would taint the objectivity we have to uphold." Seeing him frown, I doodled in my notebook.

Neil leaned closer to my desk. "Please. Bill is my roommate and best buddy. I wouldn't do anything to damage his reputation. I swear, he took off toward Faust before I could get the words out of my mouth that I was joking. I'm sorry. More than anything, I wouldn't want you to think I am mean-spirited." He looked away with a shy smile. "I respect you like my mother. Not my adoptive mother, but the picture I have in my mind of my birth mother, whom I've never met."

I hoped we were not into spilling unsolicited family secrets. I leaned back in my chair as I was getting uncomfortable with Neil. "You're adopted? I didn't know that, not that that makes any difference to me as your professor." I ignored his comparison of me to his birth mother, it was creepy.

Neil hesitated for a moment. "Did the Dean's office let you know that I've requested you for an advisor?"

I was surprised. "No, but I'm sure it's in an email or memo that I haven't yet seen. Why me? I'm sure others can guide you better for a career in archaeology. Who is your current advisor?"

Neil grimaced. "Professor Davidson, but he and I don't see eye to eye. And after Faust's death, I heard he's considering retirement."

"Let me see if he can recommend someone. I'm surprised he hasn't."

"No. No point asking him. I'm thinking of changing

directions. I've become fascinated with Hinduism. I'm sure you can help me find the right classes to get into a good grad school."

This dumbfounded me. Not seeing eye to eye with his advisor? Switching from archaeology to Hinduism? He'd be hitched to my hips for the next two years and more. "All right. Please set up a meeting with me to review the classes you've already taken, and we can come up with what you need to fill in. But are you sure of switching? It seems like a rash decision. Think it over, OK?"

Neil nodded, got up and stood to look at my desk as though trying to make up his mind. "Are you religious, Professor Rao? Sorry, maybe that is an inappropriate question." He pointed at the Bhagavad Gita on my desk. It was a gift from Ma when I left home. "May I?"

I nodded, although I didn't want his hands on it. "Well, I'd say I'm not a devout Hindu, but I believe in a supreme power that guides us. Look, I have to get ready for my next lecture. Let's talk more about your career choice when we meet next." I stood up.

Neil opened the book and turned the pages. "I know what this is, the Hindu Bible, right? Full of sage advice from God Krishna to the warrior, Arjuna." He closed it and put it back. "Professor Rao, I am an investigative reporter for the student newspaper. I plan to do a series of articles on the case. Next week, it'll be about Bill's arrest. I've Bill's permission to report it." He paused and seemed to consider something. "My source at the station tells me you have met with the police a couple of times. Can you elaborate on what you are helping them with?" He whipped out his cell phone to record my answer. "I'd like to include that in the next edition. Make you and our school look good."

He must have seen my frown, because he put the phone back in his pocket, spread his arms wide, shrugged, and smiled. "Freedom of the press, Professor Rao." And walked out of my office.

I made a quick call to Patricia. I needed to get the inside scoop on why Faust ended Bill's internship before I met with him in jail.

Patricia was more than generous with her time. "As you know, it happened the day I was sick, and a temp was managing the desk. She told me she'd asked Bill to go in and wait which she later realized was a mistake. She heard loud voices from the office and soon Bill came out, red in the face, and took off. Professor F told her never to let anyone wait inside his office, and to leave me a note that he'd terminated Bill's internship. It was strange, I tell you. I've never heard him get angry at students. I suspect he had a good reason this time, but he and McGraw are the only ones who know what transpired between them."

My questions for Bill crystallized in my mind.

~ Chapter 6 ~

Friday, March 31, 2017
Los Angeles, CA

I had an hour for my meeting with Bill. I had called first thing in the morning and an authoritative voice told me that since Bill didn't have any relatives nearby, either his godparents or I would be allowed to see him. I'd called first. I had to show proof of my faculty position at Oxy and my role as Bill's academic advisor. No problem. Our advisor-advisee relationship left me at ease to talk to him. The power of his aunt's plea gave me strength.

Men's Central Jail, under the jurisdiction of the LA County Sheriff's department, was located on Bauchet Street. A gray concrete building that looked like it was constructed of Lego blocks, it proclaimed its name in large yellow letters. After the painfully detailed security check, I was directed to the visitor's room that was as bleak as the outside. I sat down on one of the two gray chairs at a square metal table and took my notebook out of my satchel.

The door opened and Bill walked in accompanied by a guard, who pointed him to the chair across from me and took his seat near the door.

"Professor Rao, I'm so glad you could come." In his blue

prison garb, his cheeks drawn and eyes listless, he still smiled.

"Bill, they let me speak to you because you're my advisee, and your great-aunt couldn't be here. I wanted to make sure you're doing OK. I also have to ask you some questions so I can help you get out of here. How are you?"

"Not too bad. They're holding me for 48 hours while they search for evidence in my car. I'll also have to stand in a line-up for Faust's neighbor who reported seeing me in the alley near the house. I'm sure he will realize his mistake. I didn't use my car, and I was nowhere near there." Bill rubbed his palms together. "As for asking questions, go ahead, anything to get me out of here."

I was afraid that if they jailed him, I'd lose all access. He was my lone informant of how the case was evolving. Al had kept his silence ever since our heated encounter on campus. "Tell me what happened after Neil dropped you off."

"As I told the officers, I left my car at our house and went to the conference with Neil. I was low on gas. He gave me a ride to Roy's and from there, took me home to Eagle Rock. Neil put some gas in my car from a can he kept in the garage so I could take it to the gas station next morning. Before he drove off, he texted me and I responded, saying, 'thanks'. In the morning, I drove my car to the school to see you, and went to the police station. Detective Newton talked to me and everything sounded good. But after I got home, they came, took my car, and arrested me. Newton asked me why I was near Davidson's house the night Faust was killed. I told him I wasn't." He stuttered the last few words.

"So you heard Neil drive off, right?"

"Yes, it took a few minutes but when I got the text I realized the reason for the delay."

I knew that all that confirmed was that Neil had left their

apartment. It didn't tell me where he went. But unlike Bill, he had no obvious connection to Faust, looked forward to getting a student position on his next excavation, and hoped to become a graduate student in archaeology. But what about his sudden desire to switch to Hinduism? Was he involved in the theft of the Durga? "Did you notice anything different when you started your car the next morning? Were there any smudges, blood or things that didn't belong to you?"

Bill ran his fingers through his unkempt hair. "The police asked the same thing. No, the car looked the same as before."

"Did the cops question you about anything they found in your apartment?"

Bill blinked. "No, but there was nothing to find, other than textbooks, notebooks, and personal items."

"What can you tell me about Neil?" I purposely delayed asking him about what happened in Faust's office. I wanted him to be at ease when I got to it.

Bill closed his eyes for a few seconds. I scrutinized him, wanting to believe him.

"I've known Neil for two years now. He grew up on a farm and went to local schools, but got into Oxy because of his smarts and stick-to-it-iveness. Financially, he has to scrimp and save to stay in college, even with a scholarship. Brings home-grown produce to cook his meals." He stared at me for a few seconds. "You don't think he killed Professor Faust? No way would he destroy everything he'd worked for. Do you know he chose Oxy at the last minute because Faust was teaching here?"

That was an interesting piece of information. It seemed that Neil might have already narrowed down archaeology for his undergrad major before starting college. Students rarely selected that early. Most waited till the latter half of their sophomore year. Why a special interest in Faust, other than the fact that he was world-renowned in the field? I had more questions for Neil.

"Do you know where his parents live?

"In Altadena . . . it's just his mom and kid sister. I was there once during a break. Neil's mom cooked us up a great dinner. They seem to live a modest life, like my aunt."

"You think Neil held any grudges against Faust?"

Bill laughed. "No way. Neil thought Faust was God incarnate. He was hoping to impress him with his thesis proposal to get into one of his digs as a student assistant before he applied to his graduate program. He loves archaeology. Professor Faust was kind enough to meet with him a couple of times, I think." Bill lowered his eyes. "He was a great man and now he's dead. It's not fair."

"I know, Bill. We're all grieving." My heart went out to him. "Who owns your apartment? How did you come to rent it?"

Bill's face perked up. "My godparents, the Gielguds. They're antique dealers. Believe it or not, my aunt met them a couple of years ago when she took a course on antiques. They became good friends and when they found out I was going to Oxy, they offered me a condo in their rental unit at a subsidized rent. I recruited Neil for a roommate."

"Did they know the Fausts? Or the Davidsons?"

Bill leaned forward as if wanting to share a confidence with me. "I know what you're thinking, but you're wrong, Professor Rao. I don't think they knew Faust. And the Gielguds are not the type of people who engage in illegal activities. Or . . . kill others."

It would have made my quest easy if there were *types* that killed.

Bill continued. "As for Davidson, I'd seen him at their collector parties."

"What are those?"

"Well, every two years or so, they have a party for their collector friends who come to see new items they'd secured. I happened to be there once or twice. Boring." He smiled.

"Where do they live, Bill?"

"In San Marino."

"I need to know you a little better. Have you run into any problems with the police before?"

"Eh?" For a second, Bill looked like I'd flashed a light on his eyes. He clasped his restless hands and planted them on the table. "You may find this unbelievable, but I was an unruly kid, always into trouble throughout my early teens, but nothing serious. I'm so thankful my aunt didn't give up on me." He paused for a few seconds and stared straight ahead at the blank wall opposite him. "And here I am in jail accused of murder."

"Let's see if we can get you out of this mess."

The cop at the door stopped reading and looked at us.

I asked in my calmest voice, "Focus, Bill. You told me yesterday you didn't know why Faust ended your internship. Tell me again what happened last Friday in his office, without leaving anything out."

Bill looked down and fiddled with his fingers. "OK, I had only been doing the internship for a week. I was assigned to help catalog photos of the Jwalapuram microliths for a digital library. I worked mostly with his lab assistant but once a week I was supposed to meet with Professor Faust in his office, to discuss papers he'd assigned. It would've been great to have someone of his caliber give me twenty minutes of his precious time. As it turned out, I got fired at the first meeting."

The cop looked again and got back to what he was reading.

"Get to the point, Bill. What happened that day?"

Bill glanced at the cop and frowned. "I told you already, Professor Rao. The woman at the front desk told me I could go in and wait for him. I was in his office and was going to take a book from his bookshelf when he walked in. He stared at me and asked what I was doing. He was very angry. I mumbled something about my interest in archaeology. He told me he had no time to see me and to come back Monday."

I knew the layout of his office. "He has built-in bookshelves on both sides of the desk. Where were you at?"

"The one on the right."

"Which shelf was the book on?"

"The fourth from the bottom, I think." He touched his shoulder. "It was at my shoulder level. And, this might be my imagination, you know, watching *Forensic Files* and all, but I've been thinking about it all this time."

"Go on, be specific."

"See, each shelf had two rows of books with the larger ones in the inner rows. I tried to pull out the book at the left end of the inner row. I didn't remember the title when I talked to you earlier. Now I do, *Southeast Asia: From Prehistory to History*. I was interested in looking at the Table of Contents, but the book wouldn't come out. As though it was stuck to the shelf. Then, of course, Faust came in."

The cop moved to us and said, "Your time's up, son." He turned to me and said, "Sorry."

We both stood up. I said, "Is that all you can tell me about the book? Promise me you're telling the truth, Bill."

As he was led away by the guard, Bill turned to me, nodded and said, "That's all I know, honest. Please help me,

I'm no murderer."

I nodded back and walked out. I wasn't confident I could help him, but his pallid face and tremulous hands as he walked away, cemented the decision I took the night before. Nothing I had learned from him suggested Bill was a murderer. But I also knew it was too early to eliminate him as a suspect.

~ Chapter 7 ~

Saturday, April 1, 2017
Culver City, CA

The special family dinner hovered in the background like a cobra lying in wait for its prey, but I had one more errand to run. I wanted to see Ginny Faust.

I had met Ginny on several occasions at UCI when Faust arranged dinner meetings with his advisees at local restaurants. On one occasion, Ginny wanted to surprise her husband by dressing in an Indian outfit, a *sari* he'd brought back from India. I helped her pick out a turquoise silk top, matching underskirt, and helped her put them on. It brought a sparkle to Faust's eyes. I knew Ginny would remember me.

The Fausts lived in Culver City on Charles Avenue. The street had an eclectic collection of homes, each with its unique style, some left to age, and others given a new life with complete or partial remodeling. The Faust home appeared to be in the latter category, with old and new coming together sharply with no middle ground for transition. In the front yard, everything grew wild. A massive bougainvillea placed too close to a tree seemed to get its sustenance from strangling it. Jasmine bushes were overgrown with fading blooms that still exuded a rich aroma. The Fausts were no gardeners.

I rang the doorbell and knocked twice before the door opened and Ginny's head peeked out.

I said, "Hi, Ginny."

She looked confused and said, "Can you give me a few minutes, Rekha? I need to change. Have a seat, please."

I looked around the living room: shaker-style furniture, fabric Roman shades with matching carpet on a wood floor. Photos of the family adorned the walls. Kevin was everywhere, as a baby, a toddler, an awkward teenager, and a young adult with the pretense of confidence and self-esteem. This was the first time I'd had a look at him. He looked so much like his father.

At the sound of shuffling feet, I turned and saw Ginny, who gestured to me to follow her. "I am sorry to keep you waiting, Rekha." She looked around and frowned. "Kevin had promised to answer the door."

The hallway we went through led to a sliding glass door that opened into the backyard, with sand-colored paving stones leading to a redwood building in the corner. Ginny led me into a large room with a wooden floor and two windows that opened into the side yard. In the center of the ceiling, there was a rectangular skylight.

Ginny looked like she might have gained a few pounds since I saw her last, but the regal look was still there. She was in a well-tailored gray dress that fell to her mid-calf. Over it, she wore an unbuttoned navy cardigan. She had no jewelry on, other than her wedding ring that she kept twisting around and around her pale finger. Brick-red lipstick was her only make-up, a bright and cheery mask on a desolate face.

"Thanks for seeing me, Ginny. And I'm so sorry," I said as I accepted the delicate hand the woman offered.

Ginny pulled out a chair for me. I took it, resisting my

first impulse to look at the creative space where she found her inspiration. And comfort.

"How nice to see you, Rekha, I remember you well," Ginny said in a clipped British accent. Ginny lost her words for a few seconds. "This is my haven, a place where I could feel Joe's spirit." She pointed to an incomplete portrait of Faust in the center of the room. "He loved it. He used to come in when he had free time, sit for me, and watch me paint. That was our time together."

I put my hand on her shoulder. "Ginny, you know how much I respected and admired your husband as a scholar and mentor. His quiet dignity and lack of pretensions . . . I'm so sorry. Professor Faust became a father figure to me after my Dad died. I was looking forward to his continued guidance when I joined Oxy. Now both are gone." I consciously avoided bringing up the word murder.

Ginny blinked a few times and looked at me again. "Joe did tell me about your father. I'm sorry. Two good souls lost to this world." She shook her head as if denying the deaths. "I heard you were helping the police with the idol. What can I do for you, Rekha?"

I marveled at her grace, even in grief. Knowing I needed to show her the close-up photo of the Durga on Faust's back, possibly for the second time, I had taped it on to a plain piece of paper with the tapes hiding the images of Faust's tie. "Will you take another look at the photo of the idol for me? I'm sure the police showed it to you already, but I wondered if you recalled anything new since then."

I gave the photo of Durga to Ginny. "I'm sorry, but it was used to kill your husband, and the killer left it on his body."

She took the photo and stared at it for a few seconds. "Some cruel joke, I'm sure. When the detective showed it to me earlier, it was the first time I had set eyes on it. Of course, I recognize it as Durga from the Hindu religion. I took a class on world religions some time ago and Durga was a favorite of the women students. I wish I had her strength." Ginny circled the image with the fingers of her right hand, as though seeking a blessing.

"Do you think your husband knew anything about it?" I asked.

She frowned. "I am sorry, but my husband did not usually bring his work home except what was on his laptop." Ginny smiled. "But that laptop was never far from his reach. I never opened it or looked at any of his files on it. So, no, I do not know if he had it or not. I did not think Indian deities attracted his attention. Does the idol belong to the killer? The police would not tell me anything."

"The police think there might be a link between the Durga, the killer, and your husband. Since we're in the dark about the killer at this time, any connection between your husband and the idol is all we can explore. Can you think of any Indian connection your husband might have had in the past? Was there an Indian staff member or colleague who could have held a grudge against him?"

She arched her eyebrows, making lines on her forehead. "Nothing comes to my mind, Rekha. You knew Joe, he was a peacemaker, resolving issues before they became problems. He was fair-minded to a fault." She shrugged.

"Please think about it and call me if anything occurs to you." I handed Ginny my card and stood up. "Do you mind if I look around? I'm in awe of people like you who paint, something that I have no talent for."

In a split second, Ginny became energized. She got up from her chair and said, "Feel free but I have to warn you, I am not that good. Yet." She gave a faint smile with tight lips, and said, "Would you share some tea with me, Rekha? I have not eaten much today."

She was already at the door by the time I'd nodded, holding back the excuses that came to my mind.

When Ginny closed the door behind her, I took a quick tour of the space. The studio, its walls painted in cream, contained several easels on wheels with paintings in various stages of completion that could be moved around the room to get any type of lighting the artist desired.

There were landscapes, still lifes, and a few portraits. Under the skylight, there was a *plein-air* work that lit up a desolate seashore with the luminous effects of natural light. It filled me with a child-like abandon, clearly the artist's objective. My eyes drifted to an attempt at copying an abstract painting. Its original stood nearby.

Unused canvases and frames were neatly stored in open cupboards made of light grain wood. A utility sink and drying rack were in a corner. A trolley held acrylic paints in tubes and bottles, and brushes of all sizes and types. Several rolled-up canvases leaned against a cupboard. I opened a few of them and found they were sketches of Faust and Kevin in outdoor settings, drawn in ink with watercolor washes added here and there. As I leaned them back in place, I noticed a dark object tucked away behind the cupboard. I pulled it out.

It was a portfolio of five by seven photos and incomplete sketches of a man dressed informally in jeans and a short-sleeved plaid shirt. A smiling, debonair face of a middle-aged man. He looked like someone I'd met a while ago, but I couldn't quite place him. I pulled out my cell phone and took a couple of photos. I turned a few blank pages and found a few more photos toward the back of the portfolio, this time of a young boy dressed up in girl's clothes. In some, the boy was possibly four or five, and in others, maybe a couple of years older. He sported a variety of outfits, a long velvet skirt and short-sleeved blouse in one, a black sheath dress in another, and a sporty tennis dress in yet another. Was that Kevin? Why hide them if it was Kevin dressed up as a girl, as kids often did for fun? I captured a couple of them with my cell phone and made a note to ask Ginny, if not now, later.

As I put the portfolio away, Ginny returned and placed a tray of teacups, a teapot, and a plate of Marie biscuits on a small table near the chairs. She looked more relaxed as she poured me a cup of tea.

"How was your police interview?" I added some milk to my cup and sipped the tea.

"Well, the detective who came to see me made me feel I had something to do with it. I suppose that's the way they operate. Have you ever had to deal with them?"

"You wouldn't know this, but my father was also brutally murdered three years ago. It happened after your husband moved to Oxy and we lost touch. I recall the detectives asking me, my mother, and brother questions that made us uncomfortable. But we assumed that was what little we could do to help them move the case forward."

Ginny stared at me, her hand to her mouth. "Oh my God. How was he killed? How terrible. Did they find who did it?" She leaned forward and touched my forearm.

"He . . . was also bludgeoned to death. They convicted a Hispanic janitor who was found holding a bloody baseball bat. But our whole family knew the man. He worked days as a handyman and had done some work for us. I was . . . I am convinced they have the wrong man." It wasn't my plan to make my Dad's murder the center of our conversation.

"You mean . . . they were both killed the same way?" She said in a whisper.

I nodded and brought her back to the present. "Did the detective ask you about your movements during the day?"

"Yes, he did, and I told him. I always attended social events that honored my husband. There were several in the last few years. Joe understood my lack of appetite for the more scientific talks and it was OK with him if I skipped them." She stopped and started again. "But the evening of the award presentation was special for him and I attended the first part and left right after Joe's acceptance speech. His party was a guys' thing. Beer and loud talk and patting each other's backs for their achievements." She gave a feeble smile. "I was about to call the Davidsons before Joe took off for Santa Cruz." Ginny fumbled with a handkerchief. "Before I did, Bob called, and I knew right away from his somber tone that something was wrong . . . I wondered if Joe had had an accident or something. Never expected to hear the word murder. It was and still is bizarre to think someone would do that to another human being, to Joe . . . and to your father. I am sorry, Rekha." Ginny put her head in her hands and her shoulders heaved up and down.

I found a tissue box and placed it next to her and gently touched her shoulder. "I understand, Ginny. You don't need to say anything more."

She looked up in a quick motion. "No, I must. I am sorry, I am skipping around. I spent the afternoon and early evening here in my studio. I took up painting a few years ago and poor Joe was so proud of my progress." She wiped her eyes and proceeded. "I drove to the award ceremony with Shelia, a friend of mine. We had a quick chat with Joe when the ceremony ended and took off for a light meal. Sheila dropped me off at about ten and I went to bed. I read for an hour or so and fell asleep. I gave the detective her name and phone number."

"That must have satisfied him."

"That was why I was surprised when he asked if anyone saw me after I got home. How could anyone? Most of the time, there's no one else in the house. Kevin comes by occasionally, usually without notice." Her eyes widened in disbelief. "I am sure the detective thought I had something to do with the murder. Why would I want to kill my husband? I adored him."

I said, "Well, their excuse is that they've to confirm everyone's whereabouts. That's the procedure. The sooner they eliminate the family, the faster they can get to the real culprit. They don't worry about what's appropriate or not."

"I know what you mean. The detective even dug up our divorce that we had not even finalized. Yes, we were getting the paperwork done through a mediator. All our friends knew."

I said in a gentle voice, "I'm sorry to hear that. Can you tell me why, if you don't mind?"

Ginny cast her teary eyes around the room. "Joe and I had been drifting apart for a while, but we were still the best of friends. So I was surprised when two years ago he brought up the issue of a divorce. We went to therapy for a whole year. Nothing came of it. Joe was insistent. He said he wanted to settle more than half of our estate on Kevin and me. I could not for the life of me see the reason for any of it. Why not live as friends? I had no desire to find anyone else at my age."

"Did your husband?" I asked.

"Not to my knowledge, though I understand the wife is always the last to know." She grimaced. "To be honest, I did wonder if he was attracted to another woman, and being the principled man he was, he chose not to do anything with it until he obtained a divorce from me. I am struggling to find the truth, Rekha."

"Did Kevin get along with his dad?"

"Reasonably well. Joe had hoped that Kevin would follow in his footsteps into academia but they both knew it was a lost cause. Kevin is a dreamer. His nose is buried in books. I sensed that Joe had made peace with Kevin's decision to choose literature as his major and become a writer. He worried whether he could make a living after the trust fund depleted."

"How did Kevin take the impending divorce?" I asked.

"Not well. He got into an argument with Joe when he first heard about it. In his eyes, we were the ideal married couple. Children know only what they witness. He did not see the two of us sleeping apart from each other in the same bed. He asked Joe why he could not leave well enough alone."

"When was this?"

"About a month ago. Here at home during dinner. I had never heard Kevin yell at his father like he did that night. Joe tried to explain and then kept quiet. After Kevin left, Joe said to me it was good that he'd vented. He said he would under-stand if I yelled at him as well." She poured more tea into my cup in an absent-minded way.

I shook my head and asked, "Did you, at any point, fight over the divorce?"

"Yes, I was furious at first, and after that cried a lot. I am still trying to figure out what had gotten into my husband of twenty years. I truly thought there was another woman. At first, Joe denied any affairs, but he recently told me to go ahead and think that he had a mistress if that gave me comfort. Strange."

I thought about asking if *she* was having an affair but held my tongue out of respect for her grief. "Do you think Kevin would talk to me?"

"I'm sure, why would he not? He did not kill his father." This was a matter-of-fact statement. She paused. "Your father's murder, Rekha. How . . . how did you come to terms with it? Have you?"

"No, and I think I never will. That's the truth." Especially with Eduardo Lopez in prison for life.

"Why did you move from UCI? I thought it was a good fit for you."

I had no choice but to tell her the whole truth. "For two years after my Dad died, I spent all my time talking to people who knew the convicted man and his relatives, and the doctors and nurses who knew my father at work. I found some new information and tried to convince the police to reopen the case. It came to nothing, and it cost me my tenure. I had to leave. I was so happy to get a job at Oxy because your husband was there. Now I'm like a rudderless boat, without a dad or a mentor."

Ginny grabbed my hands again and looked into my eyes. "I'm so sorry, Rekha, so sorry." She quickly dropped my hands, stood up, moved away to the window, and looked out. "You know, I am now worried that Joe's murder could be related to his connection with another woman. I used to worry about his assistant Patricia. And the students who adored him. I need to know. Promise me you will tell me? That is if you find out something was going on?"

I was amazed. The hidden photo suggested *she* might be carrying on behind her husband's back, yet she wanted to know if *he* was having an affair. "I will, Ginny. One more thing. How long have your husband and Davidson known each other? Your husband once told me they go way back."

Ginny's cheeks flushed, and she stared at me. "Well, they were fellow students at Harvard, best friends from then on. Yes, Bob was disappointed he did not get the co-directorship, but accepted it after a while." She looked down for a moment and said, "Please find the killer, Rekha."

Was Ginny herself capable of plotting to have her husband murdered? The better part of me wanted to think that despite her indiscretion, she wouldn't. If not for a new relationship, what would be another motive? More money? The divorce would have guaranteed her a giant share of their savings and leave her wealthier than now, but her husband's death would give her everything. Would this gentle, cultured and elegant woman stoop to that?

~ Chapter 8 ~

Monday, April 3, 2017
Eagle Rock, Los Angeles, CA

I was in my office early Monday morning, my mind off-kilter with thoughts of Al, clashing with those of the Indian attorney, Rajeev, I'd met at Ma's special dinner.

The taste and smell of the vegetable *biriyani, baingan bharta,* and *sag paneer* that Ma and Aunty Leela had cooked up still lingered in my mouth. Dessert was *ras malai,* the only Indian sweet I liked. Despite my misgivings about the whole arranged marriage thing, I couldn't help but like Rajeev. He got high marks in my book for his genuine enjoyment of Indian food. During the short time we got to talk to each other out of earshot of the family, he left a clear impression of being gentle, respectful, and funny. I wanted to see him again, one-on-one.

I remembered Ma's advice. "Indian men know our customs, our food, and our upbringing, Rekha. So you are already starting at an advantage. With any other culture, there are so many differences to be ironed out." Maybe I could help Rajeev become more acculturated, and in turn, he could take me back to my deeper roots. As for Al, I could teach him the elements of Indian culture, and he could show me how he solved problems. Will either one turn out to be an abuser? I knew that abuse of women crossed cultural divides and was universal. Well, the way things were going, I had no idea when I'd even get the chance to get to know either of them better.

I reviewed my to-do list for the week. I'd already posted the potential list of topics for the students for their paper on the course website. My notes and slides were ready for a lecture the next afternoon. I'd fallen behind on my self-imposed time-line for my proposal for an undergraduate major in Indian Art History, but I still had a month to finish it. No way was I going to jeopardize my career this time. I'd learned the hard way that my job was also part of my dharma.

My mind back to the case, I knew exactly where to start. Davidson, who was now in charge of Faust's class, had the deepest connection with him outside the family. He was involved in the excavation, which connected him to the Durga, which in turn, connected him to the theft and possibly the murder. In my mind, he was the top suspect. Attending his lecture would please him and give me a starting point to learn more about him.

* * *

I walked over to JPM, went up to the second floor, and walked into a maze. Hallways led in three different directions. I had to ask the way to the classroom. A room in theater style, it was large enough to hold a hundred or more students, but at 12:45 in the afternoon, it held a mere handful of eager-beavers lounging in their chosen seats. They'd straggle in, I knew. For some, the last fifteen minutes before a lecture were too precious to waste sitting and waiting in a classroom. I was grateful I had smaller classes, but Faust's reputation for encouraging budding archaeologists and his acumen for securing scholarship money brought in more.

One look at the man at the podium and I had to catch my breath. I recognized the subject of Ginny's hidden sketches. So, Davidson was her paramour. Fascinated, I watched him as he advanced his first few slides and reversed them. He shined the laser beam of the pointer randomly on a slide and fiddled with the wireless microphone to attach it to his lapel. He was tall and thin, his gray jacket loose across his torso. He looked gaunt and periodically pushed up his glasses toward a receding hairline.

Looking at my watch and noticing students still straggling in, I walked up to him and said, "Professor Davidson, I'm Rekha Rao from the Art History department. I think the late Professor Faust introduced us at the inauguration of the Institute."

He looked lost for a second and then smiled. "Sure, I remember you. What can I do for you?"

"I just wanted to sit in on your lecture. Do you mind?"

My question brought some color back to his face. "Of course not. But why the interest? Want to teach this class next year?" He gave a questionable smile, halfway between happy and sad. Davidson had an authoritative guttural voice. "By all means, feel free to stay as long as you want. I usually end the lecture ten minutes to the hour. Sometimes I get carried away and forget until I see squirming in the seats." He did the thing with his glasses again and his voice softened. "Joe was special. I am mostly a field person, nowhere near as good a lecturer as he was." He gave a nervous cough and added, "I wouldn't be offended if you leave in the middle. Some students do."

"May I have a few minutes of your time after class? Unless you're busy." I asked.

"Of course. I've got an afternoon seminar, but I can give you fifteen minutes if that's OK." He patted my shoulder, looked at the students in their seats with open laptops and notebooks, and mumbled, "I'll look for you when class ends."

I turned toward the steps to look for a seat. I saw a hand making a half-hearted wave from the third row up and recognized the owner as Neil Anderson. He got out of his seat and leaned over to shake hands with me. "Professor Rao, it's nice to see you. Come to check out the class?"

As Davidson cleared his throat over the microphone, I ditched Neil and found a seat.

Davidson coughed into the microphone. "Testing, testing, can you hear me in the back?"

The seat I secured was in a meagerly populated back row and I sat down next to a student who had his binder open and his head bent down upon it. A new way to absorb information? Bob Davidson was no Faust. Compared to the erudite Faust, whom I had the good fortune to listen to many times at UCI, and at the inauguration of the Institute, Davidson was mediocre, sweeping through the slides, reading his notes into the microphone in a monotonous voice, and periodically moving the green laser beam here and there for emphasis, with no indication of stopping for questions. Maybe he had to use Faust's slides, since he'd started halfway through the semester, and they didn't work for him. Or, more likely, he'd have had a different energy if he were not grieving.

I listened with interest as Davidson elaborated on the definition of provenance and how it is established. "In most fields, the primary purpose of provenance is to confirm or gather evidence as to the time, place, and when appropriate, the person responsible for the creation, production, or discovery of the object. This will typically be accomplished

by . . . " My eyes started to glaze over. ". . . history of the object
. . ." Davidson droned on, "comparative techniques, expert
opinions . . ."

The lights came on, and I opened my eyes as Davidson
ended the lecture. A student in the front row raised his hand
and Davidson pointed to him. "I'll take just a few." Now wide
awake, I looked around the room and found several heads
bobbing up from brief naps, others furiously scribbling and a
few still typing into their laptops. A bizarre thought occurred to
me. Could any one of this bunch have plotted and committed
the murder? Did one student have a personal connection to
Faust outside the class? Their innocent demeanors didn't
fool me.

The students gathered their paraphernalia and shuffled
out, wide awake and looking for fortification before the next
class, and the tan that awaited them outside the building.
Several studious ones crowded around Davidson with questions. Davidson spent a few minutes with the group, and I
heard him say, "Meet me during my office hours. I have a
visitor to take care of," as he dismissed the group, looked at
me, smiled, and nodded.

Every student who moved away from Davidson stared at
me, notebooks clutched to their chests and pens still poised
in the air as if I were a hindrance to their thirst for intellectual exchange. Slowly they scattered as they came to the top
step that led to the doors. I heard muffled voices, "Faust . . .
investigation . . ." as some looked at me with curiosity and
exited through the door. Did they recognize me and know my
connection to the murder? The special Saturday edition of the
Oxy Weekly had not included my photo. Did the Wednesday
edition carry my photo? I kicked myself into thinking I was
being paranoid.

I stepped out of the classroom to wait for Davidson and attuned my ears to the small talk between a few remaining students who lingered in the hallway. The topic of discussion seemed to be Faust's murder and snippets of it reached my ear. Mob killing, secret past, mistaken identity. One thing was clear: their professor's killing weighed heavily on their minds and all the creative motives they came up with were plausible.

Davidson and I got into the elevator, the professor now sporting a visor and sunglasses, determined to ban all sunlight, his classroom possessions tucked into a leather briefcase. Outside, Davidson directed me to a bench in the shade and placed his bulky briefcase next to him.

"So, Professor Rao, what can I do for you?"

"Please call me Rekha. I've been asked by the police to help determine the connection between the idol and Professor Faust's murder. The problem is that the lead detective seems to have little information about the Jwalapuram excavation. Can you give me your perspective about what happened there?"

Davidson took off the visor to wipe his sweaty forehead with a handkerchief. "What can I tell you that you haven't already heard? Yes, I did see the idol in Jwalapuram, and remember Patel and Reddy taking charge of it. And I remember police checking our luggage and asking questions. Someone at the dig must have stolen it and passed it on to a middleman at the train station." He chuckled, the first expression of lightness that I'd heard from him. "Believe me, I've seen the elite display stuff like that in their homes to enhance their prestige."

"Why the rail station?"

He said gruffly, "Just a guess. There is no airport in Jwalapuram, the nearest is in Hyderabad, with a train connection. Unless someone personally collected it and spirited it away by car. I'd suspect the Indians—Patel and Reddy from the National Museum, who were there to catalog and store the artifacts. Do you know if they're being looked into?" He turned to look at me and I could see his eyelids ringed in red like he hadn't slept for days. Was he still grieving for his best friend, which would be a touching tribute, or, was he plagued by guilt for killing him?

I didn't want him to know that he was the top suspect on my list. "Of course, the police are checking on them. They should be the primary suspects since they were the first link in the Durga's transit. I heard that all of you took the train from Jwalapuram to Hyderabad for your return flights. Did you all leave together?" I asked.

"No, I left a day later than my colleagues because I wanted to do some sightseeing. But I did take the same train, the fast Venkatadri express. I tell you there was a throng of locals on the platform for that train."

I sympathized, "I bet they stared at you and other Caucasian men waiting for the train. Kurnool is not the center of tourist attraction, and foreigners would stand out in the crowd."

"Oh yes. In addition to me, there was only one other white guy on the platform. Short, overweight with a heavy backpack on his back. And we were being scrutinized by the Indians as though we were creatures from another dimension."

I laughed, to egg him on. "What did they do?" I knew I was asking the man to cast his mind back to almost a year ago.

"You know, I didn't pay that much attention because I was intent on not missing the train. The man asked me which train I was taking and nodded when I told him I was going to Hyderabad. Just then a train whistled and rumbled in. It was mine. I clambered aboard, pushing and shoving, and scrambled for a window seat for the long ride."

"Did you see where the other man went?" I asked. I noticed Davidson frown at me and realized I had reached the farthest point in my questioning.

"I watched him trying to get on board and having a hard time with the weight of his backpack. I thought he was going to drop under the train. I lost track after that. The hotel had packed me tiffin, my lunch, and I was hungry. The best part of being in India, good vegetarian food." Davidson patted his lean belly.

"Did the police ask you to identify the man from a photo?" I said.

"They didn't have any photos. I told them even if they had, I couldn't promise to ID him. It happened a while ago." He smiled at me and patted my shoulder. "But I would be more than happy to contact you if I recall anything else." He picked up his briefcase and pulled its strap over his shoulder. Instead of hurrying, he paused and looked at me with a strange expression. "This is none of my business Rekha, but why this interest? I understand your connection with Faust, and I admire your efforts to help the police. But, aren't you going a little overboard with it? I've heard you have a bright mind and the potential to become a full-time faculty here."

I was silent for a moment. I knew Davidson wouldn't understand my desperation to find Faust's killer. "I might as well tell you I have another personal reason. After my father's death, Faust was a father figure to me. I desperately want justice for him."

Davidson's voice was grave. "Aren't you concerned that whoever killed Joe might come after you? If I were your father,

I'd ask you to get back to your academic work."

My spine tingled. Was he threatening me? I changed my tactic. "I heard you and Faust go back, way back."

"Joe Faust was a good man, a brilliant mind. We were friends from the time we were at Harvard. But I can tell you many on the faculty envied the fame and adulation he got. Not that he cared."

"I can't think of anyone who would even dislike him." I hoped Davidson would lead me to some names.

"Striker for one. They were both up for the Directorship of JPM, and Striker being the Acting Director, made it clear to the selection committee that he'd leave if he weren't appointed *the* Director. But the committee wanted Joe here and decided to have co-directors. I understand they continued to be friends."

I'd not included Striker on my list. Would he be the one who had arranged to bring the Durga here? And used it to kill Faust so that he could be the sole Director of JPM? No, that was all water under the bridge. Could he be involved in the illegal trade of artifacts? I made a mental note to check him out.

Davidson's voice took on a softer tone. "I'm off to get a bite before my next appointment. Why don't you join me? I can tell you many more stories about JPM." I almost said yes, wondering if he was looking for a shoulder that his wife didn't offer.

I politely declined with a white lie but left the door open. "Sorry, I have an appointment. Maybe another day? I heard that you felt insulted when Striker didn't pick you for the co-directorship, and your friend got it?"

He turned his glance sharply at me. "I threw my name into the basket to see what would happen. I'd planned to retire at the end of this semester, and yes, it would've been nice to retire as a co-director, but it was no big deal." He shrugged. "For your information, Joe was my best friend, and friends don't kill each other." His lips tightened.

I picked up my satchel, smiled at him and said, "Thanks for your time, Professor Davidson."

* * *

Out of the corner of my eye, I noticed a young woman signaling to me from the side of the path, almost hidden by a large bush. A tall blonde, she asked me if I was the Indian professor who was helping the police. I admitted I was, once again annoyed that Neil's report or campus gossip had allowed students to connect me with the investigation. "Can my girlfriend talk to you privately? She has something to get off her chest. You need to hear it from her. She's very reluctant to talk to the police. May have nothing to do with the murder but I told her if not the police, she ought to at least talk to that nice Indian professor who is up to her knees in it." She smiled at me.

I jotted down my cell number on the back of my faculty card, gave it to the blonde and said, "Have her call me any time, night or day. I'd rather talk to her in person. If she feels better with you along for company, do that. Please."

I shook hands with the young woman and left.

~ Chapter 9 ~

Tuesday, April 4, 2017
Eagle Rock, Los Angeles, CA

"Neil Anderson?" Patricia looked at her computer and said, "Oh, yeah, Davidson was his advisor. But three weeks ago, Davidson decided for sure he wanted to retire, one hundred percent as he put it, gave up his office and student counseling. So, yes, Anderson was adrift, but I believe Striker talked to your Chair before he assigned him to you."

"It seemed so, but I wanted to check. Have you got a few minutes?"

"Sure, what's bugging you?"

Today, Patricia was cheerful. Knowing her only for a short time, I wondered if she'd divulge any departmental secrets.

I asked, "You must miss Faust. How long had you worked for him?"

Her eyes lit up. "Since he moved to the Institute. He was such a great person, Rekha. Very patient with me as I developed the vocabulary for his manuscripts and memos. I'd have died for him. Don't get me wrong. There was nothing inappropriate. I know where the line is."

I smiled, thinking of Ginny's worry over Faust's assistant. I was making some headway with Patricia. "I heard there was some friction between Faust and Davidson. Was that true?"

"Oh yeah, they both went to Harvard. Fellow grad students. Then, Davidson went to teach somewhere in the Midwest, and Professor F went to UCI. When the institute got started, it was Striker who recruited him to join him here. But when the committee selected Professor F for the other co-directorship, Davidson went berserk."

I noted that Patricia seemed to revere Faust in a way she didn't accord the others. "What do you mean?"

"I overheard him yelling at the professor the day the committee announced the decision."

"Davidson told me he patched it up with Faust."

"Yes, they were back to being buddies. Men, they don't hold grudges as we do." Patricia laughed.

"Tell me about Striker. I just learned that he was unhappy he didn't get the solo directorship. How did he treat Faust?" I sipped my coffee.

"I can't tell you of a single person who held a grudge against Professor F. Poor man, he was too nice." She cleared her throat. "Yeah, Striker was pissed when the committee suggested co-directors. He'd worked to get JPM built and wanted to be its sole owner, in a way. I sometimes laugh at what people value in their lives. Thank God, I'm not like that."

"Do you think Striker would have arranged to get the Durga? Is he a collector of any sort?"

Patricia laughed. "Him? A collector? His wife died a few years ago, and he's now married to JPM. Some of us were invited to his house after the Institute opened. I can tell you there was no collection of anything there. Except for dust."

I couldn't help smiling. "Tell me about Neil Anderson." I peeked at my phone to check the time.

"Well, he's a bit strange."

I leaned forward to ask, "What do you mean? He's brilliant, that much I can say. Very quiet in class but brilliant in his analysis and interpretation of data."

Patricia smiled. "I guess his behavior goes along with his braininess. He wanted Professor F to read his proposal for the junior thesis. And he's just finishing his sophomore year. The professor gave him a couple of meetings and suggested he talk to his advisor, Davidson."

"Well, I think Neil was dead serious about getting into Faust's next excavation. That must have been why he was so persistent."

"Maybe, but he pestered the man with emails, sent his proposal here, annoyed the heck out of him. Professor F told me to block his emails and tell him to work with Davidson or Striker. If it were up to me, I'd have reported him to the Dean for harassment."

Other than my Chair, Patricia was the only female at Oxy who paid me any attention. I could use a little solidarity. On an impulse, I hugged her and said, "Let's do lunch some time." She smiled and nodded. Before leaving, I asked for Davidson's phone number and address. I wanted to talk to him about Neil and other things. "I stopped by and saw Ginny, but wondered if Faust had more kith and kin in this area. Are his parents alive?

"No. Striker reached out to every relative we could locate. There's a niece who lives in Pasadena. Want to go see her?" She handed me a hastily scribbled address on a post-it note.

It was clear to me now that Davidson had always been in Faust's shadow. Faust got the accolades and the co-directorship. What was the tipping point that led Davidson to murder?

~ Chapter 10 ~

Wednesday, April 5, 2017.
Eagle Rock, Los Angeles, CA

I had allotted only thirty minutes on Wednesday for my advising session with Neil, but he turned out to be chatty. And annoying.

"Professor Rao, you must have already looked at my academic performance? There should be no problem there."

"Your academics are stellar, Neil. But with the change in direction you're now taking, it could get tricky to finish all the requirements and grad school applications in the next two years. Have you given it more thought?"

Neil looked down and fiddled with his jacket. "I'm sorry to do this to you, Professor Rao. The more I thought about it, the more I became certain that I should stay on in archaeology. If not for anything else, to honor Professor Faust who inspired me to consider the field."

I contained my exasperation and pretended to look through some papers I had in my folder. This kid was driving me nuts. "I'm glad that's all behind you. The coursework you completed so far seems to satisfy the prerequisites for an archaeology major. Are there any exceptional circumstances in your life that might affect your performance? No worries—we advisors are all trained to ask this question. Adverse situations can offset your academic progress."

"Well, I have a mother—and a younger sister who's still in middle school in Altadena," Neil said. "We used to live in Moorpark on a farm but moved once I got into Oxy. Mother needs help with finances, and it was too far to drive to Moorpark. Now I go home on weekends to help them out. I want my sister to come here, get a good education. Rise above the blue-collar." He frowned.

"Why, is there anything wrong with being blue-collar? What does your mom do?"

Neil looked away from me and blushed. "I'm sorry, I didn't mean to put Mother down. She works at the check-out counter at Vons. I'm grateful to her. I must tell you I've no idea who my birth mother, my real mom is. I want to find her." He drummed on his thigh with his right hand.

The conversation was going in the wrong direction. "There're ways to trace birth parents. Do that if you have the urge, but make sure not to let that preoccupy you and distract you from your academics." I gathered up the folders on my desktop to return them to the file cabinet. I hoped he'd leave. "I'd suggest that you review the courses for the next semester and come up with a list targeted toward an archaeology major. We can then meet to finalize your classes."

There was something odd about this kid. I needed to talk to his previous advisor, Davidson.

* * *

Neil's reference to his adoptive mother as "Mother," and birth mother as "Mom," made me wonder about the former. Did she not build a loving relationship with her adopted son? My desire to meet her grew stronger, but I wasn't sure how to make it happen without creating an awkward situation.

I went back to grading. I'd asked my freshmen students to write their interpretations about a self-selected panel of a painting from the murals of the Ajanta caves in India. They had to describe their first impressions of the painting, the deeper meaning it conveyed, and how it affected them emotionally. Since this was the first experience for the class analyzing Indian mural paintings, and since they had undertaken the one-page write up seriously, the lowest grade I gave was a C.

My cell phone rang. It was Rajeev. I felt guilty I hadn't contacted him as I'd promised. I'd let the events surrounding Faust's death once again lead me to ignore my priorities, my dharma.

"Rajeev, I've been thinking of calling you but . . ."

"It doesn't matter who calls whom, right? I hadn't heard from you, so I thought I'd call. What are you up to? Do you have time for a bite?" He chuckled, "I hope I don't sound overanxious."

"No, not at all. Honestly, I could use a glass of wine, some Italian food and your receptive ears. But can we do it tomorrow?"

"Sure, no problem."

I laughed. "I'll call you this time to confirm, OK?"

What a nice guy, I could use his shoulder right now. I made an entry in my phone calendar to call him the next day.

I stood up and got a bottle of water from the small fridge in the corner, walked over to the window and peered out on the small triangle of the quad seen from my office. No soul around. I looked at my watch. It was two in the afternoon. I'd grade a few more papers and go home. I reluctantly turned from the window and went back to the desk.

The phone rang. "Yes?" I said, picking it up.

A soft, barely audible and hesitant female voice came on. "Is this . . . Professor Rao?"

"Yes, what can I do for you?"

"I'm one of Professor Faust's students. I talked to you briefly at the Davidson lecture. About my friend? You remember?"

I perked up, "Yes, I remember you."

A brief laugh broke out at the other end. "I bet you thought there was no friend. Isn't that what most people do when they are in trouble? Make up a friend?"

"Some do, but you called, that's what matters. Is it for a friend or for you?"

More giggles. Then a worried voice said, "No, it's actually for my friend who doesn't want to call. She's frightened. I promised her that you'd keep the info to yourself. Sorry, but that was the only way I could get her to let me call you. I can't go to the police. She'll freak out."

"That was very clever of you . . . what's your name?"

"Sorry again, Professor, I promised her we'd keep our names out of this."

"That's fine. You're a good friend. Why me?"

"Students say you are kind. Someone who listens. We thought you could decide how serious it is and then tell the police only if necessary?"

These girls knew nothing about a police investigation. Nor about the risk I was taking, talking to them. "I need to warn you ahead of time. If I receive information that could be valuable to the police, and I don't pass it on to them, I could be found guilty of obstructing justice. Do you understand that?"

A barely audible yes came from the other end.

"Do you guys want to meet with me in person or do this on the phone?"

"Can you meet us at the Oinkster? May be get there by 1 pm? I don't want to wait too long 'cause my friend might change her mind."

"OK. I'll see you guys there."

* * *

It took me only fifteen minutes to get to Oinkster on Colorado Boulevard and find parking. Not seeing the tall blonde, I walked inside, looked around, but didn't see her inside either. I got a glass of brewed ice tea and sat down at a table near the entry and saved two chairs, as the place was filling up. I looked at the menu and decided to treat the young women.

Within ten minutes, two women walked in, their shoulders strung with heavy purses, eyes hidden by sunglasses. They came straight to my table. "Hi, Professor Rao," the taller of the two women said, waving her hand. "This is my friend. I'm sorry but she insists we keep our names from you because of what she has to tell you. She made me promise I'd keep my sunglasses on all the time." I recognized the speaker as the woman who had called me earlier, the tall blonde who had approached me after the lecture.

The short woman had her face almost hidden by the hood of her frayed gray sweatshirt. Through it, I could see pitch black straight hair trying to escape. Her frame was thin, and she couldn't have been more than a hundred pounds. She was rubbing her gloved hands together, at odds with the day that was already warming up.

"Do sit down," I said. The women sat with their backs to the afternoon crowd.

I smiled at them. "Why don't you guys order something to eat and drink? It's on me."

The tall blonde got up and said, "I'm going for an Oinksterade." Her friend nodded, meaning for her too. "Nothing to eat, we just ate lunch."

"So what is it you'd like to tell me?" I picked up my notebook from my satchel.

The gray sweatshirt shivered and looked away. She still had the hood and sunglasses on. I realized my ears alone would have to do the work that day.

Her tall companion turned to her. "Trust her. The professor will keep her word, Mon . . ." She stopped abruptly, looked at me and cupped her mouth with her hand, having realized she had almost given away her friend's name.

The hooded woman bent over her drink and blurted out, "Kevin Faust was my boyfriend for about a year. We broke it off the night of the murder."

I exhaled a deep breath. "Go on, tell me more, anything you want to get off your chest."

The young woman tilted her head down and mumbled just loud enough for me to hear. "He came to my apartment the night before the murder. Close to ten in the evening. I didn't want to let him in, but he sounded frantic and begged." She took a sip of her drink. "We've had a few problems since we started dating and I had been ignoring them."

"What kind of problems?" I asked.

"Oh, he had a temper that'd come out of nowhere. I thought at first that I was doing something to irritate him. But it didn't get any better. I also disliked him putting on my clothes. Bras and panties more than anything else. He said he found women's clothes more interesting than men's. He wasn't kinky in any other way." I nodded in understanding

— no kinky sex of any kind.

"Please go on. What happened that night after you let him in?"

"He wanted to dress up and was so insistent that I thought he might finally have gone off the deep end." I wished I could see her eyes. The woman's voice was raspy. "This time it was like he was out to prove something. He always spoke very highly of his father, but that night, I was shocked to hear him say he hated him because he was a prude. He said . . . he said he wished his father was dead. That was it. I said no, no more of this weird stuff. I kicked him out and broke it off with him. Later, when I heard about Faust, it freaked me out."

"What time was it when he left? Did he tell you where he was going?"

"It was about eleven-thirty, I'm sure. Well before midnight. I assumed he went back to his apartment." She picked up her Oinksterade. "There's nothing more to tell." She turned to her friend. "Can we go now?"

"Has Kevin threatened you any time since this happened? Was he ever violent with you?" I had to ask.

The tall blonde jabbed her friend's arm with her elbow. "For chrissakes, girl, tell her everything. That's why I dragged you out here."

Monica, which I assumed was the girl's name, took another sip of her drink and made a face as though she wondered how anyone could drink this crap. She said, "He called a few days later and told me that the police were after him and not to tell them what he had said about his father the night before the murder. He said I should know he was incapable of killing anyone, especially his father. Our little squabble, in his words, had nothing to do with the murder and was best kept between us. That was all. He never bothered me after that. Now I feel silly I had you come over for this."

The blonde shook her head at her friend, turned to me and said, "He told her to say that he was with her until morning. There, I said it for you, and that's the whole truth. Do you need to tell the police, Professor Rao?"

"I'm not sure. But if I were to do that, I'd contact you first. OK? Thank you both for coming to me."

Monica started crying, tears cascading over her pale cheeks as the two girls gathered up their belongings and made a swift exit.

Did Kevin ask his girlfriend to lie because he had killed his father after he left her apartment? Or was cross-dressing the only offense he wanted to hide? All of a sudden, he moved up in my suspect list, just below Davidson.

* * *

I wanted to confirm the story with Ginny and check out Kevin's alibi at the time of the murder. I called her before I went to bed.

"Ginny, I have something to ask you. In person. Do you have some time tomorrow?"

Ginny sounded energized. "Tomorrow? No, but if it can wait till Saturday, I can make time. I am coming up to Eagle Rock on Friday to spend the weekend with an old friend. Would late Saturday morning work for you?" Her voice went up. "What is going on, Rekha? Did something happen? Is Kevin in trouble?"

"No worries, Ginny. I'm glad you'll be in the neighborhood. Where do you want to meet?"

"I do not know the area well, but the last time I came, my friend, and I went to the Rec Center. Where there's a children's play area? I can be there in the morning at 10."

"Great, it'd be nice to see you again."

There was silence, and I wondered if she'd hung up. Her clipped voice came on again. "I also have something to tell you."

~ Chapter 11 ~

Thursday, April 5, 2017.
Eagle Rock, Los Angeles, CA

I was well on my way home when I decided to call Rajeev. "Hi Rekha, what a nice surprise."

"Wondered if you have time today to meet for dinner?"

"Sure, any day and any time for you. Where would you like to meet?"

We settled on meeting at Gale's on South Fair Oaks Avenue in Pasadena at 7 pm. That gave me time to get home, take a shower, and change. The events of the last two days had enveloped me in a cloud of doubts and worries that not even a hundred showers would scrub away. But as the hot water warmed and soothed my body, I complimented myself for the strides I'd made in controlling my stress. By the time I changed into a clean pair of jeans and an Indian cotton tunic, I could almost pretend I was fully free of my PTSD.

An hour later, I was at the restaurant and saw Rajeev, casually dressed in khakis, polo, and loafers, waiting at the entrance. My heart took a turn. Here was a nice man who clearly liked me and if I gave him a chance, he could be more than a friend. Maybe a lover and a husband. I pulled myself back from the fast-forward and greeted him with a light hug that he returned.

We sat down at a table for two that Rajeev had reserved between the phone call and his arrival. His thoughtfulness reminded me he was a lawyer, used to making quick decisions and promptly acting on them. I liked that because I was like that before I succumbed to PTSD. The choice of the restaurant was just right as Gale's served traditional northern Italian food in a bustling dining room in a building that resembled a house.

"I'm glad you like Italian," Rajeev said. "I find it a nice contrast to the Indian food. Let's order some wine and munchies." We reviewed the wine list, debated the merits of red and white, and settled on Hitching Post "Highliner" 2012, a Pinot Noir from Santa Barbara County.

I said, "When I start making more money, I'm going to become a member of the Hitching Post Winery. I love their wines."

Rajeev nodded and said, "Oh-ho, your husband better watch out for your expensive tastes." We laughed. I liked his sense of humor. If only life were always about good wine, fine food, and uncomplicated companionship.

The waiter came back with an open bottle and poured some into Rajeev's glass. Rajeev sniffed it, swirled it around in his mouth. "Good, we'll have it."

We chit-chatted about nothing, over bruschetta and eggplant Siciliana, as I pondered getting a second opinion from Rajeev on my plans to track down the killer. I knew he was too much of a gentleman to bring up the issue. "Rajeev, do you mind if I discuss a few things about the case with you? Maybe your lawyer's mind can see holes where I don't." I knew this was not illegal since the facts I knew about the case came from Al, and were likely public knowledge by then, and my speculations were my own. I did not doubt that Rajeev would keep them to himself.

He finished chewing his food and smiled. "I thought you might be working on it, but I didn't want to poke my nose in if you chose to keep it to yourself. I'm sorry about your dad's murder and now your professor's. What can I do to help?"

Once again, I felt gratitude toward this man. Even if he did not end up as my husband, I would love to have him as a friend.

We had gobbled up most of the appetizers when I said, "Let's order so we can eat and talk without interruption. I'm going to have the rosemary lamb chops. I hardly eat meat these days." I wondered what I'd do if he ordered something much less expensive.

"Well, I'll top that with a Tuscan-style steak." We gave our orders to the waiter, and I poured more wine for both of us.

"Before I get into the case, I want to tell you something. I spent two years looking into my dad's murder and it cost me my tenure and alienated me from the Indian community in Irvine. My family, except for my brother Sanjay, was outraged. I decided to move away from Irvine to Eagle Rock. Luckily, with Dr. Faust's recommendation, I was able to get an adjunct professorship. So this time around, I'm going to make sure I maintain due diligence with my job and my family relationships . . . and others . . . while doing what I can to find Faust's killer."

"I did hear about your efforts with your dad's case." He chuckled. "Some aunt or uncle warned me about you. I'm sorry it came to nothing. You followed your heart. There's nothing wrong with that. Maybe once this case is solved, we can work together to reopen it. Get help from the California Innocence Project."

"Thank you, Rajeev." I couldn't say yes or no since I'd received the very same offer from another man. "Now, I hope you don't mind listening to my theories about Faust's murder. My main suspects are his colleague Davidson, his son Kevin, and possibly his wife Ginny, who could have orchestrated the killing. In addition, it's plausible that someone unknown could have been the killer. Davidson is at the top because he was associated with the dig in India, could have arranged for the Durga's transport, and could have confronted Faust the night of the murder. He might have had to kill him to save his reputation and his illegal business. Faust and Davidson have also been close friends from their college days. There could have been some rivalry there." I paused to take a breath.

"Alternatively, Kevin Faust, who is into cross-dressing, might have angered Faust into giving him an ultimatum that led him to kill his father. With Davidson, there's a geographical connection since Faust was staying with him during the conference and died in his front yard. As far as Kevin is concerned, I don't have any link connecting him to Davidson's home that night."

"What about the wife?"

"Honestly, I don't think she has the wherewithal to find a hit man. But listen to this. Yesterday police arrested a student, Bill McGraw, who is in both my class and Faust's class.

"Why was he arrested?"

"Faust dismissed him from an internship and police think that was enough motive. I don't. He's a polite, decent young man with a bright future that he wouldn't compromise." I was automatically defensive. "But, there's something more there."

Our meal arrived, and we started in. Both of us were silent for a few moments. Rajeev must have been thinking about what I had said because he asked, picking up a piece of steak with his fork, "Tell me more about this student. Do you know him well?" He put the steak in his mouth and chewed.

I'd tried one piece of my lamb and it was exquisite. I took another. "No, only for three months. But he comes from a low-income family and has big ambitions to become an archaeologist. He comes across as downright honest and loyal. I can't think of any motive for him to kill Faust. But the day he was dismissed from his internship, something happened. He had an appointment with Faust and while waiting in his office, tried to take a book out from a bookshelf, when Faust came in, yelled at him to get out, and ended his internship. Something Bill did ticked him off. This was very atypical of the man I knew."

Rajeev called for a waiter and asked for another bottle of wine. "I'm sure you understand that people are not what they seem on the surface. I've defended many a killer, typical American men and women who swore to me they were innocent. It just turned out they hadn't told me everything. Being a public defender can be maddening, and sometimes a waste of time. Your McGraw could be pretending he's innocent to lure you into taking his side. Find out more about what he was doing at the bookshelf."

I was wordless for a moment. "I guess I need to talk to Bill again." I felt exhausted, put my fork down and sought the solace of the wine.

"Rekha, I'm only suggesting that you don't rule out anyone too early. McGraw sounds like a student you like and who you'd rather not consider as a killer. I understand that but keep talking to him to find any other connection between him and Faust. Same thing with everyone on your list. Dig deeper, talk to them and to anyone willing to talk about them. That's what I'd do in your situation. Was McGraw anywhere near the murder scene?" Rajeev certainly sounded like a lawyer, but whether for McGraw or against him, I couldn't figure out from his neutral tone.

"Well, that's an interesting question, Rajeev. McGraw and a buddy followed Faust to Roy's, a restaurant where Faust was celebrating with his friends. On top of that, at the instigation of this friend, he approached Faust as he was entering the private dining room to ask him to reinstate the internship. Faust was livid. As far as I know, Bill and his buddy took off for home soon after that. Police suggest that the dismissal and the incident at the restaurant could have enraged him. I don't believe it. Now for a wild idea, I suspect Faust might have something hidden in his bookshelf that he thought Bill had discovered. Once the office is cleared by police, I plan to look around. But for now, I need to look deeper into Bill's behavior." And Faust's, I thought.

Rajeev nodded. "Bill is connected to Faust in more than one way. Give him a closer look."

All of a sudden, I was sick of the mess I had invited into my life. I wanted to spend some quality time with Rajeev. "Thanks, Rajeev. You've given me some new directions. Let's talk about something else. What about a dessert?"

Rajeev looked into my eyes, and said, "What about us?"

~ Chapter 12 ~

Saturday, April 8, 2017
Eagle Rock, Los Angeles, CA

I had a date with Sanjay for a hike along the Eagle Rock trail as part of my dharma vow. I had to do it early because I had promised to meet Ginny later the same morning.

I drove along West Colorado Boulevard, took a left on to Patrician Way and swung left again to enter Eagle Rock View Drive. The road dead-ended almost at the foot of the giant grouping of rocks that gave the city its unique name.

Sanjay's car was there, and he was walking around gazing at the view. He looked handsome in a light blue Polo shirt, khaki shorts, and hiking boots. Contrary to how prepared he was, I had absent-mindedly come in my work clothes. Luckily, I had a pair of tennis shoes in my car and changed into them. Good enough for a short hike, which was all I was ready to do.

He waved as I got out and we hugged. I asked, "Checking the place out? Nice location to bring a date to." Caution crept into my voice. "But do it during the daytime."

He laughed. "No dates, no worries, Didi. It seems the Eagle Rock Canyon trail is a short one." He looked down at my shoes. "Your tennies should be fine."

We went through a break in a wooden fence and hit a

forked trail. "I think we can go either way. Both should bring us back here. It's supposed to be a loop." Sanjay was an experienced hiker.

I nodded, and he went ahead of me.

"What's going on?" His voice was casual.

We walked in tandem as the trail was narrow. I was behind my brother, which prevented us from making eye contact. Sanjay walked fast and I tried to catch up with him.

"I'm just going to give you a few facts and would like your take on them. Oh, and this conversation never took place, OK?"

My brother chuckled, "That sounds like lawyer-speak, Didi."

"I saw Rajeev last night. He gave me some sound advice. One of my students, Bill, was dismissed from an internship by Faust and he also caused some innocent trouble at the restaurant where Faust was. A neighbor reported seeing him in a car in an alley near the house where Faust was killed. Bill is now in jail. Granted, I've only known this boy for the last three months. He grew up poor and got to Oxy on a scholarship. He takes care of his great-aunt who lives in Ashfield, Massachusetts. Rajeev thinks that I should consider him among my top suspects. My heart says otherwise."

Sanjay was silent for a few seconds. The air was chilly, and I could hear unfamiliar bird calls from the surrounding wilderness. "Didi, you lead with your heart. That's who you are. So, if you feel he couldn't have committed this crime, there's probably something to it. I'd suggest you keep him among your list of suspects and pay close attention to what he says and does. Once you find the killer, you'd be relieved if it wasn't him."

I leaned forward to grab his ear, the punishment Ma

often doled out when as children, we misbehaved. Sanjay howled and pushed forward to get away from me. "Not you, Didi. Had enough from Ma."

I pulled him back with his Polo shirt. "How come you're so cool?"

Sanjay laughed. "Mom and Dad protected you more than me. Remember, you stayed home the first two years while going to UCI. Who does that these days? I put my foot down and said I wanted to live away from home. To learn the ways of the world and all that. Anyway, you're taking the right path to finding the killer. Don't let anyone off the hook until you find him. Or her."

"My only suspects are Davidson and possibly Faust's wife or son. Davidson could be it. Faust might have caught him with the idol on the night of the murder. He was also having an affair with Faust's wife, which she ended."

Sanjay whistled. "Maybe he was confident she'd return to him if Faust were no longer alive? Or the wife could have done it herself, I mean, hired a hit man. I see many such incidents reported on *Dateline*. Maybe she wanted a second chance at love?"

"The Fausts were divorcing, so why resort to murder?" I stopped to pull out some weeds from my shoes.

"I told you their son is at UCI and I've heard rumors that he'd had a falling out with his father. You want me to check out what he's up to?"

"You mean tail him? No way. Stay out of it, Sanju. I only need your brain, don't want you to put your body at risk. What do you mean he had a falling out?"

"His father threatened to cut off his inheritance. Not sure of the reason. I think you should look into him, but Davidson sounds like a good bet. With his connection to Faust and the

Durga. I'd find out more about Bill also."

We got back to the beginning of the loop trail. I sat down looking at the awesome rock groupings. Solid, immovable, like Faust and Dad. And Al.

"The senior detective Al pisses me off. He's always playing one-upmanship with me. He must be insecure. He cautioned me about the dangers of going out on my own to track the killer."

Sanjay stared at me, at my abrupt change of the topic. "It's Al now? Aren't you done with the police?"

"Well, I wish. I ran into him again when my student was arrested. He tried to implicate him and Faust in the theft. He has no respect for anyone."

Sanjay smiled. "He sounds the opposite of you. He's a detective, so his job is to suspect everyone. But tell me, do you dislike him . . . or like him?"

I put my head in my hands to cover my embarrassment. When I looked up, I saw Sanjay silhouetted by the rock, the trees, and the clear blue sky between the mountains beyond. Despite everything, at that moment the world was a beautiful place, and love a possibility. "I can't figure it out, Sanjay. Something about him attracts me, yet other aspects keep me at a distance, which is where I've stayed." I got up, Sanjay giving me a hand.

"Tread carefully, Didi. He's a cop, an American, OK by me. He sounds like he's somewhat older than you. How do you think our family would receive him? Don't do anything impulsive, wait to figure out if he's the man for you. Then, of course, you've no choice." There was his wisdom again.

"Let's go. Sanju. And thanks for everything. Want to get ice cream on the way?"

* * *

I took the 134 Freeway and got to the Eagle Rock recreation center on Eagle Vista Drive.

The children's play area was easy to locate. It had an exterior façade that bore the letters R, O, C, and K, each letter slanted in a different direction and painted in a different color. Just like a child beginning to pen the alphabet.

There was barely any wind, and it was hot. I saw Ginny's waving hand amidst a swarm of squirmy kids and serious-faced adults, who looked like they were there on an outing. Ginny wore tan shorts, a pink tank top with a sweatshirt tied around her waist, a visor, and running shoes. Up close, she looked more cheerful than when I had seen her last. Her facial skin was glowing. Good for her, I thought. She's learning to deal with the tragedy. Or has she hooked up with Davidson?

We found a bench away from the crowd. I eased my feet out of my shoes and wiggled my toes. I waited, hoping she'd speak first, not wanting to bring up Kevin.

"I have kept something from the police, Rekha, and you. I had been feeling guilty about it ever since Joe died. But first, tell me what you wanted to ask? Is it about Kevin?"

"Have you met Kevin's girlfriend, or maybe an ex-girlfriend now?"

Ginny's mouth fell open. "This was what you wanted to ask me? Goodness, I am relieved. Yes, of course, he has a girlfriend. I have met this one a couple of times. Seemed like a nice girl. Chinese. I think her first name is Monica. Why?"

"She broke up with him the night your husband died."

"Kevin has never had a steady girlfriend who lasted more than a few months. So what else is new? How did you find out?"

"Well, his girlfriend and a friend of hers sought me out yesterday. The girlfriend told me he called her the day after the murder and told her to say that he was with her all night. I wondered why." I didn't want to tell Ginny of Kevin's death wish for his father or his cross-dressing.

Ginny looked at me with her eyebrows raised. "Why would he ask her to lie? My son would not kill his father. But I have to share something Kevin told me last night, Rekha." She delved into her bag and pulled out a stack of what looked like index cards and handed them to me. They were the sketches of the young boy dressed in girl's clothes, the same stack that I'd found stashed behind her cupboard. I thumbed through them and pretended I was seeing them for the first time.

Ginny took back one sketch from my hand, and as her eyes took it in, she stroked it gently with her hands. "When Kevin was young, I used to dress him up in girl's clothes. I longed for a girl. But, mind you, I love my boy as much as I would have a girl." She handed the sketch back to me. "Maybe I should have stopped this habit early on. It was my fault. Kevin confessed to me last night when I told him I was coming to see you. He has been cross-dressing all this time as an adult, just for fun. He said his girlfriend kicked him out recently because she couldn't stand it. I told him I would share this information with you."

"Did your husband find out, Ginny? This is important."

"Sorry, Rekha. I asked Kevin and he wouldn't answer that question. I think he's embarrassed to tell me. Maybe Joe walked in on him and didn't tell me about it. He always tried to protect me. He would rather keep the worry to himself than include me in any problem. And then, of course, he ran out of time." She sniffled.

I remained silent.

Ginny seemed to read my thoughts. "I am sure you think Kevin might have killed his father to keep his strange habit under wraps."

"Would he?"

"I do not think so, Rekha. He is my son. He is like Joe, not a mean bone in his body. Oh yes, he can be temperamental, and now I suspect a bit weird, but he is not a criminal. He told me he was with Monica the night before Joe's murder but went home at midnight and fell asleep. I believe him."

Ginny put her head down and covered her face with her hands. She took a few deep breaths and looked up. "I have to get something off my chest, Rekha. I am ashamed of this. And guilty. Joe deserved better." She pulled some Kleenex out from her pocket and blew her nose.

"What do you mean?" I moved closer and put my hand on the woman's shoulder. "You can tell me anything."

"I have to start at the beginning. I first met Bob Davidson when he and Joe were working on their graduate degrees at Harvard. I was deeply in love with Joe at that time, and Bob was just a friend to me, charming and gallant. At times, when we were alone, he'd make me nervous by praising me to the skies. He was Joe's best friend, even after he joined him at Oxy. In the last two years as Joe and I grew apart, Bob offered a sympathetic ear." She stopped and squeezed her forehead with her right hand. "He admired my art. I do not think his wife knew, but then again there was nothing much for her to find out. Bob and I had coffee sometimes, and he did come over once or twice to see my paintings. That was when he kissed me. Took me by surprise. I was embarrassed and did not respond. He looked embarrassed, too, and maybe that was why he asked for one of my abstract paintings. It was my first one, and I was not that proud of it, but I gave it to him, anyway."

She took a sip from her water bottle. "A month before Joe's death, Bob asked me to go with him to Cambria for a weekend. Have you been? It's mostly tourists there. Right by the ocean and we didn't have to worry about running into anyone we knew. I took him up on that. Honestly, it felt good to be cared for physically."

Ginny paused, started again. "Two weeks later, Bob asked again but I couldn't do it. Somehow, once did not feel like cheating, but I was not going to repeat it. Even though Joe and I were going through a divorce, I knew it was wrong. That was how I was brought up. Now Joe's murder has put an end to all that foolhardiness, at least for me. I have developed a guilty complex over my affair with Bob. I have not talked to him since Joe's death, though he keeps trying. I am thinking of returning to England. I have family there."

Ginny's reveal opened another door for me. Had Bob Davidson been crazy enough to kill Faust or have him killed in his front yard for a second chance at romance? It was a horrible idea, but a plausible alternate motive. "Ginny, do you think Davidson is capable of killing your husband, his best friend? Is he a vengeful man?"

Ginny started shaking, and I put my hand on her shoulder. "I worried about it after Joe's murder. I got an email from Bob asking me to keep our affair a secret. Not tell the police. It was almost like he was ordering me to do it, or else. From that point on, I thought he could have killed Joe. And to think I was involved in it, unknowingly." Ginny sobbed. "Rekha, can you keep this confidential? Unless of course, it is relevant to find Joe's killer. I would not let anything stand in the way of that." She stumbled over the next few words. "Kevin would . . . hate me if he finds out. He thinks I am an angel walking the earth."

"I will warn you if the affair has to come out, Ginny," I said. I wondered what Al would have done in this situation. Take Ginny to the station to be questioned? I looked at my watch. "Listen, I have to go. Call me if you think of anything else that might give me another angle on your husband." I patted Ginny's hand in reassurance, slipped back into my shoes, and walked her to her car.

Ginny caught some hair that had escaped from her clip and tucked it back in. "Kevin says he wants to talk to you, without me. We must have both suddenly found God or something. I told him to call you and set up an appointment. Let me know if he does not."

In all honesty, I couldn't include her among my suspects. Her grief and guilt felt genuine. There was always the opposite side of the coin, that she might be faking her emotions. Let Al go there, I thought, I needed to hold on to the convictions of my heart.

~ Chapter 13 ~

Saturday, April 8, 2017
Pasadena CA

I avoided the freeway and drove on Colorado Boulevard, along the historic Colorado Street Bridge that spanned the Arroyo Seco. Today, the bridge's Beaux-Arts arches, lampposts, and railings faded into the background as I mulled over Ginny's story.

As soon as I crossed the bridge, I changed my mind and made a U-turn. I wanted to confront Davidson, make him admit the affair, and maybe reveal more about his role in the theft and murder. I was sure he was involved in one or both. I knew I was about to step into the dangerous grounds Al had warned me about, but so be it.

Davidson's home was within a mile of the Rose Bowl and looked traditional and modest. It was a two-story, with a dark brown shake roof, a stucco exterior, and casement windows. But its true worth came from a pair of charming Craftsman cottages on either side.

I parked about five feet past the entryway to the house and dialed Davidson's number. I told him I was in the area and would like to stop by for a few minutes to discuss Neil Anderson. He invited me over.

I entered the driveway and recognized it from the photo montage that I had seen in Al's office. Long and wide, it was paved with concrete and landscaped along the periphery. On the left, it led to a closed garage. On the right, yellow tape walled-off an expansive, quasi-Japanese garden with a rock pond, extending to the front entrance. The garden looked messy, like someone had trampled through it. A stone lantern lay broken and a lone Buddha statue was tipped on its side.

A rough oval outline in chalk was marked near the edge of the garden. I shivered. I knew it was the place where Faust had fallen. Dried-up red splotches led from the outline toward the entrance of the house where they abruptly stopped about three feet from the front porch. Was that where the killer first attacked? Faust's car was no longer in the driveway.

My throat went dry as I played the movie of the murder in my mind. Faust gets out of the car, takes out his briefcase and conference bag from the front passenger side and starts to close the door, but doesn't make it. He's interrupted by the killer. Did he recognize him? Most likely he did because he seemed to have turned his back on him to enter the house when the killer delivered blows to his head. I pulled my open jacket closer to my chest, tightened my belly against the real or imagined sickly sweet smell of blood, and quickly made my way to the front door. I felt for the Davidsons. Would they enjoy their Japanese garden ever again?

Davidson opened the door to my knock. "Rekha, pleasure to see you again. Come in, come in. Angela is out getting groceries. Cup of coffee?" Despite the smile, Bob's voice sounded stiff and his face still looked gaunt. I envied him the luxury of time to grieve, something I didn't have. I pulled out a water bottle from my backpack. It was empty. "No coffee for me, Professor Davidson, but maybe a glass of water? Thanks."

Davidson wore a short-sleeved, pale blue shirt and jeans. His auburn eyes, sunken with dark semicircles under them, were expressionless. I recalled first meeting him briefly at the inauguration of JPM when Faust had introduced him as his classmate, colleague, and best friend. I knew nothing of Davidson's past beyond Harvard where they both had been grad students. I was curious how their paths had diverged and finally met once again at the Institute where they had been colleagues for the last three years.

I moved around the living room that looked disorganized. The pale blue wall sported family photographs, framed certificates, and several paintings, some askew. One was a large abstract work in brilliant colors and deft brush strokes. Possibly a Kandinsky, I thought, and most likely a print. College professors earned a comfortable living, but unless they had inherited wealth or engaged in illegal activities, I knew they could not afford original art.

My eye caught another abstract painting of circles and squares, done somewhat inexpertly in pastel colors, on the center of the wall above the television. It was Ginny's, I was certain.

Davidson returned, pointed to the loveseat and sat down on the armchair, handing me a glass of water. Wondering where to start, I sat and soothed my parched throat. "How are you and Angela doing?"

"I can't believe Joe is gone. He was my best friend." He said in a strained voice, as he stared ahead with still eyes as though he were sightless.

"What happened that morning? I got very little information from the police."

He took a sip of his coffee. "Joe came here the day before around five o'clock after work with a suitcase and left for the award ceremony. He was going to stay the night after the conference, instead of driving back to Culver City where he and Ginny live. He was due to go to Santa Cruz the next afternoon. He called from the conference and told us he'd be late and not to wait up. He had a key and hadn't returned when we both went to bed about eleven . . . " He paused as though he had run out of words.

"So, what time did you discover the body?"

Davidson stared into his coffee. "Around 7:15 or so in the morning. I went out to get the newspaper, trying not to disturb Joe, who I thought was still sleeping in the guest bedroom. Then I saw him in the Japanese garden. At first, I thought he must have fainted. I went and shook him, but by then I could tell he was gone. So much blood. I felt his wrist and there was no pulse. I knew enough to not disturb the body, and waited until the paramedics arrived and pronounced him dead."

If he had killed Faust with the idol, there should be blood spatter all over his clothes. I knew there were ways of determining that. What did Al find? No point in asking him. "Did either of you hear anything during the night?"

"The police asked us about that and we understood why. A violent crime took place in our front yard and we'd slept through it." He wrung his hands. "That night was the monthly Marching Marathon that usually starts at midnight and goes on for an hour. We took sleeping pills and turned music on to drown out the street noise."

"Whatever is a Marching Marathon?"

Bob answered, "It's a take-back-the-street kind of thing done by the neighborhood watch group once a month. Volunteers march, or rather walk through sections of the neighborhood in groups. We're too old for all that, but glad someone is doing it."

I hated to take any more of his time before bringing up Neil, but I had to ask. "Professor Davidson, why didn't you attend the award ceremony and the dinner at Roy's in honor of your best friend?"

Bob's face blanched perceptibly. "Call me Bob, please. I was just recovering from a cold. I didn't want to pass anything on to him. He had a busy speaking schedule ahead. Now I regret it. I wish I could have listened to him that one last time. He was a phenomenal speaker." He struggled with the last few words.

"As I walked in, I couldn't help think how much harder it must be for both of you, continuing to live in this house."

Bob's eyes shifted to Ginny's painting. "We are talking about moving, but we love this house, the community, and of course, our friends. We've fond memories of the time Joe spent here. But, we feel guilty about not having stopped the murder from happening." He took a tissue and blew his nose. "Angela used to tend to the Japanese garden herself. We now have a gardener to do that but still, we have to pass by it many times during the day. Sitting out there as we did before? No way." He sighed, and I felt the man was genuinely grieving, not only for his lost friend but also for the home he'd had, the life he'd had, before crime violently rearranged them. It was hard to think of him as a murderer.

"I understand, Bob. My father was killed three years ago."

"Oh, my, no, I didn't know that. I'm sorry. Three years. Does time do the healing it's supposed to?" The question was rhetorical. Bob picked at his nails. "Can you guess what the worst quality is in a human being? Cowardice. I've got to admit I'm guilty of it." His eyes welled up, and he wiped them. "Forgive me, Rekha. Every day, I keep thinking I could have helped Joe."

I couldn't make sense of his reference to cowardice, and his failure to help Faust. Did he mean that if he had woken up before the murder, he'd have intervened?

Bob recovered, shifted his position in the chair, and said, "Now, about Neil. Isn't that why you came?"

"Yes, yes. I'm sorry I got sidetracked."

"Don't worry, it helps me to talk about Joe. Now, Neil, he is a strange character, but I think you can guide him well."

"What can you tell me about him? He seems to be peculiar in many ways. Brilliant without a doubt, but also somewhat lacking in social graces. Am I too judgmental? I've never met a student like him."

Davidson sat back comfortably and smiled. "Peculiar is a gentle way to put it, Rekha. He's eccentric, gets distracted easily. Goes with the brilliance, I guess. I suggested he see a therapist, but he disregarded it. If only he'd learn to harness his energy."

"I agree with you that he has tremendous potential, a very astute and creative mind. I noticed the distractibility. Please tell me how you handled him."

"He'd often drift off from what we were discussing and start talking about other subjects. Things like that, not harmful, just plain irritating. I finally ended up catching him early on and bringing the discussion back to where it started before he wasted too much time." He looked away, his eyes glazed and staring. "He's not a bad sort, Rekha. With proper guidance, he could be another Joseph Faust. I'm so sorry he didn't get the privilege to work with Joe."

"I'll certainly remember to use your advice. Did Neil ever tell you about his thesis proposal?"

Davidson laughed. "Ah, that. I wondered what that was about. One-upmanship, maybe. I told him, that like Joe, I too wouldn't have read it until all applications were in."

I got up and picked up my satchel. Davidson also got up and straightened a couple of cushions. "Sorry, the house is still a mess. Anything else?"

I pointed to the abstract painting over the TV. "I'm curious about this painting. Who's the artist?"

"Oh, I picked it up at a street fair. I do that often. Why, do you paint?"

"No, but I admire artists. When I was in Ginny's studio, I noticed a couple of unfinished versions of abstract work. She told me she was getting into abstract and was copying other people's paintings, something that beginners are always encouraged to do. I think Ginny Faust painted your abstract. Am I correct?"

Bob looked at me with tight lips. "Yes," he said in a gravelly voice. "I didn't want Angela to know because she's the jealous type." Davidson's voice rose now to a more authoritative tone. "But so what if I lied about it? It's not a capital crime, is it?"

I wondered why he'd put up the painting so brazenly. To relive his affair? I stood up and walked over to see it up close. Its colors were exquisite, shapes defied categorization and blended from one into another. Without taking my eyes off the artwork, I said, "Ginny talked to me in private. She wanted to get something off her chest. You both had a brief affair, didn't you?"

Now Davidson's face turned ashen. He stood up and started pacing.

"She told you that? I'm amazed. An affair? I'd hardly call it that. We kissed one day when we were in her studio. That's when I asked her for the painting. She was thrilled that someone would value her first . . . and I must say . . .

rather amateurish abstract work, a copy."

"Didn't you spend a weekend together in Cambria?" I asked. I was standing directly across the front door and if necessary, I knew I could run faster than Davidson out into the street. Physical confrontation was not my strength.

Davidson stopped pacing and fell silent. He looked at his watch. He put his hands in his pant pockets. It looked like he was trying to make fists. Then he let out a long sigh.

"I'm not sure why this is any of your business, but I've no problem telling the truth. You have to promise you'll keep this from Angela." I nodded. "I was attracted to Ginny ever since I met her at Harvard. But she preferred Joe, and I didn't get in between them, ever. Until that day in the studio. She shared with me that she and Joe had been drifting apart for a few years and Joe had asked for a divorce. When I suggested we go away, I was surprised at her eager acceptance. We didn't think having a weekend together under the circumstances would be an affair. After Joe died, Ginny was riddled with guilt and called off any further contact between us. And I've honored that."

"Do you think Ginny had anything to do with her husband's murder?"

Bob gave a harsh laugh. "Are you out of your mind? I guess you don't know Ginny. She's pure, without any blemish. After Cambria, she told me I should fix my own marriage or get a divorce. She'd never be a mistress even if Joe went through with the divorce. She said . . . once a cheater . . . ." To my surprise, his tone became gentle and tender as he said, "Ginny's incapable of doing or planning what happened to her husband. She lived for the man. She was old-fashioned when it came to love and loyalty. That was what I adored about her. Yes, I made a fool of myself for her, but when I realized it, I had the grace to disconnect from her." His eyes went to the painting and instantly softened, and a small smile spread across his face. "I'll always have Cambria. And her art."

"Were you and Faust rivals professionally?"

Bob answered right away. "There was hardly any rivalry between us, our specialties were different. And, to be honest, Joe always outsmarted me. He won Ginny over. We were both considered for the co-directorship of JPM with Striker, but again, it went in Joe's favor. I was bitter for a while. But I couldn't hold a grudge against a good friend." He paused and stared at me.

I was done with skirting around the issue. "Professor Davidson, I sense that you know what happened that night."

"Are you kidding? As I told the police, I was fast asleep when the murder took place. The police asked me what I was doing between midnight and 2:30 in the morning." He stared at me with a strange expression. "The last I looked at the clock, it was 11 pm and I didn't wake until 7 am. I feel if I had been there, I could have prevented his death." Bob's eyes took on a hunted expression, and he averted his face.

Seeing my frown, he added, "The police went through everything in my garage and storage unit. I'm no idol thief either. I have a modest collection of paintings I buy and sell, but no statues or artifacts. Would you like to see them, Rekha?" His voice was silky, his face flushed.

I shook my head. I was certain his garage would be pristine by now. I stood up. "No, Bob, I'm sure I have troubled you enough."

He went to the door, opened it for me, and followed me onto the front patio.

In a calm voice, I said, "If you know anything about that night, please tell me, or the police. That's the least you could do for your friend, and for your own peace of mind."

Davidson crossed his arms across his chest. "I think you've overstayed your welcome, Rekha." His voice was terse.

As I walked toward the street, I turned back to him. "Would you have divorced Angela to marry Ginny? If Ginny hadn't ended the relationship?"

Bob's eyes drifted to the Japanese garden. "What's the point of dreaming? Wondering what might have been? Angela and I will move on, living our disconnected lives here or elsewhere. I only hope this specter of murder doesn't hang over us too long." His face was devoid of all emotion as if he had put on a mask. Perhaps, I thought, he had always worn that mask for Angela.

As I got into my car, I concluded that the Bob Davidson I'd seen was grieving his loss. Could his intense grief be a cover for guilt, for stealing the Durga, and killing his best friend with it in such an inhuman way? Did his subconscious resentment for his more successful colleague, married to a woman he'd also loved, bubble up beyond containment?

~ Chapter 14 ~

Sunday, April 9, 2017
Eagle Rock, Los Angeles, CA

My goal to take care of all my dharmas was not a facetious one.

I'd spent the night fretful, a bundle of nerves. On waking, I felt an emptiness in my belly that food couldn't fill. I longed for a word, a gentle touch from another to say, I'm here, lean on me for a while. But I had no one to offer me comfort other than Ma, Grandma, and Sanjay, each in their own way. Since moving, I had cultivated no new friends other than Patricia, if I could call her a friend. I thought of Al, his strong stature and gentle handshake. I had no idea when, if at all, I'd see him again.

I went to see Ma and Grandma.

My mother's new home, a condo, was devoid of any vestige of my dad's gift as a gardener. The front yard was minimal, paved, and taken care of by the Condo Association. But the backyard held all that remained of Dad, his ashes in a jar, buried under a maple tree that Ma had planted, and tended with the same care and affection she had for her husband in life.

I went to the back through an unlocked side gate and

sat down on a flat-top rock near the growing maple tree. The lawn was small, separated from other yards by a wooden fence draped with bougainvillea, my mother's favorite flowering plant. In the fading evening light and silence, I spoke to Dad. Of my involvement with the police, of Rajeev, and my progress with Faust's murder. It sounded like a quarterly report to an HR manager and made me laugh. But I wasn't finished. I took a bold leap and brought up my love-hate feelings for Al. What did they mean? Did he ever feel that way about Ma? About another woman? I heard no answer. I realized it was up to me now to find the answers, locked inside my own conflicted psyche.

I returned to the front door and rang the bell, although I had a key. Whenever I came unannounced, I behaved like a polite visitor. Ma opened the door and beamed, surprised. "So good to see you, sweetie." She hugged me. "Skin and bones." She admonished, a comment often echoed by other family members, one that I had learned not to fight over.

"Ma, I'm starving. Just happened to be in the neighborhood." I took off my jacket and scarf and sniffed the air that never failed to contain the smells of clove, cardamom, cinnamon, and cumin.

"You don't need any excuse to drop in, Beti." Ma walked back into the kitchen and resumed chopping tomatoes. "How's work?" The standard question my family always asked.

I was uncertain whether Ma meant my college work or what I was doing for the police. I went with the former. I opened the fridge, took out a can of coconut water, and started gulping it down. "Lot of work, nature of the beast, Ma. My classes are going well. Students seem to like my teaching. And I am slowly but surely working on my proposal. Where's Grandma?"

"In her room, she must be just finishing up her prayers. I was going to make *palak paneer*, rice, and *raita*, OK?" She pointed to frozen chopped spinach thawing in a bowl and took out paneer from the fridge. "Days when I work, I am all short cuts. Luckily, Grandma is not fussy about her food. Recently she has been adventurous, asking for tacos, noodles and all." Ma laughed.

I laughed with her at the thought of Grandma, my eighty-year-old grandmother, eating noodles. Did she eat it with her hands as she ate Indian food at home? It was so good to hear Ma laugh. She must be adjusting to life without Dad. I also suspected that this mother and daughter pair were grateful for each other's company in a life that otherwise would have left each of them lonely. I doubted if my mother would remarry. Her generation didn't in India, where such a move would raise eyebrows and start juicy gossips. Women would whisper to each other at the innumerable Indian parties, why does she need a man, a woman of her age? She should be devoting her time to her children and her daily prayers. Would Ma think differently, now that the US was her home?

I knocked on Grandma's door and hearing her tremulous voice granting me entrance, walked in and found her standing in front of her homemade altar. A large oval silver platter that held figurines of Krishna, Vishnu, Ganesha, and Shiva, surrounded by fresh flower petals and an incense holder. In front of the figurines was the *diya*, a small brass oil lamp, with a flame emanating from its single oil-soaked wick. A petite woman, Grandma stood straight, her shoulders drooping a little under the weight of a midnight blue cotton shawl, draped over a tan tunic. And loose pants.

"Ah, Beti, how nice to see you," Grandma said as I came in and gave her a gentle hug, for fear I might break her frail frame. She pulled me toward the altar and said, "Let's pray together before I put out the flame." In silence, we stood with folded palms, and I prayed for a long life for Grandma and Ma. Prayer finished, Grandma held me at arm's length and looked into my eyes. "You have your father's eyes. How are you? Is work going well?"

We sat on the bed and chatted away about my teaching, the latest Bollywood movies she'd watched, and other tidbits until I said, "Grandma, I want to talk about two men that I seem to like. Did you ever have that experience?"

"No, although it seemed like I fell in love many times with characters from books and movies before my parents arranged my marriage to your papa. Once I met him, I had no doubt, I was destined for him. But those were ancient times when women never met men on their own. Tell me who you've fallen for," she chuckled.

"OK. Don't laugh. One is Rajeev, whom I met here. The other is a detective I'm working with, although I have done nothing about it because of my conflicted feelings."

"You like both, I assume. Well, you will figure out soon who you like better or love. Is the detective Indian?"

"No, Grandma. He's American and somewhat older than me."

"Oh, my," Grandma said. "Take your time. Rajeev comes from a good family, good people. Get to know him and your detective. At least you have options, unlike me. I chose the man my parents chose. He ended up being my best friend." Her eyes looked away as if to focus on an image she alone saw.

"I'll do that, Grandma." Never before had Grandma shared with me her feelings about her husband who had died almost ten years ago.

Ma called us for dinner. I left my hair loose to please Grandma. I admired her pragmatic approach to life's problems.

Halfway through the improvised yet scrumptious dinner, Ma asked the inevitable question. "Did you get a chance to meet Rajeev again, Beti?" My mother had a gentle, harmless way of asking a difficult question, reducing it to its simplest terms.

Grandma and I exchanged looks.

"Yes, Ma. We went out for dinner. I like him. We plan to get together again. One can never predict when a lawyer might come in handy." I laughed, but seeing the serious look on my mother's face, I added, "Or a life partner."

"Give him a chance, Rekha," she said.

Both Grandma and Ma never heard the details of what I went through with Matt Porter. I never wanted to feel helpless like that ever again. Any man in my life would need to prove his trustworthiness.

We lapsed into a comfortable silence interrupted by a call. I looked at my cell phone and saw it was from Sanjay. I said, "Sorry, I've got to take this." I moved over to the hallway.

"Didi, I need to see you," Sanjay said in a hushed voice. "I have something to tell you. I knocked so many times. Where are you?" God, it's true that when it rains, it pours. Family and more family.

I moved further into the hallway. "What do you mean, come in, you idiot? Where the heck are you?"

"I'm outside your house in my car. Will you please open the door before the neighbors think I'm a prowler or something?" Sanjay sounded anxious.

"You imbecile, I'm having dinner with Ma and Grandma." I couldn't help but worry. "Don't you have the key I gave you? . . . You aren't hurt or anything, are you?"

"No, nothing like that. I've something to tell you that can't wait, that's all." He was calmer now but breathing deep. "Sorry, I can't find my key."

"OK, you stay put or take a little drive and come back. It'll be an hour before I can be there." His urgency troubled me. What has he done now? Did he disobey me and confront Kevin?

I wanted to leave right away but didn't want to create panic for Ma and Grandma. "The food is great Ma, and I almost finished it. Can I take the rest home?" I laughed, hoping she didn't pick up on my anxiety.

Ma got up and said, "Wait, I'll get more. It'll only take a second."

I got some foil, wrapped up the leftover from my plate, and grabbed my satchel. I kissed them both. "No, Ma, Grandma, don't get up, please finish your dinner. I need to go." I stood still for a moment to regain my composure and to calm them.

Ma sat down again but did not attempt to eat. Grandma stared without understanding, put her left hand to her forehead and lowered her right hand that was halfway to the mouth with a ball of rice, spinach, and paneer. Turning to me, she said, "Be safe, Beti," and then to herself, "Rama, Rama."

* * *

Sanjay sat on the rocking chair on the porch, swinging back and forth, cell phone in hand. I unlocked the door and watched him move like a zombie into the living room and crumple on the sofa.

I asked, "What's going on?"

"My throat is parched. Can I have some water?"

My landline rang. I picked it up. There was only deep

breathing. I put it down.

I brought Sanjay some water and swatted him on his shoulder. "Drink it and tell me what happened. I've all the time in the world." By instinct, I took out my notebook. Just in case he had a story to tell.

Between gulps of water, my brother said, "I'm sorry, but I need to confess that I didn't listen to you. I'd been watching Kevin Faust for some time, just trying to help you." His eyes didn't meet mine.

"What the heck . . . have you lost your mind?"

"I told you he lives in a rental unit a few doors from me near the campus. Last Friday, I got home from the library near midnight, saw him in his car ready to leave, and followed him. At a safe distance, mind you."

Sanjay shifted his position and focused his eyes on the cup in his hands. "But wait till I tell you what I found out, Didi," Sanjay said, energized. "Do you know where he went? To La Descarga, the burlesque club in LA." He chuckled. "I followed him there, got a ticket and watched the show. And there he was, one of a group of men dressed up as women, and dancing, with exaggerated thrusts of their . . ." He fell silent.

My phone rang. I ignored it.

"Why don't you answer it? It might be Ma."

"Ma never calls this late. No, it's someone who calls and hangs up. I don't have the patience for it."

Sanjay's face clouded. "Who could play pranks on you? Your students?"

"No way. They wouldn't dare. Some neighborhood kids, I'm sure. Nothing to worry about, OK? Go on with your story."

"Well, I wanted to make sure it was him. So I talked to one of the bouncers and asked him for the name of the person in the red outfit. He gave me two names. Kevin Faust and Dancing Kali." He laughed and coughed as the water in his mouth took a wrong turn.

"You can get hurt doing this, Sanjay. It is not a job for the novice. Have you noticed that I'm staying put and not sneaking around and following people? Didn't you think if Kevin found out, he'd have reported you? There's a law against stalking, you bozo." I wanted to put some fear into his thick head.

"That's why I had to tell you. Listen, if he goes there every Friday, he couldn't have killed his father, because the murder happened on a Friday night. Right?"

"OK and thank you for finding that out. But we still don't have any info if he was there on the night and early morning in question."

Sanjay said, "You think I wouldn't have thought of that? I asked the bouncer about that specific date. Lied that he was my buddy, and I wanted to play a prank on him. He checked the ledger and said he was there until 2 am. Now you can thank me." He made a bow from the seated position and smiled.

"All right, thanks. I didn't think you had this in you. But promise me you won't do any more sleuthing on your own." I held out my right hand, palm up.

"OK, I'll stay away from Kevin from now on." He placed his right hand over mine, palm down. It didn't escape me that his promise was specific, about not following Kevin only. Clever guy.

The phone rang again—this time I picked it up. My body stiffened as I listened to what seemed like an electronically distorted voice at the other end. "Hey, sweetheart, how's it going?" The caller hung up. I couldn't figure out who it was.

I felt my body tremble. Was it Matt Porter? How did he get my phone number? Did that mean he knew where I lived? Or, was it Faust's killer threatening me?

"Is everything OK?" Sanjay asked, perceptive enough to detect the change in my body language.

For the first time since leaving Irvine, I felt panic, but said calmly, "Yeah, yeah, it was just a wrong number." I put the receiver down. I debated about telling Sanjay that it might be Matt Porter. That I needed him to stay the night on my couch. But I was gradually recovering from my PTSD, gaining inner strength and rediscovering courage. I didn't want to come across as wimpy to my brother. Besides, the calls were likely pranks.

My landline announced another call. Sanjay was on his way to the door and turned back to stare at me. I made no move to answer it. He shrugged and walked out. I took the phone off the hook and went to bed.

~ Chapter 15 ~

Sunday, April 9 - Monday, April 10, 2017
Eagle Rock, Los Angeles, CA

I was driving aimlessly, stepping on the gas to lose a blue Audi following me. I was about to take a right turn when the Audi hit my rear bumper, forcing me to bring my vehicle to a stop. The driver got out, and I heard him slam the door. All I could see in the pitch-black night was a shadow, silhouetted by scattered lights from homes along the road. But there was no question about this figure, a man dressed in dark clothes and wearing a mask and a cowboy hat. He had the physique of Bill, but it wasn't Bill. He held a gun in his hand and got very close to my side of the car. I couldn't make out his face in the shadows. I tried to open the door, but he blocked my way and thrust his gun into my face. His mask, up close, resembled the face of the Mahishasura. A wail rose from the depth of my bowels, primitive, soundless. I pressed my belly with both hands to generate a sound and woke up from the nightmare with a silent scream.

A cold sweat covered my body. The old house seemed to shudder from the aftershock of my scream. Was it just a dream?

I heard the door creak. Someone was inside the house.

Did I forget to set the alarm last night? Was it Matt?

Stealthy footsteps tracked the wood floor of my living room. Although my bedroom was separated from the living room only by a pocket door without either a latch or lock, I had confidently relied on the motion sensors to alert me if someone approached the door. But I knew I hadn't turned on the alarm.

I grabbed the cordless handset from the side table, crawled under the bed, found the mallet I kept there and dialed 911. The line was dead. I had taken the phone off the hook last night and never put it back. The thought of the intruder trapping me under the bed brought the taste of bile into my mouth and I softly crawled out, hammer in hand.

My cell phone, that I always kept on my nightstand, wasn't there. My heart pounded through my chest. My throat felt dry, my legs wobbly. I needed to make my way out into the living room to get my phone, even if it meant coming face to face with Matt or a stranger. As I entered the hallway, moonlight streaming in through the glass patio door fell on my cell phone on the side table, three or four strides away. I must go for it now, or I was dead.

A shadow moved past the kitchen door. The rooms were pitch black, but the shadow was no ghost, it was a tall man with a broad chest clad in a sweatshirt with the hood pulled over his head. I made a swift dash to reach the table.

I made it but knocked down the table and heard the phone hit the wood floor.

The shadow in the kitchen transformed into the man from my dream and plunged toward me. A strong force grabbed my arms and pushed me to the wall. He kept me against the wall with his left arm crushing my neck and punched my face with a tight right fist. Only bouts of deep breathing came out of the intruder's mouth, but I could feel his rage. I tried to scream, but no voice came from my throat. I twisted my body around, freed my right hand and used it to maul his face. My fingers slipped off a silky and slippery surface, and I realized a piece of cloth or plastic covered his face. Before I knew it, I was on the floor with a pair of strong gloved hands constricting my throat. I tried to fill my lungs and thrashed around trying to get free. The man was now upon me, crushing me with his full weight. God, I didn't want to be raped. With every ounce of my rapidly draining energy, I struggled to free my right leg, took a deep breath and thrust my knee at his groin. He let out a noise like a butchered pig, the only sound he had made during the entire encounter. I felt him let go of me and deliver a swift kick to my right side. I found my voice and yelled, "Help, somebody, help me." I heard noises outside the front door. He must have heard them too because, in a flash, the hooded figure lunged toward the kitchen and was gone.

I sat gasping and sobbing, unable to move my body, not knowing where my cell phone was. Someone was pounding on the front door repeatedly and I heard Al's voice calling my name. I crawled to the door like a live rag doll to open it, and fell into his arms, trembling and sobbing.

"Who was it? Was . . . it . . . Matt? Did . . . you . . . see him?" I asked hysterically, my voice croaking at a high pitch, without realizing that Matt was a stranger to Al.

Al put his arms around my shoulders, walked me over to the sofa and sat me down. He took a throw from the chair and wrapped my body with it and held me tight to stop the shaking. "It's over, Rekha. We're here to help you. And cops are looking for him." He gulped, tightened his grip and added, "I'm so glad you're OK."

The emergency response team checked me out and concluded that no bones were broken and that bruising of my face and neck were all the physical injuries I had sustained. They wanted to take me to the ER for a thorough check-up, but I insisted I was OK, that I'd go see a doctor in the morning if I felt worse. They gave me some medication to alleviate pain and to put me to sleep for a while.

I sat staring at the disarray in my living room and told the cops I'd check in the morning and call them if anything was missing. I knew in my bones that this was no burglary.

"You are safe now, Rekha. Let me get you some water," Al said and made his way to the kitchen.

In his reassuring presence, I tried to piece things together. It was two in the morning, scarcely four hours after Sanjay had said good night and left.

"What happened?" I asked, my voice back to normal.

"Why don't you relax and answer the questions for the cops. We'll talk after that." He reached for my left hand and covered it with his. I felt a surge of warmth flow into my body from his. There was no romance in it, nor did I expect it. It was the trained gesture of a detective comforting a victim, staying well on the right side of propriety. I put the water down quietly, grasped his hand tight and started to sob. For having escaped being raped or killed, for having someone whose hand I could hold.

I answered the cops' questions and described the intruder as best as I could. They dusted for fingerprints on the kitchen door, and said they didn't find any. "You were careless, Miss," said one of the cops who was taking notes. I dropped Al's hands. "You happened to leave the kitchen door unlatched, and your alarm system was off. It was easy for him to get in. Burglars don't usually break in when your car's on the patio.

Whoever did this, did it to hurt you." The young cop was almost accusatory, as though I deserved or had invited the break-in. "This isn't a favorite part of the town for thieves." He continued to scribble.

Al looked at me and felt my neck and face where the tissue was starting to swell up. "Try to get some sleep, if you can. Let the meds do their job. I will wait for these guys to finish up and then check in on you. I won't leave until you're asleep. A cop car will stay in front of the house. I can assure you the perp won't come back tonight. Let's talk in the morning. I need a list of people who might have a grudge against you."

Reluctantly I stood up and wrapped the throw around my body.

"I don't know if I can sleep but I'll try . . . and, thanks Al, for coming. But how did you get here? I didn't call you."

He hesitated, and then said, "Your brother called me last night and alerted me about the hang-up calls. He was worried it was your abusive ex-boyfriend. I promised him I'd keep an eye on your place."

"You put a cop car here?"

"No, I was here in my car, watching your front door. But the perp came in through the back. I heard movements inside, pounded on the door, and that was when you opened it."

"Thank you." That was all I could say. There were no words for the growing warmth in my chest. I walked to the bedroom and crashed onto my bed, clutching the throw like a lifeline. Exhausted, I gave in to sleep.

* * *

I woke up to a drizzling April shower and the smell of clean air, a welcome respite from the recent muggy weather. I lay in bed looking at the raindrops hit the glass window in a gentle rhythm.

It took only a second before I shot up, as a slide show of last night's events whisked by my mind. Was the intruder gone? Or was it all a dream? Was Al here? I felt a sharp pain from my neck move up to my face, and my hands found the bruises that had swelled up while I slept. I threw on a robe and made my way to the living room as fast as I could and found a sight for my sore eyes.

Sanjay was on my comfortable chair, leaning back, feet on the ottoman, shirt sleeves rolled up, eyes closed, and an open notebook resting on his belly. A blazing fire in the grate would have made it an Indian Norman Rockwell portrait.

"Hey, you," I said. Sanjay sat up, rubbed his eyes. "How did you get here?" I went over and hugged him, despite my aches, immensely relieved to have him there, my one staunch supporter.

"I called Al Newton last night after I left you." He looked at me and proceeded before I could ask him why. "Sorry, Didi, I was worried about all those hang-up calls but didn't want to scare you. I had to tell him the Matt Porter story. He said he'd keep an eye out. He called me after you went to sleep. He didn't want you to be alone. Too bad you had to go through all that shit." He peered at my face. "Are you all right? Do you want me to take you to the ER?" Then through clenched teeth, he muttered, "I bet it's that rotten loser, Matt."

"I'm OK. I'm glad you're here, Sanju. But let's not jump to conclusions. It could be someone else. I'm unsure how Matt found out where I lived."

"There are ways, Didi. A local newspaper or the Oxy Weekly might have reported your involvement with the case. He snoops around Oxy, talks to clueless students, or even professors, or follows you to find out where you live. It's not impossible."

I thought of Neil and his quest for freedom of the press. Was he indirectly responsible for the break-in? I said, "I guess you're right."

"Look, you need to see a doctor." He was already on his cell phone. "Here's an ER I can take you to."

"No, no, Sanjay. I'm fine, trust me." I said. "Just a few bruises around my throat that will subside in a day or two. I can cover them up until then," I added as Sanjay started to protest. "Honestly. There's nothing that a day's rest wouldn't cure. I have no class today."

"Do you want me to stay tonight, in case he comes back?"

"No, they don't come back the next day. Promise me nothing of this gets to Ma. She'd freak out."

Sanjay nodded. "I'll call you tomorrow. Newton suggested reinstating the restraining order against Matt. Do it please, when you get a chance?" Sanjay got up, stretched, and yawned.

"Sure, sure . . . but I wish you hadn't told Al about Matt, Sanju. Now I'm a wuss in his eyes, beaten up by my ex-boy-friend." My whole body felt itchy and dirty. The physical close-ness with the attacker still clung to me as if I'd stepped in manure. I wanted to take a long shower, peel him off and throw away my clothes.

"Being a wuss is not the worst thing." Sanjay chuckled and walked to the kitchen. "Let me make some chai."

As we sat and sipped, Sanjay said, "How involved are you with the case, Didi? What if it was someone whom you'd annoyed by asking a lot of questions? Or the killer who figured out what you were up to and came after you to scare you off?" It was a casual comment followed by, "Tell me that's not a possibility."

I thought for a moment. "I can tell you it's not because I decided to look into the murder only yesterday. All I've done so far is to attend Davidson's class and talk to him. I also talked to Ginny, whom I trust. Do you think Davidson sent someone to beat me up? Would he dare? I'm a faculty colleague. Don't read more into it."

"Well, it's no secret that you've been helping the police figure out the Durga. Maybe the killer felt that your work would reveal his identity. If Davidson stole the Durga, and heaven forbid, killed Faust, he could have felt threatened by your questions and, yes, sent someone to shut you up. Or came himself."

Fear trickled down my spine. "So you're saying I should back off? No way. What about justice for Faust and his family? What about my dharma? Is that something I put on like a cloak and take off when it gets hot? No, I can't back off, especially now."

Sanjay tapped his forehead with the fingers of his right hand as though exasperated. "Then promise me you'll keep me in the loop, tell me everything you do, so I can keep an eye on you, and make sure you're OK. I promise I won't do any more sleuthing without checking with you. Get the restraining order, please."

We did our hand over hand gesture, and Sanjay left, comforted by my promise to keep him abreast of what I did. I could use a sounding board, and he was eager and bright and had a streetwise logic, but I hated to drag him into the middle of my unauthorized, imperfect and dangerous attempt at solving Faust's murder.

I held back from him that I didn't believe in the power of a restraining order. I'd reinstate it, just as a gesture, but I knew that a piece of paper wouldn't be a barrier between trusting women and the evil that men inflicted upon them.

~ Chapter 16 ~

Monday, April 10, 2017
Eagle Rock, Los Angeles, CA

T he progression of the day brought solace as the bruises first paled, then hurt less, and my head stopped throbbing. Grateful I didn't have classes that day, I decided to summarize the thoughts about the case I'd absent-mindedly stitched together in my head.

My cell rang. I let it ring. I'd made a new habit of listening to calls before picking up the phone.

This one was from Al. "I'm in the neighborhood, Rekha."

I grabbed the phone. "Hi, sorry, I wanted to listen before answering. I'm glad it's you."

Al cleared his throat and continued. "I was wondering if I may stop by for a few minutes. I have the restraining order form. I filled it in, it just needs your signature. I can submit it for you." And after a pause, "Also wanted to make sure you're OK."

I was a mess with the bruises, but he had seen me at the worst. So I said yes. Besides, I wanted to see him. His behavior toward me last night had convinced me that there was a kind and caring person underneath his cop persona.

When he arrived, he gave me a quick once over and

smiled. "Not too bad for what happened last night. You are starting to heal. Any pain?"

I rubbed my neck where the assailant had put a choke-hold on me. Al's eyes went to my neck and then to my face where it stayed focused on my eyes. His cheeks turned pink. "I can tell you from experience that all these marks will disappear in a week or two. I am so glad he didn't break any bones or cause a head injury. You're very lucky."

I pointed to the sofa, and he sat down. "I still say you should see a doctor."

"I promise I will if I'm not feeling better by the end of the day."

"By the way, we contacted the police at the University of California San Diego with the info Sanjay gave us, and they had Porter checked out. He swore he was with his girl-friend last night, and the girlfriend confirmed it. The cops said they'll keep an eye on him.

Al said, "I almost forgot. Bill was let go this morning. I thought that would be good news for you. For us too, since we can now move on to find the real killer."

"That is wonderful, I knew he wasn't a killer. How did you guys figure it out?"

Al took out the paperwork for my restraining order and pointed to yellow sickies where I was required to sign. "We had the neighbor look at a line-up of guys including Bill, and his friend Neil. He couldn't identify either of them as the man he saw in the car in the alley near Davidson's house. He'd told us earlier that it could have been Bill, from his photograph. Eyewitness testimony is not always accurate." He got up, grabbed the papers I'd signed, and said, "I better get going."

I offered my right hand to shake, and he took it in both his hands and held it for a moment. He looked into my eyes and said, "Thank you, I learned some things from you, Rekha. To consider the character of a person in the final assessment of guilt or innocence. I have to see if it sticks."

With that, he walked out. He sounded skeptical and I understood. Police valued objectivity and impartial assessment of suspects.

* * *

I settled down to do some work and was interrupted by the ping of a text. It was from my friend at the National Museum of India, Raghunath Reddy. The message was: "The Durga was collected by a lamba, patala Gora (a tall, thin, white man) at the rail station. Hope this helps." It did not sound like the man Davidson described. Was he leading me astray?

I shrugged it off, eager to create my murder board. I pulled out a bulletin board from my storage closet and leaned it against the wall in my living room. In the center, I attached a photo of Faust as Mahishasura. I found photos of Davidson and Striker online, printed them out, and cut out the heads. I put them up on the board to begin to form a circle around Faust. I had no photos of Ginny, so I wrote her name on a post-it note and pinned it to the board. I added a tag of MM, for Mahishasura Mardini, the potential killer, to each person in the circle around Faust.

I created bidirectional arrows and connected the central figure of Faust/Mahishasura with each MM. I put blank "Motive/Relationship" tags on the arrows. Once done, I took several photos of the board and uploaded them into my laptop. My Murder Wheel.

I didn't know if Faust had had an affair or had a girl-friend before Ginny, who might have harbored hard feelings. Why would she wait to kill him or have him killed after all these years? Did they run into each other recently? It didn't make sense. Despite my skepticism, I added another MM to the circle, labeled ex-lover, and made a note to talk to Ginny and Faust's niece and find out what they knew.

I entered "love for Davidson" as Ginny's motive. For Kevin, it was fear of exposure of cross-dressing or, possibly, loss of inheritance for the same reason. Sanjay's little adventure had provided an alibi for him that I needed to confirm. As a researcher, I had always double-checked facts. Until then, he'd stay on the circle.

I considered the demon theory. Davidson and Striker would qualify as demons, i.e., Faust's rivals. I couldn't see Striker as a killer, since his motive, old ill-feelings over the co-directorship, was just that, old and weak. If Davidson stole the Durga, any threat of revelation could give him cause to kill Faust. Alternatively, or additionally, he could have been jealous of Faust's achievements, or still retain hopes that if Faust were eliminated, he'd get Ginny back. And recently, there'd been a lot of guilt both on his face and in his words. He was the only one whom I could tie to both the theft and the murder. I entered his motives.

I knew the cops were not fooled either. But why had they not arrested Davidson? I'd read of cases where police held back from an early arrest of a suspect because of a lack of physical evidence that might lead to the case being thrown out of court. I hoped years wouldn't pass before Davidson got his dues.

I wondered if I should include Bill among the MMs. Both Rajeev and Sanjay had suggested I should. I only had his word that he had stayed home. If he went back to Roy's, he had to get there before Faust left, to follow him. But looking through Faust's bookshelf and his subsequent dismissal from the internship didn't stand up as motives. What other motive might he have? Faust couldn't be his father since, according to his great-aunt, his parents had died in a car accident a long time ago. I needed to double-check the accident information with a newspaper report.

I thought of Neil, with his almost unprofessional behavior. It seemed too far-fetched that *he* could be the killer. Faust's refusal to read his thesis proposal was not fuel enough for him to kill his professor. Did he take Bill's car, put in enough gas to drive it back to Roy's and follow Faust? I had no proof to substantiate any of this.

In my heart, I couldn't envisage either of these barely twenty-something boys plotting to kill their professor. I knew I wasn't being unbiased, but I placed both outside the murder wheel for the time being. I added an Unsub with a question mark as another MM. I knew that the weakness of my theories was that I was dealing with a small number of people closely connected to Faust. The killer could very well be someone peripheral to Faust's inner circle and outside my reach.

I made a note to do several things in the next few days: find out more about the accident that killed Bill's parents; talk to Neil's mom about when he came home and about his birth father; find and read his damn thesis; look for whatever Faust had hidden in his bookshelf. I longed to get one more chance to talk to Davidson, but by now I was *persona non grata* with him.

Although not extensive, these thoughts grounded me in the work that lay ahead. My head pounded and my bruises started to throb again, but I called Faust's niece and invited myself over. I didn't care if she saw my bruises.

* * *

The address Patricia had given me was on Roxbury Drive in Pasadena. I found a modest home where remodeling was in progress, as proclaimed by the sign put up by the contractor.

Sylvia was a warm and friendly woman somewhere in her forties. She invited me to sit down and said, "Your professor was my uncle, Uncle Joe. My mother was his older sister. I used to see him often, for birthdays, at Christmas and other occasions, while I was in high school here. Uncle Joe was then at Harvard. Ginny and I got along well . . ." She trailed off.

"I'm sorry for what happened, Sylvia. Your beloved uncle was my mentor and father figure. I miss him too. I'm trying to help the police with an idol that the killer left on his body. I wondered if you knew of any stories he might have brought home from Harvard?" I decided not to take notes for this one.

Sylvia frowned, got up, and took a framed photo from a table and sat down next to me. "This is the only photo I have of my uncle when he was at Harvard." She pointed to a much younger-looking Faust standing between an older man, and a woman who resembled him. "These are my parents, No longer with us."

We sat together in silence until she said, "Uncle Joe started Harvard in his early thirties. He tried engineering for a while and switched to archaeology. I was about seventeen or so then, and would eagerly talk to him when he visited because I was enamored with schools like Harvard. He'd joke about wasting his time with his best friend Bob Davidson, instead of studying. I knew he was making little of how well he did there. To keep my hopes up to get into a good college."

"Did he have a girlfriend before he met Ginny?"

"Come to think of it, he waxed eloquent about an exotic

co-ed he was dating in the first year. I remember it because I thought that was what college would get me too, a boyfriend. Uncle Joe told me she'd left school sometime during the freshman year, and he wasn't able to locate her. He seemed despondent about it. But then he met Ginny."

"Do you by chance remember the girlfriend's name? Or anything special about her?" I leaned over and touched Sylvia's shoulder. "If you do, it'd be a huge help."

She frowned. "I'm sorry, all that happened decades ago. I went off to college in another year and lost touch with my uncle. We reconnected recently after I moved back to Pasadena. I'm sorry, I don't even remember if he told me her name in the first place. But he did say she was from India."

This revelation was a thunderbolt. Could this be the connection to the motive?

I thanked Sylvia and went home.

* * *

I checked my email and found a new one, from Bill.

"I'm free, Professor Rao, YAY. Can we meet today to go over what I missed in class last week?"

I was relieved that my convictions about this young man were not off-track. But I knew he'd still be on the police radar. Wanting to be supportive, I emailed him his reading assignment and work submissions for next week. A prompt email came back, thanking me and stating he hoped to see me the next day at a party organized by the Gielguds to celebrate his release. He was asked to bring a guest, and he chose me over his friends. I was touched. In my state of partial recovery, I wasn't sure about going, although I itched for a chance to meet the antique dealers. I knew I could cover the remnants of my bruises with clothing and make-up.

Another email sounded. It said, 'Sorry to inform you that Eduardo Lopez killed himself today by hanging. He left a note for us to contact you."

I felt like someone sucker-punched me. This was an emotional setback I didn't expect, I didn't need. The poor man must have given up hope. He must have realized that I too had stopped working on his case.

I cried myself to sleep.

~ Chapter 17 ~

Tuesday, April 11, 2017
Eagle Rock, Los Angeles, CA

Bill McGraw stopped by my office the next day, unannounced.

I had finished my late-morning lecture, my neck covered by a scarf, my arms by long sleeves, and my face made-up. I hoped no one would come close enough to suspect anything. I knew the students wouldn't, and my unusual announcement that I had no time to answer questions after the lecture but would entertain emails sealed the deal. And now I had to make sure Bill didn't suspect anything. I didn't want anyone to find out. Deep down, I felt responsible, I kicked myself that I'd let it happen.

Bill grabbed both my hands and shook them vigorously. I faked a cough and turned my face to one side. "They had to let me go. Because there wasn't any evidence to connect me with the murder." He added in a whisper, "Apparently my car was clean. They put me in a line-up and the neighbor couldn't identify me. It surprised me he identified my car in the first place. And thought my photo looked like the person who was in the car."

"There are so many similar cars. Eyewitness testimony

is often erratic. How about physical evidence like DNA and fingerprints?"

Bill smiled. "Boy, I'm glad I knew something about these procedures from TV shows. They told me not to leave town until those results came back. But I'm confident they won't be a match. I was nowhere near there."

He sat down in a chair in front of me. I got up and moved to a side table in the guise of looking for something.

"I'm glad, too, Bill. Your aunt called me. She was relieved. Are you catching up with classes?"

"Yes. Everything is back to normal. I came to find out if you're coming to the party. I hope you will. It'd mean so much to me." He brought out an invitation from his jacket pocket and gave it to me.

I hadn't given it a thought since I got his email. "Any other professors coming?"

Bill rattled off the names of a bunch including Davidson and Striker. Bill's godparents, the Gielguds, were legitimate antique dealers, but I knew that didn't exclude them from illegal activities. Might they have any connection to the Durga? Was Davidson the middleman who acquired artifacts for them? "Let me say I'll try, Bill, but I'm not sure at this time."

Bill was silent for a moment and said, "I have something to tell you. Do you remember what I told you in jail? That Professor Faust got angry because he thought I was doing something unprofessional. I thought about it and thought about it and finally realized that maybe he was worried that I might have discovered something of a personal nature that he had hidden in the bookshelf. Underneath that book that wouldn't pull out?"

I wanted to say that the same thing had crossed my mind

but played it nonchalant. "Like what?" I asked with a laugh.

"Maybe a valuable book, a memento, a love-letter, or something else he didn't want others to see, something that might damage his reputation. My aunt had a collection of glass animals, like a menagerie. She'd make sure I stayed away from where she kept them because she thought I'd drop one and break it. Even to this day, she won't let me go too close to that cabinet. Professor Faust's reaction reminded me of my aunt's frightened look when she caught me near the cabinet. Idiosyncratic maybe, but human." He laughed, and instantly his face transformed, as though he'd had a revelation. "You'll tell the police, right?"

I had no hesitation. "I don't want to sidetrack them. What if it turns out to be Faust's precious glass menagerie? We'd look very silly. Forget about it. Let the police work on their clues, they're good at it." I couldn't tell him that I was determined to find out if there was anything hidden in Faust's bookshelf.

"What if it was something connected to the murder? We'd be helping with the investigation. I can sneak in there one evening and look around." His eyes looked wild with expectation.

"No, Bill, no way." My voice was loud and his mouth fell open. "You can't do that. You're *not* doing that. That's breaking-and-entering, a punishable felony. Do you want to throw away everything you've achieved so far? And did you think what it'd do to your aunt? No way." I said all this in the most authoritative voice I'd ever used with him. I didn't want this boy to get into any more trouble. "And, this subject is off-limits from now on."

Bill lowered his eyes, played with his nails for a moment and said, "What if the police haven't yet looked there?"

"Patricia, Dr. Faust's secretary, tells me they left a huge mess in the office. Don't you think they would have found it if there was something hidden? Police have better training to look for things than we have. Maybe there was nothing underneath the book."

"I guess. I bet he moved it. I would have if I were in his position," Bill stuttered. "Sorry, I'll listen to your advice and leave well enough alone. I need to catch up with my classes, anyway."

I'd heard from Patricia that one of the cops who had searched Faust's office had let it slip that they didn't find anything suspicious there. But I knew how sloppy police searches could be. After my father's murder the Irvine police had searched my apartment. They made a big mess but failed to uncover Matt's love letters I had kept taped to the underside of my mattress to shield them from the prying fingers of my roommates. And my apartment manager who snooped around when I was away.

The moment Bill walked out, I realized I should have asked him about the accident that killed his parents. Maybe at the party.

An urgency to search Faust's office gathered momentum inside me. Although yellow tape still hung across the office door, I could squeeze inside without disturbing it. I was skinny, but how to unlock the door? Asking for the key would raise suspicion, and I had little or no experience picking locks.

~ Chapter 18 ~

Friday, April 14, 2017
San Marino, Los Angeles, CA

That morning, for the first time, I called Al at the station. I was put through to him right away.

"Well, this is a nice surprise. I've been thinking of you. What's up?"

I told him about Eduardo and remained composed. He said, "I'll still look into the case, Rekha. Eduardo's death doesn't change my promise. We should get the case reopened not just for your father's sake, but also Eduardo's. I'd love to see you, but while we both are still connected with the murder, it'd be inappropriate. I wouldn't want the Lieutenant to get wind of it. I hope you understand."

I did and told him so. "I'll keep hoping that we'll run into each other again."

* * *

I knew the Gielguds were beyond wealthy, but the first look at their home on Kewen Drive in San Marino took my breath away.

The driveway was immaculately paved with large squares of peach-colored pavers interspersed randomly with small and medium squares and rectangles of red tiles. There was a huge three-car garage at the end of the driveway and a patio to one side, designed for seating close to two dozen visitors. On the other side, several sycamore trees stood guard. The house's dimly lit exterior contrasted with the bright patches of light emanating from every room inside. I looked across from the entrance for the view the home offered and found the majestic San Gabriel Mountains staring back at me.

I approached the door, stood for a moment and breathed in the aroma of wealth that the home exuded. I had grown up in a modest house with all the essential amenities, not too much else, certainly not much luxury.

A smartly dressed woman, with a slight frown clouding her face, answered my knock on the door. "Uh, sorry, I thought we left the door open for the visitors to walk in." My gracious hostess turned out to be the woman I'd heard shouting in the police station. She smiled and offered her hand. Mrs. Antonia Gielgud wore a sheath of glittery green, with what looked like emeralds at her throat and ears. Her make-up was light, thank God, or she'd have looked garish.

"I am Rekha Rao, I came at Bill's invitation," I said, as though I needed a better excuse than others to have stepped into this home.

"Oh, yes, I thought you were Bill's professor. We've heard a lot about you. Please come in and join us. The guests are everywhere." With this she took my hand and led me further into the house, shouting for Bill.

Bill emerged from a small group in the living room and looked genuinely pleased to see me. "Professor Rao, I'm delighted to see you. I wasn't sure you'd turn up. The investigation and all. But I am happy you came."

By now, Mrs. Gielgud had let go of my hand and moved

along to another cluster of people at the bar where I noticed a mix of students and faculty. I felt relieved.

"So, Professor Rao, what'll it be for you? A glass of fine wine, maybe? I still can't believe you accepted my invitation." Bill chuckled. "Neil is somewhere around. Would you like to see the house? Most everyone who comes here for the first time asks for a tour. And the Gielguds are very proud of it." Bill said, handing me a glass of white wine. "It's Pinot something, from Italy. Mrs. Gielgud's favorite."

Noticing my hesitation, he asked, "Or would you rather say hello to the JPM faculty?"

Before I could answer, Neil was with us, saying in his soft, hesitant voice, "How are you, Professor Rao? How is the case going? My source at the PPD dried up, so I'm at a loss of how I can go on with the case report."

"I think it's best to wait like all of us are doing. Bill wants to show me the house. I'll see you a little later." I turned to Bill. "Don't you think we should ask for permission?"

"No, I'm very used to showing people around, since the Gielguds are busy meeting and greeting. It's a well-worn routine. Let's go."

He led the way, directing me to a hallway that bordered an inner courtyard surrounded by steps with a fountain in the middle. We walked along the periphery, while I tasted the wine and found it delectable.

"Do you mind if I take a few minutes here?" I asked. Bill nodded.

The space reminded me of my mother's ancestral home in Hyderabad where as a five- or six-year-old, I had run around on the steps of an identical inner courtyard, save the fountain. My mother had told me stories of growing up with the courtyard, or *ankan,* that provided a gathering place for children and adults. How she and her brothers sailed paper boats on the water that gathered in it during the monsoons. How it came alive during marriage celebrations and festivals like *Holi* and *Divali*, and how it was also the place where Ma would wait for the postman who brought letters from her beloved, my father.

Lost in my memories, I snapped to attention when Bill said, "Would you like to see our gallery in the basement? Where the Gielguds display the antiques they buy and sell?"

The word "antique" was enough for me to nod my head vigorously. "I'd love to."

He led the way through a door and down a series of steps that were illuminated automatically by a sensor. I followed Bill down as he directed me through a maze that wound between antique furniture, layers of carpets stacked one on top of another, and paintings adorning the walls. Several ancient-looking sculptures were placed randomly among this medley. None of them looked Indian.

"Wow, are all these collectors' items?" I asked and immediately felt stupid.

Bill said. "Most, I'd say. Some are cheaper reproductions that still have a market value for some collectors."

"The statues. Do the Gielguds specialize in a certain kind or a period?" I tried to keep my voice in the normal register.

"Oh," he said and laughed. "I asked them about it. They said they don't accept anything without a certificate of provenance. Also, I heard that the police were here to check these out. They thought the Durga might have come from the Gielguds' collection." He spread his hands out wide.

"Sorry, Bill, I didn't mean to cast doubt on you or your godparents. I was just curious."

We passed a hallway with several group photos on

the wall. "Who are these? Relatives?" I asked.

"No, they belong to an Antique Collectors' group. Remember, I told you about it. They get together periodically to exchange information and revel in each other's acquisitions, I guess. I sometimes come just out of sheer curiosity. Take your time, Professor Rao, please. I will run up to make sure everyone is comfortable."

The photos were the least interesting of all to me. Dated every couple of years or so for the last decade, the Gielguds were the only constant. They seemed never to age. The rest of the group appeared infrequently. I was brought up short by a group photo that had a tall thin man in it, who appeared next to Mr. Gielgud. He was Caucasian. I took my cell phone and snapped a few pictures, some up close, focused on the face of the tall thin man. He resembled Davidson but was much older. I hoped the Gielguds would be able to tell me who he was. I wasn't sure what the photo would yield since I remembered Davidson's account of a short overweight man at the Kurnool rail station. He'd even mentioned the man carrying a heavy backpack and almost falling off the train. Unless that was a lie.

My thoughts were interrupted by Bill, who came back and apologized for leaving me alone. I pointed to the framed photos on the wall, the ones I had just photographed, and asked, "You have any idea who these people are, standing with the Gielguds? This man looks familiar."

"Sorry, I'm no good with that. I don't pay attention to their friends, these groups. My godparents are very sentimental and keep the photos of fellow collectors year after year. On the wall or strewn around in the drawers. You can have a copy of the latest one." He searched around in a drawer, pulled out a five by seven taken two years ago. "They wouldn't mind."

I looked at it to make sure it included the man.

Bill said, "You want me to ask the Gielguds?"

"Oh, no. It's not important." I didn't want my enquiry to be the next topic of their cocktail conversation. "Can I ask you something, Bill?

"Sure, Professor Rao, anything."

"Your aunt told me that your parents died in a car accident. Do you have any recollections of your father?" I tried to keep my voice casual.

"Oh, that." Bill seemed surprised. "Not much. I was just five when it happened. All I've seen are photos of my parents. I have one in my wallet. Would you like to see it?"

Without waiting for my answer, he pulled out his wallet and extracted a small three by five black and white print. "Here they are. I always carry it with me because it reminds me to make them proud."

I looked at it closely. "You take after your mother, don't you?" I'd wondered if the accident story could have been a foil, if Bill's father was still alive and well, and turned out to be Faust. My hopes were shattered. Even imagining him aged, Bill's father bore no resemblance to Faust. Thank God.

A voice alerted us from the top of the stairs. "Oh, there you are, the academic and her student. I guessed Bill must have wanted to bring you down here. My husband wants to meet you, Professor Rao. Come on up." Antonia Gielgud's honeyed voice had the slightest edge of an order.

Back in the living room, I found Mr. Gielgud standing next to the piano chatting with someone I didn't recognize. After waiting and saying hello to him, I walked over to the wine table and poured myself more wine. I was dying to find out who the man in the photo was. It was a long shot, but worth a try.

I was about to ask the hostess when we were interrupted by a loud gaggle of voices in varying tones from the opposite corner of the room.

Mr. Gielgud's booming voice rose above all others. "Everyone, please listen." The room was instantaneously hushed. "I just received some sad news. Bob Davidson was killed when his truck went off a cliff. It sounds like a freak accident. We all knew and loved him. Please let's take a moment to share our thoughts. My wife and I will reach out to his wife right away."

There were exclamations and sobs.

This news was a blow. Davidson had taken with him any information he had of the Durga and Faust's murder. The last time I saw him he'd looked guilty and remorseful. Now it was too late to find out what it was about. I felt sorry for his wife. Did her husband die in an accident or was he killed? Or did he kill himself?

I couldn't trouble my hosts with the photo now. I said goodbye to Antonia, waved to my students and stepped outside.

~ Chapter 19 ~

Friday, April 24, 2017
Pasadena, CA

I wanted to talk to Angela Davidson and find out more about the man in the photo who looked familiar, but I was reluctant to show up unannounced. I had never met her, for one thing, and now was not the time to introduce myself. It would be highly insensitive to invade her private grief.

So I went to see Ginny, instead.

Ginny was visibly upset. "They said it could have been a suicide. Why? Why would Bob kill himself?" She paused. "Oh, my God. Was he punishing himself for killing Joe?"

I could only guess what the police theory was and didn't want to make postulations for anyone. "We must leave it to the police to figure out how it happened. It'll take time."

"Do you think it was murder? Did someone force him off the road into the canyon? I do not believe that. Who would do that? Police called a while ago and asked me if Bob had any motive to kill Joe. Why would Bob kill his best friend? We both loved the man."

I ventured a scenario. "I wonder if Bob might have had the Durga stashed away at home, and had arranged to hand it over to a buyer. Your husband might have caught him with it in his hands, so Bob had to kill him to cover it. And maybe he killed himself out of remorse. He was so broken up about your husband's murder."

I decided to show her the photo from the Gielguds. "Take a look at this man, Ginny. He reminded me of Bob. Can you identify him?"

Ginny peered at the photo. "Oh, that's Bob's uncle in London. He's an antique dealer, I think legitimate. When Joe and I visited London, we had dinner with him a few times. Why, is he Joe's killer?"

"Not sure, Ginny, I'm going to hand the photo over to the police. I don't have any resources to find someone in London."

If Davidson had killed himself, that would be a sign of confession, not being able to live with the guilt of the theft and the murder of his best friend. All of a sudden, Bob's words about cowardice and the remorse that had etched his countenance made sense. If his death was a homicide, then there was a third person on the scene who killed him to keep him quiet. Was that Davidson's uncle? Did he come all the way here from London to kill Faust? I had no choice but to wait until the police made a public announcement about the nature of the incident. I knew Al wouldn't open up.

* * *

As I drove home, I noticed my cell phone had a voicemail from Al. It said, "Rekha, can you come to the station, please? We need you to identify a script." A script? He thought I was a language expert?

Despite the formality in his voice, my heart filled with hope. Our paths hadn't crossed since he had come to my house to help me. I longed to see again his softer side, the part that he hid under his cop persona.

At the station, the explanation for his phone call was clear.

Al was in his office, and without any greeting, pointed to several pages of a newspaper protected by the clear plastic of an evidence bag laid out on his desk. "Can you tell us if this is an Indian language and can you narrow it down? I understand there are dozens of dialects in India."

He seemed to be in a hurry. No hello, no smile, let alone any sign of the familiarity we shared just days ago. Here was Newton the cop, not Al the human who came to my rescue.

I assumed a detached attitude. "Can you give me some context that would help me? Where was this found? And by the way, India has eighteen or nineteen true languages, each with its script, literature and spoken language. Each also has dialects."

"You can hold it, Professor Rao." Why couldn't he call me Rekha?

I shook my head. It was one of the few languages I knew, or at least the bare bones of it. A burst of adrenaline made my breath rapid and my hands tingle, but I'd learned to contain these symptoms by now.

"Where did you find this? I assume in Davidson's truck? Oh my God. He must have stolen the Durga."

Al kept a poker face. "Now, now, don't jump to conclusions. I didn't say anything of the sort. Please tell me where the newspaper might have come from."

I was starting to feel annoyed. Granted, we were in his office, door open, and other cops milling around in the squad room, but still. "Well, the script is Telugu, the language of Andhra Pradesh where Jwalapuram is. It looks like the newspaper was used to wrap something, possibly the Durga, from the soil particles in it."

"Can you get this newspaper here in this country? Could

someone have had it in their collection of Indian newspapers? Davidson, for instance?"

"I have no idea. Indians here do read their local newspapers from home to get news about their state, city or community, although these days they're all online. There's no way for me to figure out if this particular paper came from India or here. You'd need soil analysis, that's if there's something unique about the soil from that part of India. I'm no expert on that."

I'd had enough. I got up. "I assume that Davidson's death could be an accident, suicide, or murder." I was giving him the opportunity to share his conclusions with me, speaking to him in a statement, the same way he usually spoke.

He nodded. "All are possibilities. We've got to wait until we gather the evidence. You understand, don't you?" He avoided my eyes.

I debated whether to give him the photo I found. Finding Faust's killer had a greater priority than our conflicted relationship. I said, "You wouldn't help me, but I'm going to help you." I took out the print photo I'd obtained from the Gielguds' house and handed it to him.

"What's this?"

I identified the Gielguds in the photo and pointed to the tall thin man. "Ginny identified him as Bob Davidson's uncle in London, an antique collector. I suspect he could be the tall thin white man who collected the Durga at the Kurnool rail station."

This was my moment of triumph. I had legitimately obtained truthful information that the police had failed to find. But it hardly felt like a victory. I'd rather have back the tender, unofficial, caring Al than this man in his suit of formality.

He pulled out a chair and sat down to study the photo further. "How did you get this?"

"I must have been just lucky." I smiled but failed to elicit a mirror reaction from him.

"I hope you didn't do anything illegal to obtain this, Rekha." He sounded concerned.

I picked up my satchel. "That's all, Detective. Keep the photo; I've no further use for it." I turned to leave.

"Not so fast, where did you get this?" He jumped out of his chair and came after me.

"All I can tell you is that it wasn't stolen but given to me fair and square. So, why don't we trade information? You tell me how Davidson died and I'll tell you where the photo came from. And we can avoid a lengthy interrogation."

He forced a smile, or so it seemed to me. "We can't do that. And, yes, we've sufficient grounds to interrogate you further to get the info. Despite my warning, you seem bent on finding evidence on your own. Murderers are dangerous. You aren't trained to protect yourself. Like what happened with the break-in . . ." His face turned red and his voice trailed off.

I felt the blood rushing to my face. I moved close to him but kept my voice neutral. "Thank you, Detective. Yes, I don't have a gun or a bullet-proof vest like you guys. And no, I couldn't kill the man who broke into my house, but I bet his groin is still aching."

In a hushed voice, he said, "I'm sorry, Rekha, I was only thinking of your safety. You understand, don't you, I have to stay professional in my office." He sounded apologetic, and more like the man whom I'd glimpsed the night of the break-in.

I said, in as friendly a voice as I could muster, "You might want to talk to the Gielguds," and walked out, realizing that

Newton the detective would always maintain his cop persona at work. And that I should learn to accept it.

~ Chapter 20 ~

Monday, April 24, 2017
Altadena, CA

The next morning, emails from Neil bombarded my inbox. They were all about a summer internship in archaeology in Galway, Ireland, with a competitor of Faust whom he had met at the conference. Neil had returned to his first love, archaeology, and wanted to do the internship. He was confident he'd qualify for it and garner a scholarship, but the application had to be postmarked by the next day. He explained that he had completed all the paperwork, but was ill and staying home. He needed my signature on a page to verify that he was my advisee. An email from me wouldn't do it.

A frantic voicemail followed these. "Professor Rao," Neil pleaded in a hoarse voice, "Can I ask a huge favor of you to stop by my home? I've everything else ready to go. I'm afraid to send Mother out to bring the papers to you. She's bound to get lost and not get the job done. My home is not too far away from Oxy. Mother and Melissa would love to meet you. I've been talking their ears off about you. And, believe it or not, it's Mother's birthday today. Please?"

I was unsure whether to accept this invitation. Between

his illness—it sounded genuine from his voice—and the importance and urgency of the situation, I gave in, determined not to stay long. Perhaps this would give me an opportunity to talk to his mother. I pulled out a book from my shelf, an Alice Munro collection, *Dear Life: Stories*, new and unread, and tucked it in my satchel. I didn't want to go empty-handed to a home where a mother's birthday was being celebrated.

Neil's address was in Altadena, on Craig Street. A single-story house set back from the road. The front yard had a central brick pathway, bordered by squares of mowed lawn. A modest home that created a brilliant, ambitious student.

I knocked on the front door. No answer. I knocked again, and the house was still unresponsive. There was a carport to the left but no car in it. I knocked on the side door that led from the carport. No response. I looked at my cell phone to make sure of the address, date and the approximate time I'd given Neil for my arrival. I decided to wait and sat down on a wooden bench in the carport.

As the minutes passed, I started to feel foolish that I had agreed to Neil's request, and thinking of it again, I wondered if he'd contrived it to get me here. For what ulterior motive? He had told me he had spoken so much about me to his mother that she wanted to meet me. Neil's request was not unlike Bill's invitation to the Gielgud home.

I was about to give up when I saw a young girl ride up to the house on a bike. She wore a lemon and pink flowery skirt, a red top and a pink embroidered sweater. She got down from the bike, secured it to a bike stand in the carport and took off her helmet and a bulging backpack. She placed the backpack on the doorstep, shook her curly blonde locks, and they fell in place. There was no resemblance to Neil, but this must be the sister he'd mentioned in a conversation. Did she take after the other parent? I got up from the bench. "Are you Melissa? Melissa Anderson?"

The girl turned to me with an angelic smile "Yeah, I'm Melissa. Who're you? Were you waiting for me?" She pulled out a key tied to a ribbon around her neck and opened the front door and stood there watching me with quizzical eyes.

"Is all that homework?" I asked, smiling and pointing to the backpack that Melissa picked up from the doorstep.

The girl laughed out loud. "No, no way I've that much homework on a Thursday. But I'm in the Magnet program and they bring us books from the central library. Our school library sucks. I keep the books with me so I can read when I get free time. Want to see?" She unzipped her backpack and pulled out two hardcover books.

"This one I like the best. It's called *The Lion, the Witch and the Wardrobe*. The other one is OK, a Nancy Drew mystery I'm not much into. But I love Harry Potter. Have you read any of them?"

Before I could answer, she made a wry face and said, "I'm sorry, but who're you? I'm not allowed to talk to strangers." The girl was still guarding the front door.

I said, "I'm Neil's teacher from Oxy, Occidental College. I'm here to sign off on his application for a summer internship. And he has been asking me to come and meet you and your mother. Today's her birthday, right?" I tried to keep a distance from the child, recalling the admonitions from my parents about not taking candy from strangers. I had no intention of helping Melissa break any rules.

"Listen, let me check on Neil. He has been sick. And if he can see you now, I can let you in." She disappeared, making sure to shut the front door.

If he can see me? What the heck? Neil must rule this

household.

Melissa was back. "Sorry, he doesn't answer his door. He might be napping. Can you please wait? I can't let you in the house until Mom comes back."

She took out half of a cereal bar from her pocket, broke it, and offered me half.

I shook my head.

Melissa asked, "Do you have a badge or something that says you are from the University?"

Clever girl, it was obvious her mother had trained her well. I was thankful that I was still in my office gear and pulled out my faculty card for Melissa, wondering if she had ever seen a card like it before. She scrutinized it, read both sides and said, "OK, you're all right. I can talk to you until Mom comes. She'll hound me about homework, but I've done it already." Melissa sat down on the bench and I followed suit.

"Neil talks about you with pride, Melissa. You want to go to college?"

"I'd love to. Neil wants me to go to Oxy too. He took me there once to show me what a big university looked like. We went into the classroom where he studies. Like a theater. Learning in a place like that must be like watching plays or movies." She paused and looked at me. "Maybe you taught in that room?"

"I might have, but the University has many rooms like that. Is your mother or father coming home soon?"

"Mother, not father. Yeah, she gets home soon after I get back from school."

"Maybe it's best for me to wait in my car till she gets here. You go on in and lock the door. You do that always, don't you?" I could imagine what Al would say. *It's unlawful to accost a minor without an adult present.*

Melissa hesitated, nodded, picked up her backpack and disappeared through the door, followed by the creak of a bolt slid in place.

I stepped out to the curb when I saw a woman entering the carport, rolling a bicycle with a full grocery bag behind the seat and a purse strung from her shoulder. She looked at me, got down from the bike, and said, "You must be Professor Rao, right? I'm sorry I kept you waiting. Neil told me you offered to come and sign his application. How nice of you."

Melissa poked her head out the door and said, "She was here when I came back from school, mom. She's Neil's teacher, showed me her badge. I knocked on Neil's door but he didn't answer." Melissa was preempting her mother's scolding.

"You do your homework, Melissa." The woman gave a sharp look at the girl and pointed to the door, making Melissa retreat. She parked her bike and retrieved the grocery bag. "I'm Alice, Neil's mother. I recognize you from your picture in the college directory Neil showed me. Please come in. He told us to expect you today." She frowned. "I wonder why he didn't respond to Melissa's knock. He has it terrible, coughing and sneezing, but had the wherewithal to finish the paperwork. Oh, here it is. He must have left it out before taking a nap."

Alice handed me a manila folder with a printed form clipped to it. It was an Oxy standard form that formalized a student-advisor relationship. She pointed me to a clean, worn sofa, and sat down in an armchair with torn padded arms, took off her sneakers, and slipped into a pair of flats.

I was mystified. Was Neil that ill that he couldn't hand me the form in person? Then I recalled what Davidson had said about him. An odd fish.

I shrugged, signed it, and gave the package back to Alice.

"Here, it's all done. Make sure you mail it right away. He told me tomorrow was the last day to postmark it. Some schools require signed papers still."

Melissa was hanging about in the hallway, trying to be part of the conversation. Alice glared at her daughter, pointed to the grocery bag and said, "Put this away and get to your homework."

"I already did it, mom." The child gave a whimsical look at me that said, I'd rather be out there with you, took up the grocery bag and disappeared.

"Professor Rao, I'm honored you came here. Neil adores you and when he told me you'd agreed to come and drop something off, I dismissed it as his usual bravado. Can I offer you something? I just made some cookies this morning. For my birthday." Alice sighed. "I hope Neil will wake up before you leave. I'm embarrassed he hasn't come out of his room yet."

"No worries, Alice. He must be ill. By the way, happy birthday." I said cheerfully and took the unwrapped book from my satchel. "Neil talks about you and Melissa." Despite the woman's hand-me-down clothes and sparsely furnished house, she spoke a language that left no doubt Alice was educated. I was glad that I chose a book for her. I handed it to her.

Alice took the book and looked at it with a big smile. "Thank you. There was no need, but I appreciate it. I love to read."

I followed her into the kitchen, and she beckoned me to sit at a small table. The kitchen was old-fashioned with a linoleum floor and melamine counters. The countertop and floor shone, pots and pans were neatly put away in the rack, and there wasn't a crumb anywhere. The room smelled of lemon.

I watched Alice pour boiling water from a kettle into a teapot, add tea leaves, stir, and cover it. "Did Neil tell you about his professor who died?"

"Yes, he was murdered, wasn't he? Neil was hoping to do his doctoral study with him. Professor Faust, right?" Alice went to the kitchen counter and came back with a large platter of cookies, teapot, two cups and saucers, and napkins.

"Yes," I took a cookie. "Faust was my mentor while I was at UCI."

Alice laughed. "What a coincidence." She poured tea into cups, moved the creamer and sugar toward me. "I was trying to avoid sugar. It sometimes works and sometimes doesn't. But birthdays are exceptions."

I wanted to avoid sugar, too, but didn't want to be rude. Besides, the cookies looked scrumptious. I broke off a piece of one and chewed. It smelled and tasted of peanut butter, vanilla, and sugar. "These are delicious, Alice. How did Neil react to the murder? Faust was not just a great teacher, he was also a great man. We, the faculty who knew and respected him, are devastated."

Alice took a cookie and bit into it. "Neil was upset, more than upset. Shut himself up in his room the whole next day. Didn't talk to me about it. He doesn't open up with me anymore. We used to be very close when he was a little boy." Alice frowned and looked at the hallway. "But now that I've told him he's adopted, he's bent on finding his real parents. I don't blame him."

"He did tell me he was adopted. How about Melissa?" I asked.

"She's my niece. Her mom, my sister, died from cancer, and there was no father in the picture. So we adopted her. My husband, who is no more, didn't want to, but I told him family is family."

I sat back, having finished my tea. "It sounded like she

worships Neil, Alice. You're very lucky."

"Isn't that a blessing?"

I wasn't sure whether I should probe into Neil's adoption but gave it a try. "When did you adopt Neil, Alice?"

Alice's face brightened with a big smile. "As a newborn, barely a week old. I still remember my first look at his face. A beautiful boy with the complexion of caramel."

"What about the birth mother or father?"

"No, I had no information about them since it was a closed adoption. But now that Neil is an adult, he or the birth parents can write to the agency and find out. I have a suspicion Neil has already done it. But not a word to me."

Alice got up with her cup still in her hand. "Sorry to bore you with all this. I get carried away."

I took another cookie. "Thanks for the tea, Alice. You should be proud of your son. He's an outstanding student in my class and across the board. By the way, when did you find out about the murder?"

Alice put her cup down. "The next day, from Neil. He came home late the night the professor was killed. Stayed shut up in his room the whole next day. Never came out, never ate. When I asked him, through the closed door, he mumbled that his professor was killed, and could I leave him alone. I felt bad for him, this happening just as he was working on a proposal to give him. Melissa took some food for him but brought it back and said her brother wasn't hungry. He left the next morning before I got up. I assumed he went back to his classes."

We walked into the family room and I picked up my satchel. "Neil must have known as a child that he was adopted?"

"No, I told him when he turned eighteen, before he went to college. That was his birth mother's wish. So he has known for a couple of years. He's been angry with me ever since. What could I do? I could have kept it a secret but, morally, I would have felt terrible if I hadn't followed the birth mother's wishes."

Alice sighed and stared into the hallway again. "Melissa, come out here. The professor is leaving. You want to say goodbye?"

"One more thing, Alice. You said Neil came home late the night of the murder. Do you remember the time? Closer to midnight or later?"

Alice's face hardened. "Very close to midnight. I heard the door open and looked at my clock."

Melissa had come out and stood smiling at me. "Before you go, would you like to see my book collection?" She turned to her mom, "Mom, please, just for a few minutes?"

I intervened. "I'd love to see it. Alice, may I?"

Alice shrugged, shook my hand and said, "Knock on his door once more, Melissa," and went back to the kitchen.

Melissa crooked her finger, beckoning me to follow her and bounced her way into a tiny room at the end of the hallway. It was matchbox size, but pretty. The room had a twin bed that sported a pink cover with white ruffled border, a freestanding rickety metal bookcase and a chest of drawers of weathered oak. "This is where I hang out after school until Mama comes home." On the chest several small elephants of varying sizes, made of different materials, were arranged in a parade. A family of ceramic, plastic, wood, metal, and glass pachyderms.

"You collect elephants? These sure are pretty," I said.

Melissa smiled. "I love elephants. Neil gave me some of them. And here are my books." The bookshelf was tightly packed, with more books in cardboard boxes placed on end to create small cubes, and even more on the floor in neat stacks. I picked out a couple and said, "I remember reading these." I turned to a photo on Melissa's desk. "That's your brother and you, right?" I said, smiling.

Alice appeared at the door. "Melissa. Let the professor go. I'm sure she has better things to do."

"OK, Mom, but can I walk her to her car?'

"*May I*, Melissa. Not *can I*. What do they teach you in school?" Alice looked at me with tired eyes. "Thanks for coming, Professor Rao. I apologize for Neil not getting up. I knocked on his door again. He grumbled something like . . . go away. If you'll excuse me, I need to start the laundry." Alice walked back to the kitchen.

Melissa nodded and skipped over to the next room, tossing her curls about. "This is Mama's room." Slightly larger than Melissa's, this room held a full-size bed covered with a plain red bed cover. "Mama's very clean. Always makes her bed before she leaves for work. I sometimes forget in the morning but try to do it before she gets home."

"Good girl," I laughed.

On the other side of the family room, there was a third bedroom that Melissa announced was her brother's. "This is locked. That's the way he likes it. No one can go in without his permission. When he's home, he lets Mama go in to clean it. Not lately though. Let me knock one more time. Maybe he's awake now and will want to thank you." She knocked on the door three times in rapid succession. "No luck."

I stepped out of the house into the carport accompanied by Melissa.

"You and your brother seem to have a special relationship, Melissa. How about your mama and Neil?"

"Oh, Neil gets into fights with her. He calls her names

and I don't like that. I've told him so."

"What do they fight over?"

"Mostly money, that's what I think. Mama sometimes makes mistakes with the bills and Neil gets real mad over it because he gets calls at the university about them. He told me he has to manage our money or I'll never get to college."

"You're a bright little girl, Melissa. You'll go to college."

I got in my car and closed the door. I rolled the window down, seeing Melissa gesturing to me. "When I get to college, I hope I don't get a teacher like . . . what was the name of the dead professor?

"Why Melissa?" I looked at the girl. "What makes you say that?"

"After the professor died, Neil told me he deserved what he got because he didn't bother to read some paper or something Neil wrote. I hope you don't treat your students like that?"

"Well, we're all busy, Melissa, and the professor who died was even more so. He might not have had the time. It's not because he was mean."

Alice called out, "Melissa, come back in here."

Melissa took off like a greyhound, turning back to wave at me.

I drove off, thinking that although Melissa had volunteered the information, I had done something to coerce the child. I shook off the feeling and realized that I needed to read Neil's proposal. That was the only link I could find between him and Faust. It was preposterous to think that it would reveal a motive for the murder. But I had only a few potential suspects to work with, and I needed to do due diligence with them.

* * *

Driving home, I chewed over Neil's discourteous behavior. Why didn't he respond to Melissa's knock? Was he avoiding me or playing a game with me, and if so why? Maybe he was sick and was thoughtful enough not to transfer his germs to me. He sure was a strange character.

Preoccupied, I had failed to notice a blue Audi in my rearview mirror, staying at a respectable distance behind me. With a jolt, I recognized it as the car from my dream but calmed myself enough to keep watch on its movements. It stopped when I did, made the same turns I made. I speeded up a little to lose it, but it persisted in tailing me. I knew the best strategy was to drive into a busy parking lot. I turned into the Pavilions lot and parked my car near the Starbucks. The Audi went past me and turned to the left and stopped in front of the dry cleaners. For a minute, I sat and watched and saw no one getting out. Relieved that the driver was there to pick someone up, I walked over to the Starbucks. Today, I needed a strong coffee. Besides, I never liked store-bought chai.

I ordered and sat down, checked my email and voice-mails, when I saw him come in and sit at a table in the corner facing me. Matt Porter. He must have been in the Audi that followed me, watched me enter Starbucks and followed me in. As always, he looked sharp in a pale blue shirt, a multi-colored paisley tie loosened at his throat, and clean Levi pants. A pair of black tennis shoes completed his attire. He looked fit and handsome as ever.

We locked eyes, and I felt sweat breaking out under my armpits. I felt dirty and my hands flew to my throat, where his arm had crushed me as he held me against the wall. I looked away, aghast that this could happen, despite all my efforts to stay hidden from his eyes. I felt the ground under my feet, and reminded myself that this was a public place. That he wouldn't dare hurt me here, physically at least. I had the power to embarrass him, at the risk of being arrested for a misdemeanor. I took the risk.

I heard someone call out that my order was ready. I picked it up, walked to his table and sat in front of him. He narrowed his eyes, smiled, and said, "Hello, there, my love." He started to grab my hand that I'd placed on the table as bait, and I quickly snatched it back. He wasn't flustered. "Still angry with me? I read all about your police work. My, my, never give up, do you? First your father's murder and now your professor's."

"Listen, scumbag. I'm going to say this once and once only. Keep away from me. The police have you on their radar. How dare you break into my house and attack me? Go find another paramour, I'm sure there are many vying to take the position I vacated."

He laughed so loud that many eyes turned toward us. He leaned forward and tried again to grab my hand. "Oh, I'm sure you don't mean that, Rekha. I can tell you still love me. By the way, you look even more stunning than the last time I saw you. Come on, let's give it another try." He whispered in a seductive voice that I knew so well and never wanted to hear again.

I was done. I took a deep breath, got up, my ice coffee in my right hand, leaned over and poured it over his head, all of it. I saw him shudder at the coldness of it, and the surprise and humiliation. He struggled to stand up, threw his arms out in a defensive posture and yelled, "Somebody call the police. This woman just assaulted me." No one in the café moved, although all eyes were trained on us. One lone woman in the opposite corner stood up and clapped. Not loud and energetic, but slow and barely perceptible as though she of all the customers understood me and understood him. I nodded my thanks at her, grabbed my satchel, turned around and walked toward the door, not looking back at Matt. As I exited, I thought I heard suppressed laughter coming from the inside.

Never in my life had I felt more powerful or in control of myself than at that moment. Here was a part of my dharma that had been unfulfilled until today.

I went home, poured myself a glass of red wine and turned on the TV. I couldn't focus on the picture or the sound.

~ Chapter 21 ~

Tuesday, April 25, 2017
Eagle Rock, Los Angeles, CA

The yellow tape was off Faust's office door, and Patricia was standing at the entrance, hands on hips. "What a mess the cops made. *They* should clean this up, not me. But I would, for Professor F's sake."

"I can help. I have a couple of hours before my class. One thing, Patricia, when was the last time Neil wanted to set up another meeting with Faust?"

"Well, let me think. The boy barged in here the day of the professor's award ceremony and insisted he meet with him without an appointment. Good luck, I told him. Professor F had canceled all meetings to get his presentation ready." Patricia laughed. "A smooth talker, that fellow, Anderson. He praised me for my looks and I almost thought he was going to ask me out. Yeah, that was, of course, the day before Professor F's murder."

"Did he worry he wouldn't get into the dig the legitimate way? I find that hard to believe."

"I told you he's a bit strange. I think he was trying to preempt not getting one of the two student positions on the next dig by asking the professor to review his proposal early.

To dazzle him with a preview of his brilliance."

I laughed. "I guess he figures there are hundreds of brilliant students out there and wanted to stand out from the crowd."

Patricia looked at her manicured nails. "Rekha, students apply from all over the world for a position. Professor F has to turn down many of them. Besides, this fellow wasn't even ready for consideration. There was no way I was going to let him take up the professor's precious time. So I told him that when he gets to his junior year, to go through the proper channels and submit his application, like everyone else."

"Did you keep a copy of his proposal?"

"No. I gave it back to him. And told him I wasn't going to give it to Professor F when he'd already declined to read it." Patricia laughed. "What happened between you and the dapper detective?"

I laughed. "Nothing, nothing at all."

"Why, is he too old for you?"

I didn't want to tell her that age was not my issue.

Patricia extended her hand with a couple of keys in a keyring. "I need to get back to the desk. It'd be great if you can start to make a dent, Rekha. Keep the key and return it to me when you leave. I'll come in on Saturday to finish it."

She walked out, stopped, and turned back to look at me, her right arm raised in a fist. "I hope you'll find the bastard who killed him."

I hadn't planned on spending time in Faust's office and was behind with my class preparation. But I decided to take a quick look around.

I picked my way gingerly through a maze bordered by stacks of journals, papers, and books all over the floor. More books and papers filled ceiling-high bookshelves on two walls.

The age-old oak floor looked badly in need of refinishing, but was redeemed in part by a splendid Persian carpet with multicolored flowers and vines on an off-white background.

This must have been a much loved, much-used room, his haven within the crazy world of academia. Would he have also used it to hide personal papers or objects that he didn't want his family to see? I looked for the bookshelf Bill had referred to, the one on the right. It and its counterpart on the opposite wall were jam-packed with books, several taken out and left on the floor, likely by the cops who believed in a sample search, not an exhaustive one.

There was no way I could look for a secret compartment with the limited time I had. Besides, every other minute, someone walked by the office, and some even stopped and peeked inside through the glass window. Pretending to clean up was fine, but anything more than that would attract attention. So I picked up several books the cops had left on the floor and put them back into the sparsely populated shelf at the bottom level. I looked for the tall book that Bill had talked about being stuck on the fourth shelf from the bottom. I couldn't find any that offered resistance. Where was it? Did Faust disengage it from the secret compartment?

I decided to come back at night, to look for the hidden object, if there was one. There will be less foot traffic outside and more obscurity inside. With the decision made, I moved to one of the two desks to do some honest uncluttering of the desktop. I picked up an ornate metal frame that held a headshot of a strikingly beautiful woman in her thirties, her dark hair in soft waves, eyes expectant and lips curved in a shy smile of a trusting and loved child. I easily recognized Ginny Faust, a few wrinkles less. I held up the photo to my eye level and noted an engraving at the bottom of the frame.

"To my darling husband of ten years. Without your love, I would be nothing." The photo spoke of uncomplicated love and trust. I couldn't even fathom how people stayed together for that long. Yet I knew many, including my parents, and now the Fausts, who remained married for decades. What kept their love stable, their trust unquestioned, and hopes ever sustained? I knew my parents quarreled, but they also managed to keep a united front for their children. And here I was, thirty-two, with no hope in sight for an enduring romance, attracted to an older Caucasian man who kept his true self close to his vest.

I walked back to Patricia's desk to leave her a note and saw *her* note admonishing everyone that she'd taken her one afternoon off and will return tomorrow. My note told her I came to return the key, but since she was gone, I didn't want to leave it on her desk unattended. I'd return it the next day.

I texted Sanjay that I was going to search Faust's office, but there was no reply.

It was all up to me now.

~ Chapter 22 ~

Wednesday, April 16, 2017
Eagle Rock, Los Angeles

It was 5 pm when my discussion session ended. I kept myself busy in my office until the light faded and the campus business seemed finished for the day. As I made my way to Faust's office, only the odd person or two walked by, a student or faculty member. At the door, I looked to both sides and not seeing anyone, unlocked the office, my body covering what my hands were doing. I closed the door behind me and stood leaning on it, praying that nobody had seen me.

I made a beeline to the shelf on the right side of the desk, the same one I'd looked through before. Using the beam of a tiny flashlight, I searched the row at my shoulder level again. I pulled out the books closer to the end, in the inner row, and they came out with ease. None stuck to the base. It was likely that Bill's snooping, as Faust had interpreted it, would have prompted him to remove whatever he had hidden there and hide it elsewhere.

Exasperated, I started pulling out the books from the row above my shoulder level, slid them out in sections and looked and felt behind them for whatever might be hidden there. I looked between the books. Nothing. I climbed on a chair and went one row up, with the same result.

I sat down on the floor, tired and confounded. The risk I had taken to enter the office at night had left me drained.

I heard a scuffling noise and saw the glare of a large flashlight shining through the glass plate of the office window. Damn it, the security officer was making his periodic round of the area. My heart thudded in my chest and my throat was bone-dry. I was glad I'd sat down, and now I crouched on the floor as flat as I could. I held my breath, my armpits moist, and hoped he wouldn't come in.

The officer tried the door, presumably to ensure it was locked, looked in through the glass window, and must have been satisfied, because he walked away, whistling. I took a few deep breaths, and downed sips of water from my water bottle. My efforts to find what was hidden in Faust's bookshelf had been so far an utter failure. I looked around the room and realized there was another bookshelf, a mirror image of the one I had searched, on the opposite side of the office. I could have mixed up right and left, or Bill could have. Right and left reversed if you were entering the office, or leaving it.

I decided to look through the other bookshelf, just in case. It was worth a try.

Pay dirt. On the fourth shelf, I met with some resistance at the end of the row. The last few books seemed stuck. I loosened them and pulled them out one by one, trying not to damage them. These books were all frayed along the bottom as though they might have been removed and put back regularly. My heart raced as I got to the last book and looked at its title. *Southeast Asia: From Prehistory to History.*

The very book Bill had discovered. And like Bill, I couldn't lift it from the shelf.

A closer look revealed that the book was secured to a

panel, about five by seven that was constructed to be slid back, but it was locked. I needed the key. My heart sank. How was I going to get into the compartment covered by the panel? My brother held all the mechanical abilities in my household. I was a klutz.

I moved to Faust's desk and quietly opened the drawers looking for any keys the police might have left behind. Several large ones wouldn't fit the keyhole in the panel. A few smaller ones did fit, but didn't turn the lock. I knew I had to force the lock open. I grabbed a paper clip, opened it up and tried, but to no avail. Scrounging around, I found a letter-opener with a pointed, although not sharp, tip, and I pushed it in the keyhole and turned it first in one direction and then the other. After several attempts, the keyhole broke, and the panel sprung open along with the attached book.

This revealed an opening big enough for me to push my hand through, but with not enough space to manipulate my fingers. With the tips of my fingers, I felt something solid, about an inch thick and shorter than the full depth of the panel. My right hand was now stuck inside the compartment along with the object that seemed to be a small book. Leaving my thumb and index finger around the object, I dragged out my other fingers one by one, with some difficulty. I pushed my thumb and index finger as far down as they'd go, held tight to the slippery object and pulled in a vertical direction. The crude edges of the compartment scraped my skin, but I held on and gave another firm pull that brought my fingers and the object out of the compartment.

It was a hardcover notebook, about six inches by four inches, and half an inch thick, with rounded corners. It was covered in Moleskin, of an earth-brown color, and secured with an elastic closure band. Panting with the emotional and physical effort it had cost me, I opened it right there. I found ivory-colored pages covered in meticulous rounded hand-writing. I didn't have the time to read it, end to end. Instead, I put it in my satchel and crept out, making sure to lock the door behind me. Once on the campus lawn, I walked along nonchalantly, pretending to have stayed late in my office. I wondered if Dad would have approved my actions.

My satchel burned with its precious cargo. The cops had turned the room back over to the department, having finished their search. I had found the notebook having entered the room with keys given to me by Patricia. I was sure I hadn't committed a crime. Besides, I planned to turn the book over to Al the next morning.

I drove home riddled with guilt, doubts, and questions. But I could barely contain the excitement ramping up within.

* * *

Once home, I couldn't wait. I sat down in my chair to explore the book.

With no label, no lock and no frayed edges, it looked new. The first page said,

"Joseph Faust, January 2015."

On the next page:

"I AM GAY."

And below that,

"I have always been gay. I was a coward not to admit it, and now I'll hurt two innocent lives by revealing it. But I no longer have a choice."

He seemed to have torn out several pages. Several other

pages contained phrases and brief sentences, all scratched out, as though he was in a thought process, drafting what followed.

The next several pages contained a letter. I took a deep breath.

January 1, 2017

Dear Ginny,

You are my inspiration for putting into words the feelings and thoughts that I had concealed inside me for as long as I can remember. I do this to honor your unfailing love for me and Kevin. This is my last gift to you, my best friend, before we part ways.

Since the age of thirteen, I knew I was different. Outwardly, I pretended to like girls, dated them, brought them home to meet my parents, while my heart experienced strange feelings for boys. I was confused but there was no one to talk to. My parents were strict Catholics who had created a solid structure for my life based on schoolwork, church services, Bible classes and volunteering. At eighteen, I learned that my favorite cousin had packed up and left home, and no one would tell me why. I later heard whispers about his unnatural sexual orientation, that he was gay. I never knew if he left of his own accord or was thrown out. I swore that I'd do nothing to risk breaking the bonds with my parents, my sister and my extended family, no matter what. But a suspicion that I too was gay was never far from my mind, although I never experimented with it. I continued to date girls. Keeping up appearances was drilled into my marrow by my parents.

The AIDS epidemic scared the hell out of me. If this was what happened to gay men, I would not be a part of it. I saw men wither away before their time, morph into skeletons of their former selves, and die, alone and neglected. There was no cure, only prevention by using protection, or staying straight. I chose the latter. In college, I shed most of my external manifestations of being a devout Christian, but promised to God that I would remain a good man. I'd forever be humble, compassionate, dutiful, and walk the straight and narrow path, the righteous path defined by my values and morals. I never strayed.

I thought I knew what love was, darling Ginny, what you and I had shared for over two decades. What I saw my friends as couples experience in their lives. A chance encounter two years ago changed me, when, at a bar at a conference in New York, a male colleague I'd collaborated with for years, leaned into me, eyes lit like torches, and whispered, "I love you, Joe." My carefully constructed facade fractured into a before and an after. I felt my heart expand to make room for this remarkable new sensation I'd never experienced before. My heart danced with such lightness that I felt I could fly. There was no going back, although nothing more happened. I told him, "I love you too" in the way friends tell each other. I couldn't taint the sacred bond I had with you by indulging in a physical expression of the new feeling. My love for you never changed. My heart has enough space to hold on to it, and my newfound feelings.

Upon my return, I kept re-living my New York moment. I could recall with clarity every second of what I saw, felt and learned. This time, I could not let go of it. I wanted to touch base with my colleague and tell him that I have always loved him since we first met. But I held back, hoping that if he truly loved me, his love would sustain.

The time is here now for me to do the right thing.

I must separate my life from yours, seek a divorce after two decades of marriage, shed the last ounce of fear that has shackled me as long as I can remember, and live a life of truth. When I finally told you about my need to separate, you blamed me for having an affair. Coward still, I let you hold on to that suspicion, assuring you I still loved you, will always love you. I couldn't find the words to tell you then that I have always been gay. I am sorry.

I have made legal arrangements for a divorce, left all my savings essentially to you and Kevin. I haven't yet considered what the future of my profession will be, how my colleagues will treat me when they find out. I've been good to them, and now they have the choice to return the favor. Some will, and some won't.

But times have changed, and I'm now ready to tell the world who I truly am. I am worried about your future, dearest Ginny. Will you find love in the remainder of your life? Will you be happy? Will you accept me as I am now, or shun me for the rest of my life? Without a doubt, wherever I end up, I'll stay in touch with you, if you allow me. I'll always be here as a loyal friend.

I'm unsure of Kevin. A month ago, I paid him a surprise visit and caught him dressed up as a woman. He assured me it was just a fad, a phase, nothing more serious. I wanted to believe him, but I also wondered if he's taking the path I did, being gay or even transgender but not willing or courageous enough to admit it. I didn't want that for my son. I want him to come to terms with who he truly is and live the truth. I wanted to shout at him, don't you understand how much easier it is for you now, compared to what I'd gone through? I made him promise he'd go and see a psychiatrist and find out the real meaning of his extraordinary hobby. Earlier tonight,

I called him to ask if he'd been to see the psychiatrist. He told me no, and in no uncertain terms told me he was not gay, and he'd take care of his problem in his way. What could I do? I can cut him off from my will, but I'm sure it would hurt you, Ginny. Hopefully, my coming out will help him figure out his truth.

My darling Ginny, I love you as I've always loved you. You accepted me, a shy young man with my intellectual nose buried in books, guided me to blossom and fully experience the world. I am forever grateful to you. It is because of you, your love and kindness, that I'm now able to reveal my secret and come out into the open. I can never thank you enough. I hope that after we separate, you will rebuild your life, find love and joy again. I'll always be here whenever you need me. That is my promise to you.

These ramblings are for you alone. It'd be your choice to share it with Kevin. Everyone else will learn my truth in due time.

Tomorrow, I start a two-week lecture tour in Northern California, ending in San Francisco. I've made an appointment with a psychiatrist there, Dr. Alan Lambert, who specializes in counseling men who come out late in life.

When I return, I plan to give you this letter and help you understand my decision. I need your blessing to start my new life.

Yours always,

Joe

Tears streamed down my cheeks as I thought about the anguish my mentor must have suffered prior to taking the bold step of writing this letter.

It was obvious now why he'd dismissed Bill. He worried

that Bill might have located the book. So, why did he leave it in the same place? Maybe that was when he locked up the secret compartment?

The notebook had a value far above rubies, and now weighed over a hundred pounds in my hands, and substantially more on my mind. Should I have read it? I could justify my action with the reasoning that it could have contained information related to the murder, as Bill McGraw had feared. After reading it, I realized that it was a personal journal, with no names or facts connected to the murder.

Then the unthinkable occurred to me. What if Faust's delayed acceptance of his homosexuality was at the root of the murder? What if his gay colleague killed him? What if Faust spurned another gay man? Could it have been Bill? Is this the motive I missed? I had no answer.

I Googled Dr. Lambert and confirmed he was a psychiatrist in San Francisco who himself had come to terms late in life with admitting that he was gay. From then on, he had focused his work on helping other men in a similar situation. I noted down his address and telephone number.

I knew I had a moral responsibility not to withhold my find from the police. Deeply disturbed by the dilemma weighing on my mind, I went to bed, but could not sleep.

My cell phone rang.

"Hey, where were you? I got your text when I was in class. Tried to call later, but you'd turned your phone off. I got worried." It was Sanjay. "Sorry I said that. I know I'm not your keeper."

"It's OK, I'm glad to hear your voice." I had brought the diary to my bedside, and reaching with my hand, I felt it, to make sure it wasn't all another dream. It was there.

"We've a date at Roy's tomorrow night. Remember, you're

the one who wanted to meet there? Retracing the criminal's path and all that?" Sanjay laughed.

I'd forgotten my dinner date with him. "Sure. It's still on. See you tomorrow, bro."

My date had a dual purpose. To spend time with my brother, who had an uncanny ability to understand me, and, to talk to the waiters who'd served dinner to the Faust party on the fateful night. From my prior experience, I knew that they'd open up more with me than with the cops.

I swore to Dad's soul that regardless of what I found out at Roy's the next evening, I'd give the diary to Al the following morning. I'd had enough, dancing at the edge of the law.

~ Chapter 23 ~

Thursday, April 27, 2017
Pasadena, CA

I got to Roy's in my work clothes. It was the end of a normal day, following an extraordinary night.

Sanjay was at a table inside, sipping a glass of beer. He got up, hugged me, and pulled out a chair for me.

I said, "Hi, sorry I'm late. Was working on something and got carried away."

Sanjay looked at the waiter who approached our table, pad in hand, to take the order. "We need a few more minutes." He looked at me closely. "Are you OK? You look like you've seen a ghost."

I had, the ghost of my mentor, in his journal. "I'm OK, don't worry. I took a nap, which is not the norm for me. I'm still a bit groggy." I looked around the room, wondering which waiters had served Faust's dinner in the private room. Were they even here tonight?

"So, did you manage to sneak into Faust's office? Did you find anything? Yeah, you did, you've guilt written all over you."

"I did find something, Sanjay, but give me a day to figure it out." I checked my satchel for the journal inside. It was there. I asked, "Aren't we eating?"

"Shall I get some appetizers and a pinot for you?" Sanjay asked, probably prompted by my continued distraction and change of subject. I nodded.

We attacked a canoe appetizer that included Szechuan ribs, spicy tuna roll and lobster potstickers, washing them down with a wonderful pinot that I didn't even scrutinize.

Sanjay asked, "How's your theory about the Durga shaping up? I bet that's what's on your mind."

By now, the Durga and its possible connection to the murder were public knowledge. The police were unsure how the story had leaked out but once it was in the reporter's hands, they held a press conference to confirm it, giving out only minimal details of the idol. Al had questioned me about my possible role in the leak.

I sipped my wine. "I guess the killer used the Durga because it happened to be there. He was going to kill Faust one way or the other. The best I can come up with as a specific motive is the theft. I think the person who stole the idol got caught with it by Faust. And killed him to keep it quiet." I didn't want to say Davidson's name out loud in the context of the Durga.

Sanjay smiled. "You think it was the same person who drove Davidson off the cliff?" I was still conflicted over the journal, my guilt in keeping it. I toyed with the idea of bringing it up with Sanjay but discarded it. Not because I didn't trust him, but I didn't want him to accuse me of withholding information. And, I didn't want to incriminate him.

A heavy-set, attractive waitress approached the table for our dinner selections. It seemed she'd heard the tail-end of our conversation, because she became chatty. "I heard you say Durga. Are you guys with the police?"

I disregarded that comment while Sanjay laughed and

directed his right index and middle fingers at my eyes. "Yeah, she's the culprit. She's helping the police. But she's harmless." The woman gave a hearty laugh.

She continued. "You need some more time, it looks like. I'll be back. By the way, if you're talking about the professor's murder, you ought to talk to Linda. She was here the night of the dinner and thought something strange went on here, but she was gone on vacation when the detective came to talk to us. When she got back, she refused to go to the police. Something on her record or some such thing."

My ears perked up. Hope soared, tempered with caution that this might be another red herring. "Is she here tonight?"

Our waitress nodded.

I told Sanjay. "Go ahead and order," and turned to the waitress. "Will you tell Linda I'd love to have a few minutes of her time? Please tell her I'm not the police."

"OK, she's on the shift until 12. You want to see her now?"

I nodded, took a few minutes with the menu and ordered something, I don't remember what it was. A slip of a woman in her early thirties approached our table. She had hazel eyes and platinum blond hair pulled back into a ponytail. She wore minimal makeup. She introduced herself as Linda, and looking around at the lively, full and loud tables around us, suggested we go to the outdoor seating area.

Sanjay said, "You want me to start?"

I nodded.

The heat torches were lit in the outdoor patio and a pleasant sensation of warmth diffused out from them. I studied Linda who sat across from me in a waitress uniform with an honest look on her face. I knew initial impressions could often be wrong, but I felt I could trust her.

Linda took her feet out of her shoes and flexed and extended them. She looked relieved to be sitting down for a change.

"Linda, I was told you might have seen something on the night of the Faust party."

The waitress sipped a glass of water she'd brought with her and sighed.

I patted her hand resting on the table, "You can tell me. I won't repeat it unless it's important to solve the murder, OK? I'm not the police and you're not in any trouble."

"OK. It's just that I hope I'm not wasting your time." She was silent for a moment. "I'd left on my vacation the morning after the celebratory dinner for the professor. Sorry, I don't remember his name. I heard about the murder only after I got back. I told myself the police must have questioned every waiter who served that night and there was nothing more I knew. So I didn't volunteer to go talk to them." She paused and played with her fingernails. "Besides, I had a prior misdemeanor charge that was dropped, but I was scared it would be brought up again and I might lose my job."

"I understand your predicament, Linda. Why don't you tell me what's been on your mind and I promise to keep it quiet?"

"I hope I can trust you. I remember I was assigned to the back area of the restaurant, serving the second evening shift from ten on. I heard the commotion caused by the student who tried to talk to the professor but didn't see quite what happened. We all knew about the special dinner in the private room. Just before it broke up, a young man came in and wanted to be seated near the rear door and kept getting up and sitting back down until I realized he was trying to get a good view of the party room. I teased him about it, and he admitted that he was a fan of the professor and just wanted to see him. He asked me to tell him when the party broke up. When it did, I looked for him, but he was gone."

I kept my voice casual, but a familiar sensation took hold of my spine. Was there another young man besides Bill and Neil at Roy's? Was it Kevin? The guy at the burlesque could have been protecting Kevin. I had never double-checked his alibi.

"Can you describe him, Linda?"

"Average height, thin, wore short sleeves and jeans. Had a baseball cap that hid his hair. Couldn't see his eyes. Polite. Anxious. Sat watching the party room, sipping water, not ordering anything. If it wasn't near closing time, I'd have chased him off. I went back to get another order, and he was gone. Must have taken off as soon as the party broke up."

I pulled up photos of Bill and Kevin I had on my iPhone. "Was it one of these guys?" My pulse raced, I prayed she wouldn't identify either one. An unknown perp was far better than anyone I knew.

"No, neither of these. He was very different. Not as smartly dressed like these two. More scruffy, like a construction worker or something."

My heart dropped at yet another false lead. But who was this mysterious scruffy young man? Did he have any connection to the murder?

Possibly not a college student, but I wished I had photos of everyone from Faust's class, and photos of his lab staff. "I'd suggest you consider dropping by at the station, Linda. They might want you to identify him from more photos. Or help the police create a sketch of the young man. It'd be a big help to find a ruthless killer." I appealed to her sense of justice.

Linda got up, waving her hands. "I don't want to talk to

the police. That's why I was willing to talk to you, Miss. Don't you get me into trouble. If they come to question me, I swear I'll deny everything, honest." Her voice rose and her eyes were wide open. "Now I need to get back to my work."

She turned to walk away when I interrupted. "Can you look at some more photos?" There was no answer as Linda quickly made her way back to the kitchen.

I felt I was close to identifying the killer if I could only get Linda to the police station. Alternatively, I could send her a few more photos from my office. I found the head waiter, explained my predicament, and said, "I'd like Linda to look at a couple more photos. Can I send them to you? If she doesn't want to respond, that's OK." He nodded and gave me his cell number.

I returned to my table and found Sanjay engrossed in some magazine article and sipping coffee. "Sorry, bro. I didn't mean to take this long and leave you alone with your magazine."

He laughed. "No problem. Was she helpful?"

"Well, she did have something new to offer, but I need to go back to my office and find some photos. Might pay off, might not. I'm sorry I was so preoccupied tonight. I promise to tell you how *this* herring turns out."

Sanjay got up. "Hopefully, it's not a red one." He laughed.

* * *

On my way back home, I stopped at my office. I didn't have photos of every student from Faust's class, or his staff, but had those of my three advisees including Neil, who also attended Faust's class. I knew Neil had left with Bill just before the dinner party broke up, and Alice had confirmed that he'd arrived home close to midnight, which made it impossible that he was the late-comer Linda described. I sent them all to the head waiter to pass on to Linda. But I didn't think anything would come of it.

I went home, my mind troubled by Linda's revelation. And my helplessness in tracking the young man down. Could this be the third person on the scene? The Unsub? I'd no choice but to inform the police of what they'd missed and let them search for him. They had tools I lacked, like creating a sketch with Linda's help, and releasing it to the public. I tried to tell myself that this was by no means my moment of failure. Had I not talked to Linda, we'd never have known about this young man. Maybe this is where my dharma ends, and I should be grateful for what I'd been able to achieve. Hopefully, Al would pick up the trail.

I heard the ping of a text message on my cell phone. I sat up, like a dummy that had come to life, and grabbed my phone. It was from the waiter at Roy's. "Linda says that's him, the guy who came in late and left without ordering." The waiter had sent back the photo of Neil Anderson.

I sat still, frozen, staring at my phone, all air in my lungs sucked out in a deep expiration. Neil? He'd told me he drove Bill home, put gas in Bill's car, and went home to Altadena. Alice had told me he was home by midnight. Both had to be lies. My head was spinning. Did the quirky, mild-mannered, intellectual geek of a guy follow Faust to Davidson's home and killed him? Sweat broke out all over my body.

By now, I was fully awake with no intention of going back to sleep. My neurons were firing. Why, why, why kill a professor over his not reading an unsolicited thesis proposal? It made no sense, even for an odd character like Neil. Was it a front to gain access to Faust for the real motive? How would I get at the real motive?

I felt that Neil alone held that key. Did his adoption play a role? Was Faust perhaps his birth father? If so, he must look more like his birth mother, as he bore no resemblance to Faust.

I needed to dig into Faust's past before I confronted Neil.

~ Chapter 24 ~

Friday, April 28, 2017
Culver City, CA

Ginny, as always, gave me a warm welcome. "Come on in. It's so nice to see you again," Ginny said, as she let me in the house. She had bags beneath her eyes that spoke of sleeplessness or fatigue. Her grief, like mine, would have its ebbs and flows but would forever remain an integral part of her soul.

She led me into her kitchen and waved me to a chair at the dinette table, moving several small photo albums aside. "I am trying to assemble our old photos. Anything new about Bob's death? What an awful tragedy. Just starting to accept Joe's death, and now I've to mourn all over again. You don't think he killed Joe, do you?"

"It's one theory the police are entertaining. They have to consider everyone connected with the murder as potential suspects. But with Bob gone, they cannot get answers from him. Maybe you could help, Ginny?"

Ginny stared at me. "You suggest that I come out in the open about our affair? Even if Bob killed Joe, it was not because of me. I had given him a firm no, now and forever." She paced, wringing her hands, her face twisted in anguish.

"That wasn't what I was suggesting. We don't want to ruin the reputations of three good human beings—you, Bob and your husband. That's why I need to ask you some questions about the past. Your early years with Bob and Joe."

"That's a relief." She gave a bleak smile and pointed to the albums. "These old photos take me back." She joined me at the table.

"Please, Ginny, listen to me."

She nodded. "Go ahead, Rekha, ask me anything."

I sipped from my water bottle. "You met Joe at Harvard, right?" I didn't wait for an answer I already had. "When was that? Was it 1996 or 1997?" Subtracting twenty years from Neil's life made it possible that Faust could be his father.

"I was an administrative assistant in the Classics department in 1996. Joe and Bob took language courses required for graduate students in the first term of their freshman year. Both used to stop by my desk more often than was necessary." She smiled.

"When did you and Joe hook up?"

"His second term. On May, 10, 1997, to be exact. I could not date him while he was taking courses from the department. It would not have been . . . as you say here . . . cool."

"Did Joe see anyone else before you guys started dating?"

"I did not care about his past love history. For me it was essential that once we were serious that he honored his commitment. And he did. Joe was not a womanizer. Though I knew he had several admirers."

"How were you so sure?" I asked.

"One is never sure. You go with the general impressions you get of a man's integrity and listen to your friends. A friend of mine lived with two other grad students and she told me Joe was seeing one of them for several months in his freshman year. The girls thought the world of both of them and were disappointed when the relationship fell through."

"Did you find out the girlfriend's name?"

"No, I never asked. I heard that she moved away very soon after and no one knew where she went. Why this sudden interest in Joe's love life? Is that relevant to the murder?" Ginny sounded curious.

"Nothing about a murdered man's past is irrelevant, Ginny. Some details won't be connected to Joe's death, but others might be. I am sorry if I upset you."

Ginny sat down, was silent and stared at the wall.

I put my notebook down and leaned forward. "How are you holding up? Sometimes in the frenzy of finding the killer, we forget there's grieving going on. How's Kevin?"

Ginny moved some hair that had fallen over her face. "At some point, grieving becomes a chore for the bereaved. We have a lot of support but ultimately, it is for us to deal with it in our way. Kevin is focusing on his classes. Comes by more often than he did before his father's death. The poor boy is uncertain what to do with me or say to me. But he sits with me, and we look at old albums, and listen to music that Joe liked. I wish Joe could have seen what a good son we raised." Ginny took a clean white handkerchief with floral embroidery from her pants pocket and dabbed her eyes, one at a time. "He is not a suspect, I hope."

I shook my head. I didn't want to give her any of the details.

"Anything else, Rekha? I want you and the police to find who did this to Joe . . . and Bob."

This reaffirmation relieved me. "Ginny, do you by chance have your husband's old Harvard files tucked away somewhere?"

"Do I ever? Joe has a filing cabinet full of old files that he kept threatening to organize. I never looked at them. Would you like to see them?"

"That would be wonderful." I hoped there'd be a memento or two linking him to the girlfriend.

Ginny walked into the study and I heard the sounds of drawers being opened and closed. She soon reappeared with a dust-laden and weathered blue plastic folder that bulged with papers, held together by rubber bands. She dusted it off with a kitchen towel, sat down and opened it.

"My, my," she said, a gratifying smile spreading across her face. "This is it, what he had saved from his Harvard days. This brings back memories." She took out a notebook, opened it, leafed through it, and held it to her chest. "Had forgotten all about his diary. He was never a diary writer. A few lines here and there and then gave up on it. Cannot believe it was over twenty years ago. Now Joe and Bob are both gone." She put the diary back, closed the folder and handed it to me. And wiped her eyes.

"Don't you want to keep his diary? As a keepsake?" I asked.

"No, Rekha. The past is what it is, done and finished. I need to look forward, for Kevin." She blinked to contain tears, but tiny rivulets flowed down her cheeks.

"Do you think I can borrow this for a couple of days? It'd make my job so much easier. I promise to keep it safe and return it to you. If you want me to make a list of the papers inside, I can do that right now."

Ginny gave a tiny laugh. "Take it, Rekha. What use is it sitting there and rotting in his study? If anyone will find something useful in it to help the investigation, you would, I am sure." She paused for a moment. "I changed my mind.

Please . . . return his diary to me and feel free to dispose of the rest after you are done." She knit her eyebrows. "I'm curious, what are you looking for?"

"Ginny, I need to find out more about his first girlfriend."

She was silent for a moment. "I remember Bob talked about her once early on when we met, in a reverential tone, about how beautiful the young woman was. He used the words ethereal, exotic. Everyone was falling for her, but she picked Joe. I bet Bob was in love with her too, but he did the right thing. I don't remember her name."

"What happened to her? Who broke it off?"

"Not quite sure. She supposedly left college sometime during the first year. According to Bob, Joe couldn't locate her and gave up on her. She was an international student with no relatives in the US. Look in the folder, there may be something in Joe's diary. And maybe old photos. He was the sentimental kind," Ginny stood up as though her job was done. "Sorry, I need to lie down, Rekha. This has taken a toll on me. Will you show yourself out?"

"Maybe you can contact your old friend?" I became hopeful again. I felt that Ginny wanted to help.

"Give me a few days. I have not kept up with her but I bet other friends might have. So it will take a chain of telephone calls. My friend might have married and have a different last name by now. Lives change after you graduate, correct?"

"Of course, take your time. Call me one way or the other, will you?"

* * *

I got into the car, buoyant with my new find. I knew in my bones that what happened in 1996-1997 in a distant academic town in Cambridge, Massachusetts, between an aspiring archaeology student and his exotic lover would provide the last link in the connection between Faust and Neil.

I sat down with the folder at my dining table, with my faithful companion, a cup of chai. I removed the rubber bands and placed the contents of the folder on the table. I sorted out the stuff into as many categories as I could, stacking photos, certificates, and notebooks into separate piles.

The certificates were self-explanatory, but the photos were what I thought would yield the most information. There were many with his classmates, many more with Bob hanging out at local bars and stadiums. There was an occasional one of an older woman who could have been his mother. And several of Bob and Joe, with a well-dressed woman who had her hand on Bob's shoulder. I assumed she must be Bob's girlfriend, and now his wife. To my despair, there was none of Joe and his girlfriend.

The three notebooks were my last hope. One was quite thick, his class notebook from a basic archaeology class he took in freshman year, possibly the one that evoked his thirst for a deeper understanding of the subject. The second one contained his financial record spanning the four years at Harvard. Faust was a meticulous record-keeper who never overspent. The third one, the one Ginny took a brief look at, was his diary from his Harvard days. My heart accelerated with hope and excitement that was quickly dashed when I read its pages. She was right. Faust was no diary keeper. Sparsely filled and hastily scribbled, it lasted only the first term of his study and had been abandoned after that. It chronicled his love of the subjects he studied, a blossoming friendship with Bob, and their activities together in and out of college. No mention of a girlfriend except for flowery embellishments of the letters JV and JF scattered through the latter pages of the book. Was JV Faust's girlfriend?

It was midnight, but I was determined to review them all one more time. The same results. Then I noticed that two of the three notebooks had basic book covers but the third one was wrapped in blue and white striped fabric and taped to the paper cover. This was his diary, and although he abandoned it, he'd given it a personal touch. I recalled how as a youngster, I'd hide tantalizing letters from boyfriends and confidential ones from girlfriends inside book covers. I felt through the fabric on both sides and felt a sharp border of something hidden inside the back cover. Impatiently, I ripped off the fabric and a four by six photo fell out.

My first thought was it was likely to be some X-rated magazine picture, safeguarded from the prying eyes of others. I was wrong. It was a photo of four young people, two men and two women, leaning against a wooden gate that came up to their waist. I could easily recognize Faust and Bob Davidson. One of the women was from the previous photos, the one I'd assumed was Bob's girlfriend, but the other took my breath away. She looked angelic, like a waif who floated out of the surrounding woods, with her pitch-black curly hair arranged into two long braids that fell to her waist. She stood next to Faust whose right arm held her right shoulder. She wore a long, loose yellow top and a red and yellow shawl around her neck. Her complexion was a pale brown, her eyes almond-shaped, eyebrows beautifully arched, and her small nose, that bore a diamond stud on one nostril, tipped up at its end. Her lips were full even when parted in a broad smile. I was looking at a female version of Neil Anderson.

Staring at the young woman, I forgot to breathe. I turned the photo over and read the inscription, in Faust's careful, rounded script, "JV and I with our closest friends, Bob and

Angela. I couldn't ask for more" December 1996, Harvard University.

Five months before he met Ginny.

The first thing that struck me was how non-Caucasian she looked. No wonder I didn't, even in my wildest dreams, consider the possibility that Neil could be Faust's son. I was almost certain now, but still had no proof. I moved the photo to prevent it from getting wet from my tears.

I placed it on the table where I'd kept the photo of the Durga beneath my dad's. I now had the first and last initial of Faust's girlfriend, and the year she was at Harvard. I needed to find out what had happened to her. Did she have any connection to the Durga? How could I confirm she was Neil's mother?

I'd have to call Harvard in the morning. I wasn't sure any official would release information on a student from years ago to a perfect stranger unrelated to her.

~ Chapter 25 ~

Friday, April 28, 2017
Eagle Rock, Los Angeles, CA

The next morning I called the information number for Harvard University. A very British, almost upper-crust voice answered promptly, to my surprise. I enquired about the registrar's office and asked about the possibility of getting help to locate archived files. The man told me to hold on while he transferred me to the right department.

Getting historical records from a prestigious university was easier than I had imagined. It appeared nobody cared about what had happened twenty years ago, only to realize later how wrong I was. I told the registrar's assistant that I was looking for a female grad student who was doing a doctorate who had left the university possibly at the end of the first term in 1996-1997 and failed to return. I didn't have her field of study but gave her the initials, J.V. The assistant sounded skeptical but asked me to hold on while she checked her microfiche archives. She apologized that they had not digitized files older than fifteen years.

I drummed with my fingers on my desk. I was surprised that the college didn't ask for a court order. I hoped she had a comprehensive database of all graduate students who matriculated in 1996 that she could sort by the first or the last initial, or both. I hoped there wouldn't be hundreds of matches. How was I going to wade through them over the phone?

It was about fifteen minutes when I heard a cough that announced that the assistant was back. "Sorry for the delay. I had to sort through several databases. You said 1996-1997, right? Unfortunately, I'm unable to search without the full name. English doctorate was offered through the GSAS, the Graduate School of Arts and Sciences. Let me see, there were three female students who dropped out at the end of the fall term before taking the finals. Of these, only one failed to return. She must be the one you're looking for. But unfortunately I cannot give you her name without a written request with authentication that you are related to her." Why didn't she say this at the beginning? My hopes plummeted.

She mumbled after this as though talking to herself. "You're the second person to ask about this. Almost a couple of years ago, a young man stopped by and enquired about the same student. I remember him clearly because he was a little strange. He almost accused me for not having any record of what happened to her. Kept asking me if I thought she had died or worse yet, had been killed. I told him that wasn't part of our business and to check police records. I felt real sorry for him."

I was devastated. The strange young man who had enquired about JV had to be Neil. Did he find out she was his mother? And, how did he figure out that Faust was his father? Under the guise of the thesis proposal, was he harassing Faust to accept him as his son? Did Faust refuse, not suspecting that his first girlfriend had borne his first child? All questions and no answers.

* * *

I called Ginny with the hope that she might have connected the dots and found her old roommate.

Ginny had, and sounded more cheerful than before. "I was just about to call you, Rekha. As luck would have it, I was able to find my old friend Nora's phone number and address. She now lives in LA. She said she'd be happy to talk to you about her roommate. I suggest you go alone. We reminisced and planned a reunion next week. Here is her address and phone number."

Gathering my satchel and cell phone, I ran to my car, almost tripping over the water hose left near the front steps. I was desperate to prove that Neil was not a killer, despite his strange behavior, and hang on to my crumbling, perhaps ill-placed beliefs in humanity. But if Neil killed Faust, I'd afford no special concession for him. My dharma would align with the law.

I drove over the speed limit and prayed a cop wouldn't stop me. I was grateful Ginny's friend was home and chose to open her door to a stranger. She looked like she was in her late forties, her black hair speckled with gray. She smiled, deepening the crow's feet at the outer corners of her eyes. Listening to my self-introduction, she waved me in, saying, "Ginny told me who you are. I'm Nora. I heard of the murder and can't believe there could be a connection between it and the young woman I knew decades ago."

We sat down, face to face in a cozy living room decorated in earthy colors with lots of oak. For once, we got straight to the business at hand. "Nora, I'm looking for a woman with the initials JV. Was she one of your roommates in 1996-1997?" I spoke fast without time to breathe. This woman was my last chance.

"Yes, you must be talking about Jaya Varma. In 1996-97, three of us college students lived together in Boston. One of us, Jaya Varma, went to Harvard. My other friend and I were at Lesley."

I felt a mild electric shock coursing through my body. "What can you tell me about Jaya? Anything and everything you remember about her. Please."

Nora took out an old frayed photo album and opened a bookmarked page. "After Ginny called, I dug this up from a trunk of college mementos. Three of us girls shared an apartment. Don't we look innocent? Or maybe clueless." She laughed as she handed it to me. "Those were the good days, I tell you. We were wild. We followed some of our parental rules but were determined to have a good time."

From the photo, three young, starry-eyed faces smiled at me, one a younger version of Nora, another I didn't recognize, and the third, a flawless and glowing face. I knew that was Jaya. I pointed at her and the woman nodded.

"What can you tell me about her? Did she have a boyfriend?" I smiled for the first time in two days. The information was within my grasp now.

"Jaya was very private. She had come from India with a full scholarship to study literature. Boy, was she brilliant, quoting Shelley and Shakespeare. She mingled with us but mostly kept to herself and her books. She had no relatives in the US, no one called her until midway through the first term when she got calls from a young man that would perk her up. But she never told us who it was until one evening when a handsome guy came to pick her up. She asked us to keep it a secret. She was not supposed to date anyone other than an upper class Indian, because her family was related to the last Maharaja of the State. She had promised her parents, and that was why she could come to the US."

I pulled out the photo I found in Faust's college diary and offered it to her. "Do you see the young woman and her boyfriend in this picture?"

The woman took the photo, looked at it and smiled. "Yes, sure, that's Jaya, and the young man on her left was her boyfriend, Joe. Wasn't she beautiful?"

She looked again at the photo I gave her and her face paled. "Was . . . was . . . Joe the professor who was killed? She never told us his last name. I found out only several years later when I reconnected with Ginny. By then, she was married to him. When I heard about the murder, I wondered if it was the same Joe who had dated Jaya. I called Ginny but didn't bring up Jaya. That was all in the past."

"The murdered professor was Joseph Faust. I heard that Jaya left the University at the end of the first term. Did you hear what happened to her?"

"She never told us why she was dropping out. She planned to move out of our apartment around the same time, saying she needed a change. Asked me if I'd want to keep her bonsai collection. I knew something else was up, but she wouldn't tell me. She was so depressed. I suggested she see a therapist, but she dismissed the idea. Then the day before she left, I heard her throwing up." The woman's eyes misted over, even after all these years. She touched the photo with the tips of her index finger. "Poor thing."

"She was pregnant. Did you ask her?"

"No. I felt so bad for her. Imagine coming to a foreign country, not being able to blend in, and then discovering you were pregnant. I waited outside the bathroom and when she came out, I asked her if I could help. Nothing more."

"What did she say?"

Nora wiped her eyes and looked down at the photo again. "She said she was moving in with a distant family friend. Asked me to promise not to tell anyone, especially her boyfriend. She said she couldn't bring disgrace to his family, or hers. Nor could she kill her baby. She wanted to give the child up for adoption. I still remember how sad and frightened she looked."

"Did you keep in touch with her after she left?"

"No, she didn't want me to. I wanted to, but all I knew was that she'd moved away. What's this all about?" She held out the photo for me.

"One last question, Nora. Can you tell me if she had a middle name?"

She laughed. "Yes, how did you guess she had one? It was Durga. She kept it hidden from most people, feeling that others would expect her to be always good and pure like the Goddess."

"Thanks so much for speaking with me, Nora. I'm sorry I have to rush. I'll tell you all about it if my hunch proves to be right. I promise I'll be back." I hugged her and made my way to my car.

* * *

I still had no information on what had happened to Jaya Durga Varma, and no proof that she was Neil's mother. But the puzzle was coming together. Neil had to be Jaya Varma's son, born out of her relationship with Faust. I suspected that Neil killed his father but what became of his mother? Did she return to India? I knew who might help me. Neil himself.

Before that, I had one more truth to confirm. That Neil came home later than midnight the night of the murder. That Alice lied to me to cover for her son. I wouldn't blame her.

~ Chapter 26 ~

Friday, April 28, 2017
Altadena, CA

This time I didn't have to wait on Neil's porch for someone to come home. Alice, a mug in hand, answered my knock on the door. "Come in, Professor Rao." She led me to the kitchen, like an old friend.

I said, "Sorry to barge in. Alice. But it's important. I want answers to some questions." I looked around. Everything in the kitchen was in the same place as I remembered. Melissa was missing, most probably in school where she should be at that time of the day.

Alice sat down, a frown on her brow, and put her mug down on the table. She indicated I should take a chair. "Something wrong? You looked worried. What is it?"

"I need some information about Neil, Alice. About his adoption."

Alice examined her hands. "My daughter wouldn't stop talking about you, Professor Rao, after you left last time. She yelled at Neil for not getting up to say hello to you when you came over. He got irritated with her." Alice shook her head. "One never knows what ticks him off these days. Does this have to do with the professor's murder?"

I nodded. "You said last time that Neil came home around midnight the night of the murder and was shut up here for a day. Do you remember the exact time he arrived?"

Alice buried her face in her hands. She looked up, her eyes teary. "Is that important? Neil always came home on Friday nights in time for dinner. Although why he'd eat with us, I had no idea, because he had taken to being very formal and distant with me ever since he found out about his adoption. He'd call me Mother, not Mom anymore."

"When did you see or hear him come home that night, Alice? This is important." My voice rose although I had no intention of threatening or admonishing her. In my mind, she was a mother protecting her child.

She looked away as though ashamed. "I'm sorry. I lied the first time. Neil asked me to. He wasn't here for dinner that Friday. He came after Melissa and I went to bed. I couldn't fall asleep, so I was reading, and heard Neil's car come in and the front door open and close. I looked at the clock and it was 3 in the morning. I didn't want to confront him and ask where he'd been. I must have fallen asleep soon after that because the next I knew my alarm was going off."

"Did Neil try to find his birth parents?"

"He took it on as his mission for the year after he graduated from high school. Did his college applications, got into a couple of good schools but told them he'd be deferring for a year. Wasn't around very much, distanced himself from us, and wouldn't talk about what he was up to, either to Melissa or to me. I felt he'd hardly talked to me at all from that point on. What did I do wrong?"

"Alice, you did nothing wrong. And I'm sorry to ask you all these questions. Did Neil ever go to Cambridge, Massachusetts, during his year off from school?"

She stood up and started walking around the tiny kitchen. "I'm not sure. I couldn't keep track of his comings and goings. He told Melissa he needed to do some research on the East Coast and was gone several months that year."

"Did he change the college he wanted to go to, at the end of that year?"

Alice stared at me. "How did you know, Professor Rao? Yes, he did. He was already accepted at Berkeley and UCLA, but applied to Oxy at the last minute. He got in."

I'd guessed right. Once Neil found out where Faust was, his goal was to get into the same school. Being brilliant, getting into Oxy at the last minute was a piece of cake.

I made an impetuous decision, but kept my voice neutral. "Listen to me, Alice. I need to go inside Neil's room. Now, before Melissa comes back. Please help me."

She nodded. "Neil is in trouble, isn't he?"

"But we can help him, Alice, if we act fast. Please hurry."

Alice went to a kitchen drawer and returned with a key ring. "He'd be livid, but I want to help him. At heart, he's a good boy." She isolated one key from among a bunch of them. "He thinks I don't have a key, but I always did. I've never gone in there except to clean it, that too only when he was home." She walked into the hallway and I followed and watched her unlock the door to Neil's sanctum.

I stood with bated breath, eyes mesmerized by the sight I beheld. On the wall across from the door, there were two bulletin boards mounted side by side. On the left one, there was a large black-and-white photo of Faust, the face slashed with multiple knife cuts. Smaller photos, all partially beheaded surrounded this. The board on the right contained dozens of pictures of Durga, in various forms including the Mahishasura Mardini, arranged in a circle. A large eight-armed one was in the center, and her Mahisha's head was replaced with Faust's head. At the tip of her trident there was a dried crusty red material that I knew was blood. Faust's blood. I took several photos of the boards.

I sensed Alice shaking and saw her point at something on a small table below the displays. It looked like a book. Another journal?

"That book. The poor soul, his young mother had left it with us, to give to him on his eighteenth birthday. I couldn't help but look inside, Professor Rao. It is about some Indian ritual . . . some *Puja*." She paused and stared at me. "I couldn't understand the connection. Did he kill an innocent man because of it?" Alice wept.

I moved to her, enfolded her in my arms and held her tight.

"He did it, didn't he? He killed the professor." She started to wail. "But why?"

I knew I mustn't touch anything because it was evidence, but I needed a look at the book. Titled *Durga Puja, with notes and illustrations,* by Pratapa Chandra Ghosha, B. A., it was a 2015 reprint of an original text published in 1871 in Calcutta. Close to two hundred pages long, it recounted the rites and ceremonies of the ritual. The inside of the cover bore a hand-written note. I captured it with my phone and put the book down where it was.

I led a shaken Alice out of the room and locked the door. I returned the key to her and she tightly clasped it in her hand. I sat Alice down and gave her the lukewarm liquid left in her mug and watched her heaving subside to something closer to normal breathing.

I hugged her and got up. "I need to go, Alice. Stay inside and keep the door locked. Make sure Melissa stays inside.

Don't let Neil in if he comes here. I will find him on campus, talk to him, and ask him to turn himself in. I'll come back and explain everything. I promise, but I have to run."

Alice followed me as I moved toward the front door, her face sagging. "Please help him. I think he's insane." She opened the door and almost shoved me out. "Please, please, do what you need to do, before he destroys more lives."

The moment I got to the car, I knew I had to protect Alice. Neal wouldn't hesitate to kill her. I couldn't call Al because he'd question where I was, what I was doing and order me not to interfere with his work. I called the PPD and left an anonymous message that I had seen someone loudly arguing with an older woman outside a house. I gave Alice's address.

I looked back as I turned the car, and found Alice standing on the porch, leaning on the pillar, sobbing.

~ Chapter 27 ~

Friday, April 28, 2017
Eagle Rock, Los Angeles

I hurried to my office, locked my door, and checked the time. It was 2.30 pm. I knew I had to act right away to prevent Neil from going home and punishing his mother for betraying him. For the first time, I felt fear for Alice and Melissa. And for me.

I retrieved the photo of the writing from the inside of the book. It said, *"Harvard University. Cambridge, MA. August 10, 1997. To my son Neel, with all my love, Jaya D. Varma."* A brief verse followed the dedication:

> *Oh, came a magic cloak into my hands*
> *To carry me to distant lands,*
> *I should not trade it for the choicest gown,*
> *Nor for the cloak and garments of the crown.*

I wasn't familiar with it, but realized it must contain a special meaning for Jaya, something she wanted to convey to her son. The date could be Neil's date of birth. I didn't have the time to research it, so I focused on the task at hand.

I wasn't ready to share my information with the police until I had heard from Neil that Faust was his father and that he had killed him and Bob Davidson. If I called Al now, he and his team would close in on Neil to arrest him. They would be merciless, as cops are, as cops have to be. But I had a different purpose. I wanted to hear Neil confess to the murders since I had no evidence that he committed the acts. I doubted if Al had, or he'd have arrested him by now.

I needed a one-on-one meeting with Neil, something that Al would oppose. His cautionary words about dangerous criminals echoed from the walls of my office. Would Neil lose sight of his humanity altogether and attack me? Someone whom he seemed to respect and even consider a mother figure?

Where was my dharma taking me? Was I once again lost on the wrong path, as I'd been when I worked on Dad's murder? I was grappling with questions and received no answers.

At the thought of facing Neil alone, my heart plummeted. Anxiety and uncertainty propelled me around and around the small room. My eyes fell on the Bhagavad Gita and I took it and held it in my hands. I thought of God Krishna's advice to Arjuna on the battlefield of Kurukshetra, that fighting his brothers was his only righteous action. And how Arjuna followed his dharma and brought peace to the world. Although a mere mortal, I too had no choice but to confront Neil, to prevent further destruction of lives and restore a small measure of justice to the families. Even if it endangered my life, this was the path of my dharma.

I sat down at my desk and emailed Neil to meet me in my office as soon as he could, citing an emergency as the reason. I contacted the registrar's office and requested that they get him for me. And, after some debate, I left Al out of it. My call would cause Al to force the truth out of me, order me not to meet with Neil, even threaten to arrest me for obstruction of justice. I wanted a confession.

I worried about my safety, although my foolish sixth sense told me that Neil would not hurt me. I went with it.

There was a knock on my office door.

I opened the door and Neil walked in. As always, shuffling a little, with a half-smile, eyebrows raised. "What is it, Professor Rao? Did anything happen to Melissa? Or Mother?" He dropped his backpack on the floor near the door and stared at me. My face must have been an open book, because he turned into a Neil I'd never seen before.

With a smirk on his face, he folded his arms across his chest. "I see. So you've solved it. I knew you would before the stupid police did. Bravo, bravo." He clapped.

I got back to the safety of my chair behind the desk and sat down. I needed to play it cool. My only saving grace was that I had turned my cell phone on, and left it in my jacket pocket, to record Neil's words.

Neil walked around in some inner turmoil, clenching and unclenching his hands, and sat down in a chair across from my desk. He seemed calm, but I knew a volcano was picking up heat inside him, ready to erupt any minute. Having killed before, I believed he wouldn't hesitate to do it again. Maybe he didn't have a gun, but he could overpower and strangle me. He might have a knife and cut me to pieces. I knew I was in the presence of evil.

The only weapon I possessed was words, to keep him talking, gloat about his achievements that now included the murders. Before I could put my plan into action, Neil leaned over and grabbed the murder book I had laid open on my desk, the one where I'd written down my findings and hypotheses, and created a rough sketch of my murder wheel.

"You better give it back to me, Neil. It's mine. You can't read it without my permission."

He disregarded me, thumbing through the pages, smiled and shook his head now and then. "Cute, Professor Rao, real cute. Not as good as my thesis proposal. But the way you drew diagrams to solve the murder. I have to hand it to you, you found the truth that an entire army of cops couldn't. That's because you're brilliant, like me, we're two peas in a pod. You could have been my mother."

I grimaced as he threw the book on the table. "Tell me about your thesis proposal, Neil. Do you still have a copy? I'd love to read it."

Neil stared into space. "Sorry, Professor, I kept only one hard copy, and I destroyed it."

Another dead end. As time ticked by, I wondered how this encounter I'd choreographed would end. "I confess, Neil, I'm no detective. I just used logic to figure out the killer and the motives. Tell me, did you kill Faust? I think I can guess the answer, but I would like to hear it from you. After all, it's your *coup de grâce*." I heard a light footfall outside the window but managed not to turn my head. Was that the police? How did Al find out?

The young man burst out laughing, took the receiver of my office phone and put it aside.

"Give me your cell phone. I want to make sure no one interrupts us." I had no choice but to hand it over. He chuckled, seeing that I had been recording what he was saying. "You were taking notes for Al? Don't associate with him, Professor Rao. You and I, we're above all that scum." He paused for a second, eyes gleaming at something he alone saw. "So were my birth mother and my father."

"Faust was your father, right?"

Neil pulled up another chair and put his feet up. "Relax, I won't hurt you. I have you up on a pedestal, although I didn't expect you'd trick me into getting me here. Why did you do that? You could have turned it all over to the police."

Here was my chance to get him to open up. "Neil, you are a brilliant young man, and had the potential to achieve as many high goals as your father did. But you chose the wrong path. I want to get you help, so you can understand why what you did was wrong."

Neil scratched behind his ear, looked away from me and said, "Good luck. Let's do this. You tell me what you figured out and I will fix your mistakes. The tables are turned. I'm now the professor, and you, my student who seeks the truth from me." He laughed a full, vibrant, belly laugh that took me by surprise. I shuddered. How could he be joyous about killing his father?

"I agree, but before I do that, I want you to promise that you'll surrender to the police and confess. That might result in a lesser sentence, I can't promise. And maybe, court-ordered psychiatric help to deal with your problems."

"There you go, you should have been a psychologist." He looked away, and when he looked at me again, his eyes had turned stony. Cold, flat, hard. "But you are dead wrong." He almost yelled these words. "I hoped he'd claim me as his son, but he never responded to my emails, pleading with him to do the right thing. I told him I wanted to honor him by taking up archaeology and follow in his footsteps. I'd heard that his other son, whatever his name is, didn't want to do that. What a disappointment for my father. But even then, he wouldn't accept me. The last time we met, he told me he'd report me to the Dean if I approached him again. For an accomplished man, he was a fool. He didn't think I'd kill him."

"How long had you been pestering him? Dr. Faust was a compassionate man. He thought you would realize the error of your ways and stop bothering him. He gave you more chances than anyone else would have. And look what he got." Tears wet my eyelids.

"I decided to wait awhile when I started at Oxy. I wanted to find out the type of person he was. I talked to students and his assistant, and all I heard was high praise. That made me doubt if my assumptions could be wrong. I am methodical, Professor Rao. I did not act on an impulse. I weighed all my evidence and concluded that under that garb of humility and love for his students lay a cold-blooded killer. I emailed him, talked to him a couple of times, yet he wouldn't accept the truth. He tried to steer me toward counseling and then refused to see me or read my emails. I decided I had no choice but to kill him because that was what he deserved. It was my duty."

I laid my head down on the desk, unable to meet his eyes, as I assimilated his warped interpretation of dharma.

"Am I boring you, or are you horrified? My father didn't deserve to walk this earth after what he did to my mother. Why she killed herself because of him, I don't understand."

I was aghast. Another piece of the puzzle I'd failed to find. "Neil. I'm so very sorry. How was Faust responsible?"

"He didn't own up to being the father, the coward. And my mom killed herself rather than live with the shame of it."

"What if he didn't know there was a child? The man I knew would have taken responsibility for it." I heard whispering voices outside my door and realized the cops were here.

"If he had looked at the facts I had with me, and acknowledged me, I wouldn't have killed him. I gave him the dates, wanted to show him the book my birth mother had left for me.

How I found him using the verse my mom wrote in the book. He stared at me as though I was crazy. He left the room, and his assistant came in and told me to leave. She threatened to call the police. I had to leave. After that he refused all contact."

Neil got up and started walking, his hands in his pockets, his steps steady and firm, back and forth in front of my desk. What plot was he conjuring up in his insane mind? Kill me and kill himself?

I held on to my belief. "You could have demanded a paternity test, Neil, instead of killing him. Your mother couldn't believe—

"—My *adoptive* mother." He yelled. "She never even told me about it until I was eighteen."

"That was your birth mother's wish. She might have wanted you to have a normal childhood and be old enough to handle the information."

"Oh yeah, this was her excuse too, and you bought it, the whole shipload. It was never written down anywhere in my mother's handwriting."

"How did you find out she killed herself?"

"My birth mother had left a book for me, a book about Durga Puja, with the entry, Harvard University, Cambridge, August 10, 1997. My birth date. I knew nothing more about her until I got to Harvard—"

This time there was the unmistakable shuffle of footsteps outside, and Neil sprang up. "There are people outside." He took a couple of strides and was behind my desk, close to me.

I got up, unsure of what was going to happen now. I turned to Neil and touched his shoulder. "Neil, don't resist arrest, give yourself up and confess to what you did. You can get psychiatric help. Do that for Melissa."

Neil sighed. "For Melissa . . . and you, Professor Rao. You're the only person I loved like my mother. There're times I'd wished you *were* my mother and I could hug you."

I was relieved that Neil's creepy familiarity with me during our meetings stemmed from his love for a mother he never knew, and not any misplaced romantic fantasy. How ironic that he chose to distance the one person who'd offered him that love and would have continued to do so. Alice.

Neil turned to me and said, "Thank you, Professor Rao. May I hug you?"

I flinched, but nodded, how could I not? Even the most wretched deserved compassion.

His eyes red and moist, Neil caught me in a gentle embrace, with his head on my left shoulder and arms at my waist. We stayed like that for what seemed forever. Then he broke off, wiped his eyes and said, "Yes, I killed Faust and Davidson. But I'm not sorry, they got what they deserved. And I'll take what's coming to me."

"Open the door." Al's voice boomed outside. As I opened the door, several armed men came running in and a flood of relief poured over me. I felt Neil's body stiffen beside me and I held my hand on his back until a uniform handcuffed him. As another pair of cops led him out, Neil turned to lock eyes with me until he could no longer see me.

Al hurried over to me, placed his hands on my shoulders and said, "Thank God you are not hurt, Rekha. I listened to the anonymous phone call left at the station. I knew it was you. We went to Neil's house and questioned his mother. She told us you were going to talk to Neil to give himself up. We took a chance that the two of you were in your office."

I let go and could no longer hold back my sobs. "I didn't . . . I'm sorry . . . I tried . . ." Tears came fast wetting Al's shirt, and I grabbed on to it as if hanging onto a ledge from which I could fall to my death.

Al tightened his left hand on my shoulder, took out a handkerchief, lifted my face and gently mopped it. I could see that his eyes were glistening. "You are OK, Rekha. You are safe now." Officers were filing out, seeing no further danger lurking in the room, and waiting for instructions.

I pulled back from the comfort of Al's arm, worrying how many eyes had seen us.

I walked out on my own, leaving Al to follow me. I held my head high not letting anyone see the last ounce of fear still trapped inside me. Dad would have been proud. Ma and Sanjay would be proud. I wanted to get away from the murkiness of it all, back in the safety and comfort of my home, my family.

Outside was a jungle of men and women bearing weapons. From behind them, one figure moved toward me, my brother Sanjay. Was I ecstatic to see him.

He hugged me and between tears and laughter, said, "Well done, professor. I am glad you're safe."

He took off his coat and put it on my trembling shoulders.

"Take me home, please." I said.

"It looks like you need to go with this dude first." He pointed to a uniform standing near us. "He's going to take you to the station for your statement. Someone will bring your car. I'll wait there and personally escort you home." He made a bow.

* * *

I noticed that cops filled the squad room almost to capacity. Everyone was looking at me with smiles on their faces, some high-fiving each other.

The officers parted as a small disheveled figure and an older woman tumbled out of a nearby room, and Melissa fell into my arms. She clutched me, her little fingers digging into my skin. "Professor Rao, they told me you were safe, but I had to see you to believe it. I am so glad you are OK." The little girl started weeping, drying her tears with her hands. "I am sorry, so sorry about what Neil did to your professor. I hope he didn't hurt you."

She let go, moved back and leaned against Alice. She paused to consider something. "He'll always be my brother, I guess." What a smart kid. I hoped she'd rebuild her faith in human beings.

I knelt and looked at her sad eyes. "Melissa, Neil can never bully your mother again." My eyes shifted to Alice who hesitated for a moment and clasped me in her arms.

"He'll go to jail, won't he?" Alice asked, her voice breaking.

"Will he be OK?" Melissa asked.

"Neil needs a lot of help. The judge will make sure he gets it."

I patted Melissa's head and kissed her forehead before an officer led her and Alice away into an interrogation room.

I was led to another.

~ Chapter 28 ~

Saturday, April 29, 2017
Pasadena, CA.

I was back at the PPD after a good night's sleep. Sanjay dropped me off since my car was at the station.

"We have your statement, Professor Rao, but there are a few unanswered questions," Lieutenant Bigsby said. I'd been introduced to her early on by Al. This woman in a tailored suit and slicked-back hair exuded dignity and strength. "That's why we need to talk to you."

"Not sure if I can answer them all, Lieutenant. There are a few holes in the story that I think only Neil can fill. But what would you like me to tell you?"

"How did Neil find out what happened to his birth mother?"

"Neil told me he was distraught that Harvard had no additional information about what had happened to her. I assume that he searched the registry of vital records or some other resource and found out that Jaya Varma gave birth to a boy and hanged herself after that. But that's pure speculation on my part. I think that could be why he turned Faust's tie around to the back to mimic a noose."

Al asked, "How did he find out Faust was his father?" He

flipped through the book that I'd seen in Neil's room. "There's nothing here to suggest his father's name. Just a verse from a poem I don't find relevant." He shrugged.

I answered, "Neil must have found its source. I told you he's brilliant. How he did it, he'll have to tell us."

"Did he tell you what happened to Faust after he got to Davidson's home?" The lieutenant got up and stretched her back.

"No, Lieutenant. I accomplished what I wanted. To hear from him that he killed Faust, who he suspected was his father. And killed Davidson to shut him up. I'd guessed the latter simply because Davidson was the only other person with a connection to the Durga. I leave it to you to find out exactly what transpired in Davidson's front yard." I leaned back in my chair.

Bigsby sat down, and turned to Al, "Tell her."

Al said, "Ah, we've something new for you. We located Davidson's brother and found out about his art restoration business. Davidson would procure arts and artifacts through underground channels and his brother would alter them just enough to sell them. The brother arrived a few minutes after the murder. He was supposed to find a new artifact, clearly the Durga, waiting for him. He walked into the fresh murder scene, got scared, and split. Davidson's wife led us to him. He had a computer in his apartment with all the transactions, including the date and time for picking up the Durga. It did come from Faust's excavation in Jwalapuram. The Indian police told us that Davidson worked in cahoots with one Dileep Patel, a staff member from the National Museum of India to procure it."

I was glad that Reddy's suspicions were right on target. "Was it the brother's car the neighbor reported was Bill's?"

Al nodded. "Possibly, but we haven't sorted it all out. Rekha, are you willing to sit in and discuss the murder with Neil? With me? You might be able to get him to talk so we can complete the picture. We've arranged this for later in the afternoon. Before that . . ." He broke off. "You have a visitor. Bill McGraw is waiting for you. He says he has something urgent to tell you." Al got up and stepped toward the door.

I didn't move. "Hold on. There's something else I have to tell you. Bill can wait." I put my hand into my satchel and pulled out Faust's journal and held on to it.

"What's this?" Al asked and sat down moving his chair closer to me. "It looks like a memo book. Neil's? Where did you find it?"

"Faust's journal. The reason for him to dismiss Bill. When Faust came into his office, he saw Bill at the bookshelf in proximity to where he'd hidden the journal. He assumed Bill had opened it, but Bill swears he didn't. And I believe him."

"Why do you believe him? Maybe he found it and black-mailed Faust for whatever is in it. Both felonies and punishable." Al said in a stiff voice.

"Listen, I'm the one who deserves the punishment because I was the one who found the book. Bill could not have done it because I had to get into Faust's office, pry open a secret compartment, wedge my hand inside and pull it out. It took time, effort, and some damage." I raised the thumb and index finger of my right hand that still displayed red scratches from the adventure.

Al's eyes were like daggers directed at me. "You, Rekha? You broke in and took it? You realize that's against the law."

"No, no, no. I didn't break in. I had a key to the office that the assistant gave me, to start cleaning up the room, but yes, I found the compartment and forced it open. But it was after your guys finished your search and turned the office back over to the department. So I'm not answerable to you but to the JPM co-director, Dr. Striker."

Al looked visibly shaken. "I'm amazed our people didn't find it. What's in it?"

I handed it to him.

"When did you find it? And why didn't you give it to us earlier? You knew it was evidence." He flipped through the pages of the small notebook.

"The last entry will make the most sense to you. It was an appointment Faust had made to see a Dr. Alan Lambert in San Francisco after his lecture tour." I swallowed. "Lambert specializes in counseling adults who transition to homo-sexuality late in life."

A hush fell in the room, filling every crack and crevice, broken by Al clearing his throat.

"What does that mean, Rekha?"

"The journal, although brief, chronicles that Faust accepted that he was gay a couple of years ago. That he had been gay all his life."

Al sat frozen for a few seconds, coughed, and asked, "How long have you had this?"

"I found it yesterday. The book has no names other than of his family, no dates of events. It's a private chronicle that he didn't want anyone to see. I stumbled upon it. I don't think even Ginny knew. After I read it, I worried if Faust's homo-sexuality might have had something to do with his murder. Maybe there was a lover whom he'd rejected. But the next day, the waitress Linda led me to Neil, who filled in most of the missing pieces."

The Lieutenant's face was grave. "In this day and age,

he hesitated to come out? What torment he must have gone through."

"How can it be that we missed this waitress Linda?" asked Al. "We'd questioned everyone who served that night. There was nothing suspicious we could find."

"It so happened she was on vacation when your people questioned the staff. She had reasons not to come forward, but she consented to talk to me. No coercion involved."

Al looked away for a moment, turned back, and made a gesture for me to carry on.

"Do what you must do. The only person who has a right to this book is Ginny. I was going to hold on to it until the case was solved before giving it to her . . . but . . ."

I held out the journal to Al. "I trust you, Al. Please read it to confirm there is nothing in it that would have helped the case. Then kindly return it to me. It belongs to Ginny alone."

Al took it and put it in his briefcase. "I promise to give it back to you. Now, shall we go and see Bill?" With a serious face, he led the way out of the room and turned into the one next to it.

* * *

I'd already made the decision not to tell Bill that he'd misdirected me to the wrong bookshelf. I was sure it wasn't on purpose, and everything had worked out.

Inside the small room with just one window, Bill sat at a table. He sprang up and came forward. "It's so nice to see you, Professor Rao. I'm sorry about Neil. Did he kill Faust?"

I looked at Al for the answer and he said in a gentle voice, "We've got to interview him before we accuse him of anything, son."

Bill nodded. "Thank you, Detective. It's nice to see you

also, but may I have a few minutes alone with Professor Rao?"

Al looked surprised. "Oh sure, sure," he said very slowly, and looked at me. "Shall I wait for you? I can give you a ride to the jail."

I didn't want to disappoint him, but anticipating what awaited us at the jail, I just wanted to get it over with, go home, and be alone. "Thanks, Detective, I think I'll take my car. So I can get home right after we finish."

Al's shoulders dropped, and he shut his mouth tight and turned to the door. I hoped he'd understand and ask me another time, another occasion.

I turned to Bill. "I'm so glad you came, Bill, but what's so urgent?" I motioned him to sit, and I took the other chair.

Bill had his arms folded across his chest. "Professor Rao, I kept something from you." He started to stutter. "Remember I told you how I suspected there was a secret compartment in the bookshelf in Professor Faust's office, I didn't tell you the whole truth. It came open when I tried to pull out the tall book. I swear I felt something inside, like a book, but before I could take it out, I heard footsteps . . . forced it down and closed the compartment. I suspect Professor Faust saw the tail end of my movement."

He hung his head.

I touched his hand briefly to comfort him. "Look, Bill. You did nothing wrong. The compartment sprung open, so it wasn't locked. You didn't persist in finding out what was in it. We would never learn what Faust saw, but it's possible he felt unsafe with your proximity to whatever was in the compartment."

Bill leaned closer to my face. "What if what was in there would have revealed the killer's identity? The police would have arrested him, and we'd all have been spared a lot of anguish. I feel responsible for Neil's standoff with you."

I laughed, with the explicit purpose of having Bill think he was on the wrong track. "Yes, Bill, Neil was angry, but I knew he'd never hurt me physically. I was confident about that because all I've ever done was to help him. But thank you for worrying about me."

"Did you find out what was in the compartment, Professor Rao? Was it a clue?"

I knew I couldn't give him an honest answer, but wanted to set his mind at ease. I put my hand on his shoulder. "What I can tell you is that the object in the compartment was personal to Faust and didn't have any connection to the murder or the killer. Something that he chose not to display in public. A more private treasure than your aunt's glass menagerie."

Bill smiled. "Thanks for telling me this." He stood up as I rose from my chair. "One more thing, and this is pure speculation on my part."

"Go on."

"Remember, Neil gave me a ride home from Roy's and put gas in my car. When you asked me if there was anything different about the car, I couldn't quite figure it out. But later I realized that my tank was half full. I'm sure we didn't store that much gas."

"I see," I was beginning to understand where he was going.

Bill started to stutter. "I suspect he used my car to go back to Roy's and follow Professor Faust. He must have gone to a gas station to replenish my tank before that. I'm not sure, but I wondered if it was my car the neighbor saw, with Neil at the wheel. But he didn't identify Neil either in the line-up. I am confused."

"Don't worry about it, Bill. I'll pass it on to the police.

Listen, get back to your studies and stay in touch with your aunt. Move on, that's all we can do."

Bill hesitated, moved to shake my hands, and I gave him a gentle hug.

~ Chapter 29 ~

Saturday, April 29, 2017
Los Angeles, CA

It was a defiant Neil Anderson we encountered in the LA Men's Jail.

I was familiar with the place, having visited Bill almost a month ago. I heard that Neil was on suicide watch and would be moved to the prison after our meeting with him. He sat on a chair in the interrogation room, heavily shackled, with two hefty guards behind him.

Al and I sat down. Al turned his recorder on, placed it on the table, and signaled he was ready to start the interview.

Neil looked at Al and avoided my eyes. "Is my sister all right, Detective? Where is she?"

I answered. "I saw Melissa at the station last night, Neil, with Alice. She's OK, but is worried. Kept asking if you were OK."

I saw Neil's eyes soften. "I'll miss her. She's a good kid." His voice became gruff. "Let's get on with this."

I repeated the story I had told the police earlier in the day and Neil listened carefully to every word I uttered, sometimes indulging in a smile. "You got your story mixed up a little, Professor Rao. Is this the best you could do? You should stick to art history, although I can't imagine how much this motley crew would've done without your help." He pointed to Al with a smile.

I knew Neil was taunting the police and goading me. So I played with him. "Tell us where we went wrong, Neil. Are you suggesting that you didn't kill Faust? That wasn't what you told me in my office."

Al said, "We found a whole host of evidence under the new tree you planted behind your house. Your sister Melissa told us about it, although she didn't know what we'd find underneath."

That they found evidence under a tree was news to me. Kudos to Melissa.

"Professor Rao," Neil said. "You asked me for my thesis proposal a while ago. It's there. Have a go at it." He laughed.

I made a mental note to see it after the police had processed it. "You went back to Roy's after dropping Bill off, followed Faust to Davidson's home, right?"

I pulled out from my satchel the two faded photos of Jaya Varma, one with her roommates, and the other with Faust and the Davidsons. I had shared them with Al earlier and put them in a plain envelope. I now placed the envelope on the table close to me. "Tell us what happened in Davidson's front yard, Neil."

Neil looked at the envelope. "What do you have here? More evidence to taunt me?"

I looked at Al for a signal, but his face was impassive as though he was waiting for my next move. "Neil, You're very clever—no—brilliant. You covered your tracks well. We know some of what happened that night but not all. Well, if you fill us in, I'll give you something valuable in return." I felt wretched trading his mother's photos like a market commodity, but I knew I had to match his ugliness to get the missing answers.

"What is it?" His eyes opened wide, and he stretched out his cuffed hands as close to the envelope as physically possible.

"You have to trust me on this, Neil. First the information, then the reward." I moved the envelope closer to me.

"OK, I'll play along." He smiled at both of us in turn. "Well, let me see. I followed Faust to Davidson's home. I just wanted to talk to him, to hear him say he'd do the right thing. A DNA test. But he refused. Again. I was furious beyond belief. I had given him many chances to own up. He turned his back on me, grabbed his stuff from the car and was about to go inside, when lo-and-behold, Davidson comes out of the house."

I glanced at Al and he was staring at Neil.

I said, "Go on."

"He was holding something in his gloved hands. He froze seeing me but came down to the driveway near Faust as if to alert him. Faust turned to go inside, stopped, and turned to look at me, as though he wasn't sure what to do. I was too quick for both of them. I grabbed what Davidson was holding. It was wrapped in plastic and was heavy. I lifted it and beat my father's head with it. I don't remember how many times. I could hear the plastic tear." Neil was dispassionate in his storytelling. "I'd already decided to strangle him and had gloves on."

"Once he fell and failed to move, I asked Davidson what was in the package. He hesitated but told me it was a stone idol of Durga he'd brought over from Jwalapuram, from my father's excavation. I knew right then that Davidson had stolen it and was coming out to hand it over to the buyer. Just as my father returned from the conference." Neil chuckled.

"Did you ever think Faust could have been the buyer?"

Neil exploded. "No, not my father. He had great integrity, even though he let my mother die, and failed to accept me as his son. After talking to you yesterday, Professor Rao, I've been thinking. I'm prepared to give him the benefit of the doubt that he never knew about my mother's suicide. I might have judged him too harshly."

"I'm glad to hear that. What happened then, Neil?" I asked.

He shrugged. "I had the Durga still in my hand and threatened Davidson with it. I asked him to get back inside and not come out."

Al said, "Davidson watched you kill Faust and did nothing?"

"Yeah, he pleaded with me to let him call 911. He offered me a deal, that if I left, he'd not tell anyone who killed Faust. He so wanted to save his buddy. I turned him down and told him he could call 911 in the morning and pretend he had just discovered the body. I told him not to reveal anything to the police, or I'd report him for the theft and accuse him of the murder." Neil's voice held no remorse. He was rattling off facts with clinical precision.

I now understood the depth of Davidson's grief and why he confessed to me of his cowardice. Because, once inside, he could have called 911 to save his friend. But he was too frightened of Neil. "Why did you move the body, Neil?" It was a small part of the story but I needed an explanation.

"I dragged him into the Japanese garden for one reason. My mom had left a twig of a Japanese Maple Bonsai tree inside the book." He tapped his chest. "I've been carrying it close to my chest ever since I found it, but like everything else, they took it from me as evidence." He laughed. "I had no use for the idol and left it on my father's body."

Al asked, "Why did you force Davidson's truck over the cliff and kill him?"

Neil seemed startled that Al had a voice. He looked at him briefly and focused back on me. "I didn't trust him. I had to kill him to keep him quiet. Even with Faust dead, I had a bright future elsewhere. I knew he'd ruin it. So he had to go."

I asked, "You took Bill's car to Roy's and to follow Faust, right? Why?"

Neil nodded, "Yeah, I did. Bill is such an innocent and I liked playing pranks on him. When I brought his car back, the tank was half-full. He must have freaked out. But, I bet you didn't find any blood inside. I'd brought new clothes to change into, and a plastic bag for the ones I wore. And the gloves."

I looked at my notes and then at Neil. "I have a few more questions, Neil. Did you mean to turn Faust's tie around to the back or did it happen while you dragged him?"

Al nodded at me, as though he too had thought of the same question.

Neil smiled. If a smile could embody evil, this was it. "On purpose, of course." He looked down at his rather large hands, leaned forward and put them on the table.

"On my computer, Professor Rao, you'll come across a death certificate for my mother dated the day after I was born. Three years ago when I went to Cambridge, I obtained it from the Massachusetts Document Retrieval office. It was an easy process. The certificate noted that her death was a suicide and the manner of suicide was by hanging. It happened in Chelsea, where my mother had moved to. I was able to locate her burial site, and spent a couple of days there. I wanted to hang Faust too, at least figuratively.

You see the connection, don't you?"

I couldn't fathom the evil on his mind. "Lastly, how did you figure out Faust was your father? You might have killed an innocent man for nothing."

"No, no. You cannot charge me with sloppy work. I did thorough research. After adoption, my Amended Birth Certificate only listed my adoptive parents. In Massachusetts, I applied for my original birth certificate. I learned that I was born in Chelsea, not Cambridge. But wouldn't you know my mother had left no information about my father. I was not given a last name either. So, I looked through the book my mom had left for me to see if there were any clues. If you can get it from my room, I can explain what I found in it."

I said, "I saw it, Neil. Alice opened your room for me."

Neil laughed. "Go figure."

Al pulled out the book from his briefcase and gave it to Neil. "You can open it. It has your fingerprints all over it, anyway."

Neil opened the book and showed us what was written on the inside of the cover in neat sharp, slanted handwriting.

I said, "We've all read it, Neil. What does it mean?"

Neil decided to read it out loud.

Oh, came a magic cloak into my hands
To carry me to distant lands,
I should not trade it for the choicest gown,
Nor for the cloak and garments of the crown.

"An inscription fit for her tombstone. She was a literature major," Neil said.

"I have to confess, Neil, I don't see the connection to your father."

Once again, Neil was full of pride. "My mother was also

a bright woman. Instead of giving me his name, she left a clue for me in this book. I researched the verse and found out it was from a tragic play called *Faust,* by Johann Wolfgang von Goethe. At Harvard, I altered my original birth certificate by adding Faust as my last name to claim that I was looking for information about my father. Luckily, Joseph Faust was among the students who matriculated in Fall 1996. A calculation based on my birthdate."

Neil continued. "*Faust* was a highly successful scholar who was dissatisfied with his life, and made a pact with the Devil, exchanging his soul for unlimited knowledge and worldly pleasures. Sound like somebody we knew?"

Only in your distorted mind, I thought, but said, "No, the Faust I knew didn't fit the bill."

"Come on, Professor, stop being so righteous. I'm sure my mother wasn't sullying his name, only leading me to it. She must have selected this particular verse because it alludes to what lay beyond her death. Comforting me in a way that she was going to be OK."

I wanted to get away from the evil Neil embodied, but I had one more question. "Did you come after me? Did you break into my house and attack me?"

"Wow, wow, hold on. Don't accuse me of things I didn't do. Come after you? No. Break in? I had nothing to do with it, I swear. I respect you. I'm sorry I terrified you in your office. I didn't mean to. It was an issue of survival."

I looked at Al. I knew he was thinking the same thing. If it wasn't Neil who broke into my house, it had to be Matt Porter.

"Is there anything else you've left out?" I fingered the envelope.

Neil's eyes gleamed. "No, that's all. Now what am

I getting in return?"

"In this envelope, I've two photos of your birth mother. One with her roommates and the other with your father and the Davidsons." I looked at Al. He nodded.

Neil started to tremble. "You mean you've seen what she looked like? At Harvard, all I saw was a postage stamp size black-and-white photo, blurred over time."

"Your unique coloring came from her, Neil. She was from India. I was surprised at how she spelled your name in the book. It was Neel, meaning blue. But you never used that spelling. Why?"

Neil's eyes filled. "Dr., Rao, I'm sure you're aware that Neel is the color of Vishnu, Rama, and Krishna. The purity of gods. By the time I was eighteen and got the book, I knew I could never live up to my given name. So I stayed with Neil."

He held out his hand for the photos.

I put them on the table and gazed at the beautiful woman who died not knowing she'd created a monster. I pushed both photos toward Neil.

I got up, noticing that Al had shut off his recorder.

Neil leaned forward, his eyes glazed by the photos of his birth mother. The cops who'd brought him in moved toward him. He said, "Just a minute. May I keep my mother's photos? Please." He tried to pick up the photos with his cuffed hands, but couldn't do it.

Neil blinked furiously and tears dropped on to his cheek. He did nothing to control his silent grief. I looked at Al and saw him nod. The photos were not evidence, and they rightfully belonged to Neil. I put them back in the envelope and handed it to him. He held it against his chest with his cuffed hands.

I said, "One thing you didn't find out, Neil. Your mother's middle initial, D, stood for Durga. That was why she left you the book of Durga Puja."

Neil's eyes bulged, and he tugged at his cuffs and stamped on the floor with his chained feet. His face twisted into a vicious expression. "I killed my father with a Durga. Don't you see the relevance? In essence, my mother killed him. How appropriate." He laughed out loud, and kept at it, as the guards grabbed him to take him back.

Neil looked at me again. "Professor Rao, will you keep an eye on Melissa . . . and Mom . . . for me? They like you and trust you. They'll be all alone now. Will you make sure Melissa goes to college?"

I wasn't sure if I'd ever heard him refer to Alice as his mom. It was always Mother. "I'll do whatever I can for your family." I hesitated for a moment. "Would you like me to come and see you when I can?"

I saw Al glare at me.

Neil nodded and shuffled away.

* * *

I said my goodbyes and walked quickly to the parking lot.

I heard footsteps behind me and saw Al striding across to catch up with me.

"Slow down, Rekha. What's the hurry?"

I said, "I need to get away from all this." I kept going, Al by my side.

We walked together in silence across the parking lot that was almost deserted. I wondered if this would be the last time we would be together. What reason would I have now to see him? Instead of being relieved, I was sad that I no longer had any need for the Pasadena police.

"Thanks, Al," I said and opened my car door. "That's it, I guess."

Al held the car door, allowing me to get in and sit.

"Yes, I think once we get Neil to sign his confession, you're officially off the case."

"I thought I was never officially on it." I laughed.

"True, But you helped us, Rekha. Without you, this might have turned into a cold case. Or we might have wrongly concluded that Davidson killed Faust. Thank you. Even though he was an idol thief, it'd be a relief to his family to hear that he was not a murderer." He paused and looked up at the night sky. "Now that your work is over, what about a cup of coffee one of these days?"

Taken aback, I couldn't find any smart-aleck comeback. "Sure, I need to get the journal back, right?"

Al's smile lit up the dark corners inside my heart. He said, "I'll hang on to it with my life."

~ Chapter 30 ~

Saturday, May 6, 2017
Eagle Rock, Los Angeles, CA

In *this* relationship, I opted to take control. Before Al had a chance to call me up for coffee, I decided to invite him over for dinner. I told him that it was an age-old Indian custom to invite people whom you met, even for a short time, for a home-cooked meal. There was some truth to it. I'd heard from Ma and Dad how they felt isolated during their early days in the US, and would invite casual acquaintances to a meal at home. I had invited Sanjay too, to make the situation less awkward. Maybe it was divine intervention, but my brother couldn't make it.

Mundane chores for prepping the dinner took up most of my morning. In the early afternoon, I took a shower and changed into an ankle-length taupe linen skirt and a green silk blouse.

I opened a bottle of 2008 Au Bon Climat Pinot Noir, recommended by a friend, and set the bottle aside. The wine claimed to be "non-pretentious, well balanced, nicely textured, brightly fruity," and to go with everything from salmon to quail to chicken. I was no expert on wines and trusted those with well-endowed noses and palates.

I put on Nusrat Fateh Ali Khan's *Nightsong* on my DVD player, grabbed my apron and set to work to get the chicken ready. I sautéed the marinated chicken in olive oil and removed the browned pieces to a plate. Peering at the recipe, I added diced onions, minced ginger and garlic, followed by a thick paste of coriander, turmeric and cumin powders and just a pinch of cayenne powder. When the roasted spices exuded a rich aroma, I tossed in the chicken pieces, mixed everything, and added enough stock to cover them. The recipe then called for salt to taste, bringing the curry to a boil just once, turning down the heat and leaving it covered to cook. Once the chicken was tender, I would add the leftover yogurt marinade and turn off the heat. If yogurt boiled, it'd curdle. I had learned this the sad way.

I was going to take a short-cut on the vegetable, like Ma did on her busy days. I cooked frozen chopped spinach lightly with salt and pepper, placed two tablespoons of grated coconut mixed with pinches of turmeric and cumin powders in a well at the bottom of the pan, and covered it with the cooked spinach. I put the lid back on the pan and left it for a few minutes to steam the coconut. I tempered the dish with black mustard and cumin seeds, and a crumbled dried red chili pepper, all roasted in ghee. According to Ma, tempering or *tadka* was an essential step to enhance and blend the flavors and help with digestion. I started rice in a rice cooker.

I sat down, tasted the Au Bon Climat, and leaned back and closed my eyes to enjoy the first full sip, in the company of Fateh Ali Khan. The doorbell chirped causing me to jump. I wiped my hands on a towel, peeked in the hall mirror and opened the door.

"Hi," said Al, holding a small bunch of flowers in one hand, and a package in the other. "Am I too early?"

He was exactly on time. "Oh, no, you're . . . right on time. Please . . . come in." I flushed, feeling self-conscious, and pointed him to the single comfortable cushioned chair I had. "Please sit down, Can I get you some wine?" I saw Al nod and went into the kitchen. My heartbeat accelerated, and my hands were sweaty.

I put the flowers in a vase and placed it on the dining table and brought two glasses of wine. Outside the context of the murder, I wasn't sure how to talk to him. "Did you get time to clear up your desk? I can tell from your office that you are an organizer." I moved a small side table that had a plate of roasted cashews on it and placed it between us. "Have some, they're seasoned with lime and chili."

Al picked up a few and munched. "Starting to clean up, before another case swallows me. Whew, this has a kick. Before I forget, I brought you a couple of things."

I opened the package and took a few minutes to look at each. One was a photo of the Durga signed by Al and Lieutenant Bigsby. The other was Faust's journal that he'd promised to keep safe. "Thank you. I guess I must now be in your good books."

"You certainly are. Without you, we wouldn't have narrowed the case down to Neil. By the way, we arrested Matt Porter for assaulting his girlfriend. And she owned up and said she'd lied for him the night of your attack. We are building a case against him."

"That's a relief, Al. I'm sure it was Matt who broke into my house. And did you figure out how the Durga got here?"

"Yeah, once we knew Davidson was the one who arranged to get it, it was obvious that one of the Indian staff at the dig had to be involved. The Indian police arrested Dileep Patel."

I still had so many questions. "Who was the man in the

car that Faust's neighbor mistook for Bill?"

"That was Davidson's brother, who had arrived at the crime scene to collect the Durga. He took off scared. Wouldn't you know his car was the same make and model of Bill's except newer."

"It's interesting how all the pieces fall into place once you identify the killer."

I saw Al quietly taking in the modest décor of my small living room with an Indian tapestry on one wall, a print of Picasso's *Girl Before the Mirror* on another, and a collection of family photos on the wall behind the dining table. He walked over to the family photos. I joined him.

"Your parents?" Al asked.

"Yes," I said and touched the large black-and-white photo of my parents placed in the center of the wall. "This was taken soon after their wedding, close to thirty-five years ago." I pointed to a smaller photo and said, "This is my father a couple of years before his murder. And this is one of my mother taken recently. The group photo is a family portrait taken before my dad's death. The last time our family was intact."

Al stood transfixed, his eyes on the figures in the photos.

I said, "My father told me the story about this wedding photo. My mother was dressed in a heavy silk gold-embroidered *sari*, her hair pulled back into a bun at the back of her head. It was customary to put a large *bindi* on the forehead of the woman." I pointed to the round mark just above where my mother's eyebrows started. "Jewelry was a big deal. Look at her diamond earrings, gold necklaces, and bangles." My father wore a long shirt or *kurta*, matching loose pants and a shawl over one shoulder. He had a wide forehead, thick black hair, and a round chin. His large teak brown eyes were focused straight ahead.

"They look happy on their wedding day. Were they, in marriage?"

"Theirs was what we called in India at that time a love marriage. They went against conventions. I've never seen two people more in love than these two," I said recalling the playfulness between my parents I had witnessed throughout the years.

"What would your father say now if he were alive? Would he be happy for you or chastise you?"

I smiled at Al. "He would have been ever so proud. And he would convince my mother it was my duty to get involved."

"Your eyes," said Al, looking at me, then at the photos and back into my eyes. "You've your father's eyes and forehead and your mother's nose and mouth. I bet you'd look fabulous in your traditional costume. You still wear it?"

I said, with a shade of pride, "Yes, for the right occasion. Let me get the meal on the table. I'm sorry but it's just a simple dinner, nothing fancy."

Al came over to the kitchen and stood watching me make the final touches to the meal. "What a relief, with Neil owning up, although I'd have loved to have seen him roast in prison waiting for the trial. It'd be a slam dunk now for the prosecution with all the hard evidence. For a real bright guy, he was stupid to put his bloody clothes, gloves, and even his thesis proposal at the bottom of the tree he planted."

"I've always felt he was weird. This might sound morbid, but once you finish processing his thesis proposal, will you give it to me to read? He made such a fuss of Faust not reading it. I'm curious about what it contains."

Al laughed. "By all means. I looked through it. It was an autobiography of his life laid out like a story. Nothing more than what we heard from his mouth."

"How did you guys let him off so quickly early in the investigation?" I transferred the warm food into serving dishes. Outside my kitchen window, darkness shrouded the trees and shrubs into partial invisibility. What I could see of the sky was studded with brilliant stars. I took it as a good omen, coaxing me to get out of the cell I'd imprisoned myself in, where there was no sun, moon, or stars. More and more, Rajeev was fading while Al was clearly in focus.

Al said, "There were no prints on the plastic. We now know why. They're doing blood typing and DNA analysis, but with the bloody clothes and the confession, it'll be pretty hard for the defense to overthrow."

I put serving spoons into the dishes. "I can only hope that Neil will get a thorough psychiatric evaluation."

"Yes, and we're working with the London police to arrest the uncle for his illegal dealings."

I brought the food to the table. I stirred the chicken curry with a spoon and said, "Ouch, this pot's hot, be careful." To keep the conversation oriented toward the case, I added, "I wonder why I didn't suspect Neil except toward the end. He seemed so brainy, awkward and innocuous. Please go ahead, eat. We don't say any prayers or anything, so dig in."

"I've had Indian food a few times but it didn't look like this. You have to tell me what all these are." Al said.

I explained each item of food on the table. "In our family, my mother would serve the guest and keep adding more even if the guest says no. She'd sit down to eat only after the guest is served. That's an Indian thing, but I oppose forced feeding."

Al took bird-sized portions and said, "Let me do a taste of everything first before I have more. I'm allowed to have seconds or thirds, right?" He laughed, a genuine laugh that I hadn't heard before. I brought the warmed *rotis*, flat wheat bread, to the table covered by a cloth napkin and placed one on each side plate.

Al's eyes widened. "Do you eat this like a tortilla? Use your hands?" He asked pointing to the roti.

I said, "Feel free to use your hands. Tear up a piece, put some curry on it, fold it and eat it. See, like this."

He copied my action, spilling chicken gravy on his plate. For a while there was only chewing, clinking, drinking, and laughter.

Al put his fork down and said, "Rekha, this stuff's good. Did you make it mild for me? I'll be brave now to try the spicier version." He laughed. "That aside, I'd love to learn more about your culture. I might come across as a typical American, but I am a fast learner."

This was a pleasant surprise. "Sure, whenever you want to. I'm a good teacher."

My phone rang. I stiffened and excused myself.

"Hi Aunty, *aap kaisi hai?* I tried your recipe today." Al bobbed his head up and down with his mouth full, and with his free hand, gave me a thumbs up. I beamed. "Everyone thinks it's great. Thanks for the tips." I paused, listening. "Next week for dinner? I'll have to check if I can make it. Who is he? Why didn't you tell me earlier?" Annoyance crept into my voice. I wanted to get back to Al, who had finished the small first serving he took and was politely waiting for me. "He can call me at home, not on my cell. I can only do it if he can drive over here. It'd have to be a coffee shop in Eagle Rock. I'm not sure if there's an Indian restaurant in Eagle Rock for *pukka sahibs.*" I listened for a few more minutes and then said goodbye.

"What's up? Al looked at me with a smile. "None of my business, but it sounded like you have a date."

"Yeah. I hope I wasn't too rude to my aunt. As always, she's set me up with someone. She tries to juggle around at least three potential matches for me at any one time until I decline all or accept one. The acceptance hasn't happened yet." I giggled.

"I bet you'll find a guy who thinks that you and what you're doing, all of it, are commendable." His eyes met mine.

"Hopefully. Please have seconds or I'll think you hate my cooking." I waited for Al to get seconds and refilled the wine glasses.

I went to the kitchen to get the dessert. I never cared for Indian desserts, except the mouth-watering *ras malai* that Ma made, but I never learned how to prepare it. So I had made cookies using Alice's recipe that I got when I went to see her and Melissa after Neil's arrest. I put the cookies out and made fresh hot cardamom chai.

Al offered to clean up, but I declined. "Let's sit out on the porch, I hardly do that. It's a beautiful night." I draped my stole around my shoulders and moved to the front porch and sat down with Al. We had a plate of cookies between us and our chai to sip.

"Sanjay seems like a well-balanced young man. Do you worry about him?"

"Yeah, I've told him he needs to attend to his studies and not get distracted with what I do. With no Dad, I need to stay on top of him to make sure he graduates. With honors." I laughed. "Mom was easier on us, after Dad died."

"So you are a taskmaster?" Al asked.

"It's tough love, Al. You must recognize it. By the way, you haven't told me anything about your life, while mine has been an open book. So, do tell."

Al had pulled his chair toward me and sat very close.

I could see his dark brown eyes and the wrinkles at the corners of his eyes.

"What's to tell? I didn't grow up in an exotic culture, don't have my parents living, and have no kids or siblings. There it is. The chai is great, by the way."

"You're not playing fair. I saw the photo of a beautiful woman on your desk. Tell me about her, please." I bit into a cookie and thought it didn't taste as good as Alice's. What did I leave out?

Al put his chai down and leaned back in the chair. "OK, I'm dragging my feet. But here goes. I was married for three years to a wonderful woman who died without any warning from an aneurysm five years ago. She had had no symptoms. I seem to be stuck in the past, unable to move on since Mary's death. We had no children, by choice, and that made it even more difficult. I feel like nothing tangible remained of our marriage except for mementos in a trunk in the attic. Now I've got to dig with a pitchfork to remember the details of our day-to-day life and even my mental image of Mary herself."

Al's honesty touched me. "They say that's very common. Why do you think I keep the large photo of my dad in front of my eyes? I worry I'd forget his face." I wanted to ask if Al had a happy marriage, if he ever thought of marrying again, or looked for a companion to take Mary's place.

I got up to put a new CD on the player. A Mozart clarinet concerto with its delightful, fast-paced first orchestral movement came on.

Al asked, "So, what is on your plate now that your first murder mystery is solved? Find another mystery?" His voice was casual and conversational, but I felt his eyes below the bushy eyebrows honing in on me. Is he asking about my personal life? I wondered.

"Not sure right now. Of course, I will continue at Oxy if they don't fire me over the case. My Chair was very pleased with the first draft of my proposal for a major in Indian Art History, and she's going to push it forward to the administration. If it goes through, I might be able to hire a teaching assistant, and oversee the program. As for solving any more mysteries . . . more chai for you, Al?"

"Sure," Al said. "You have an intuitive appreciation of human psychology that's an asset to solving cases, Rekha. By the way, what does your name mean?" He leaned forward and took my hand in his, sending a surge of warmth throughout my body.

"Well, you won't be surprised. It means a line, straight, unbending, sticking to principles, however you want to interpret it. In Hindu mythology, it also means a line that you should not cross."

Al laughed. "It fits you, Rekha. I've always thought you were a straight-shooter. Have you given any thought to studying criminal psychology? The lieutenant was the one to suggest it. She thought with some training in the field, we might be able to hire you as a consultant. What do you say?"

"I'm only half time at Oxy, so I'd have the time. But this case has hit me hard. I'm still struggling to understand why a bright young man with a promising future would kill someone like Faust. These things are certainly ordinary events for you, but I need time to come to terms with it."

"Sure, you need a break from the case, but give it some thought. Maybe the case will motivate you to understand the criminal mind."

"I promise I will consider it, Al." I wondered if my dharma was directing me to my next path. Al still had my hand in his in a gentle grip that conveyed something more than friendship.

"Well, in that case, may I ask you out for dinner one of these days to help you move forward? Or not?" He smiled.

I retrieved my hand. How am I to explain my fear of men's cruelty and control? But I liked him, maybe even begun to fall in love with him. "Well, dinner would be great. You, good food, and a glass of wine. I am willing to try if you are." The image of a slightly round, funny Indian lawyer flashed in and out of my mind's frame. Time will tell, I comforted myself.

"I'll call," Al said, and leaned forward and kissed me, a soft lingering kiss that took me by surprise. We sat hand in hand, smiling at each other with our newfound truths built on mutual admiration, a growing affection, and hope for the future.

~ Chapter 31 ~

Sunday, April 30, 2017
Culver City, CA

My job wasn't done. I had the responsibility of telling Ginny the truth about Faust. And handing over the journal.

Ginny had called my cell and left several frantic messages, hearing about Neil's arrest. She had no idea who Neil Anderson was or why he killed her husband.

I met with her alone, in her home. She assured me it was best for her to tell Kevin later.

As she opened the front door to let me in, I noticed her face was drawn, cheeks pale. Her hands trembled as she reached out to grab mine as we sat side by side on the sofa.

"Tell me why Joe was killed. I want to hear that he was not at fault. Please." She grasped my right hand firmly with both of hers.

I looked at her eyes and felt comforted that I didn't have any horrible truth to unfold. Faust was not a killer, nor a womanizer, not even a bad father, even though Kevin's cross-dressing had troubled him. He was a good man, a supreme professional, and a caring husband, who had accepted his true sexuality late in life and wanted to live a life of truth. He was unaware that he already had a first-born. Ever since Neil confessed, I had wondered if Faust took Neil's claim seriously. Knowing the principled man my mentor was, I was sure he would have looked into it to uncover the truth. "Ginny, you knew your husband had a girlfriend before he met you."

Ginny's face brightened. "Yes, I did not know much more than that. I told you, Rekha that we chose not to dwell on the past and only looked to the future." Her eyes widened. "What did she do?" It was my turn to hold her hand, which was soft and smooth like a baby's. "Tell me, do not keep it back anymore." This was a command in a high-pitched voice that came close to cracking. "How was she involved? Why did this Neil Anderson kill my husband?"

I pulled up Neil's photo on my phone. "Your husband's girlfriend was one Jaya Durga Varma, a grad student in the literature program. She became pregnant and left Harvard without telling your husband. According to Bob, he tried his best to find her but couldn't. She gave birth to Neil, who was adopted by the Andersons. This is the son Joe never knew he had." I pointed at the photo on my phone. "Neil Anderson, a student in both his and my classes."

Her jaw grew slack, her mouth fell open. She stared at me like I was an alien. "But . . . but why would a son kill his father? That does not make any sense, Rekha." Her nails dug into the palm of my hand.

"Neil is a disturbed young man, Ginny. Brilliant like your husband, but with a pathological mind. He tried to convince your husband he was his son. Professor Faust must have thought it was a joke, an insult. Maybe he should have listened, but Neil had no proof to offer. It would take a paternity test to find out. Neil's accusation was based on information his mother had left for him, that was given to him on his eighteenth birthday. Instead of asking for a paternity test, he chose to harass your husband. Neil followed him from Roy's to the Davidsons' home and killed him to get revenge for his mother, who had hanged herself the day after giving birth. I'm sorry to have to tell you all this."

The grief-stricken woman seemed to consider something. "But that doesn't explain why Joe wanted a divorce. There was no way he could get back with his girlfriend because you said she killed herself. Poor thing." She buried her head in her hands for a moment, and then jerked up, her hands covering her mouth. "Why, Rekha? Tell me. There is no need to spare me now."

I took the journal from my purse. "Ginny, Professor Faust kept this in his office, and I happened to find it after his death. It has brief entries, made over the last year and a half."

Ginny leaned forward. "Was he having an affair?"

I gave it to her. "No."

She held it in her hands gently, as if it were a delicate object that would shatter with touch. "You must have read it, Rekha, right? What is in it? Why keep it in his office?"

I once again took her hands in mine. "Ginny, believe it or not, your husband of two decades came to the realization that he was gay . . . had always been gay, and had suppressed his true sexuality. The journal contains a letter to you about his conflict and grief over it, the pain he knew he'd cause you and Kevin, and thoughts on how to deal with it the best way possible. The last entry was a meeting he'd scheduled with a psychiatrist in San Francisco at the end of his tour. I looked him up. He specializes in helping men who realize they're gay late in life."

Ginny looked away, intertwining her fingers. "How is that possible? We had sex . . . I mean, we behaved like a man and a woman all these years. We even have a child to bear proof. How could he suddenly become gay?" She shouted the last sentence even as tears poured from her eyes.

"Ginny, there are many reported instances of this happening to older males. It is not their fault, just as this was not your husband's fault, and you must believe that. Every one of these men goes through severe mental torment with the discovery or acceptance, and I'm sure that was what your husband recorded in his journal. With the realization came the urgent need to separate his life from yours and create an authentic life for himself. And the only way he knew to do it was through a divorce. He anguished over your future happiness."

Ginny opened her mouth and closed it.

I said, "What is it? You can ask me."

In a soft voice, she asked, "Did he have a lover all this time? I would not blame him for that."

I shook my head. "Not to my knowledge."

She mumbled, "I wish he had told me. I even wondered if he had a medical condition like impotence when we started to sleep apart from each other in the same bed for more than a year. I was going to ask him if we should seek out a physician. I would have helped him. Why did he not share it with me? We were best friends. Oh God, how much he must have suffered." She got up and walked around the room, her hands wildly moving around all over her body, to her neck, shoulders, down her thighs and to her head like a choreiform dance of torment. I watched, not sure what to do other than to let her grieve in her way.

In a few minutes, she returned to the sofa and sat down by my side again. "Rekha, how can I thank you for everything you have done for Kevin and me? I will talk to him later today, just the two of us." She tapped the journal she clutched in her hand. "I'll read this after you leave—I have to do it alone—and decide if I need to share it with him. He will be devastated, but then again, he is a different generation and might come to terms with it better than I can." She paused and wiped her eyes. "Do you think I should go and see that therapist? He might be able to help me."

I was relieved that after the shock, she was looking for practical solutions. "I think it's an excellent idea. I have his number and address. He might even suggest someone local—"

"—No, if Joe wanted to see him, I want to see him as well. Maybe Kevin might go with me. Since Joe's and Bob's murders, I have been in a state of mental paralysis, about how to move on. But now, I realize Kevin and I have to rebuild a future for ourselves. Joe would have wanted that."

I nodded. "I need to thank your friend Nora. She gave me valuable information about Neil's birth mother."

"Don't worry, I'll do that for you, Rekha. Before the news broke, she and I planned to meet for lunch in a couple of days." She paused, and she stared into the distance. "What is . . . if any . . . my obligation to Joe's son? Should I go and see him? Kevin might refuse, but I do not have a problem with it."

I had witnessed Ginny's grace under dire circumstances before, and so her question didn't floor me. "Why don't we give it some time. Let's wait until the trial is over. I, too, had promised to go see him. Maybe we can do it together, but we need to make sure he's OK with a visit from you. Do you understand?"

Ginny hugged me and held on to me while whispering "Yes, yes . . . I understand . . . I understand. Everything."

~ Chapter 32 ~

Sunday, May 8, 2017

Sanjay and I drove to Ma's place for another special dinner. This time, it was to celebrate my brother's birthday, a week late.

The air in the car was thick, and I worried about my brother. After learning about Faust, I'd been thinking about Sanjay. What if he was gay? I wouldn't want him to go through what Faust did. Marry a girl under family pressure and learn years later that what he needed was a male companion. Should I bring it up with him? I had spent the last week muddled about it, inspired by Faust's story of struggle.

Sanjay talked randomly about everything and everyone under the sun as though pre-empting any topic I might have brought up. I was sure he had read about Faust.

I said, "Sanju, you can tell me anything, even a secret you're keeping to yourself."

My brother stared at me, and his voice went up. "What do you mean?"

I let it go. If he was gay, I hoped he'd feel free to share it with me at some point. My family would have to accept it. And he'd have a staunch supporter in his Didi.

"So what are you going to do with Al?"

Caught off guard, I said, "He came over for dinner yesterday. We had a nice time. I'm going to see him again."

"Ooh la la. What about Rajeev?"

"I am confused about it. Rajeev, although I've met him only twice, offers familiarity, a common culture and upbringing. In Al, I see new wonders and experiences. Which is right for me?"

"What are you scared of?"

"I'm unsure if my heart can withstand another break."

"I read somewhere that broken hearts get stronger when they're mended."

I made the gesture of swatting him.

"Are you going to tell Ma about him?" Sanjay asked.

"No. But I am determined to do one thing. I'm going to tell all of them that, much as I love them, I want them to leave me alone to find my future husband."

My brother said, "Wow." Under his breath, he added, "Me too."

THE END

Acknowledgments

Writing this novel took almost seven years as I switched from decades of commitment to science to a brand new world of fiction writing. I call this, "A journey from the left side of my brain to the right." I plan to continue it for the rest of my life.

Grace Peirce (Great Life Press): Grace, you held my hand through this process with patience and professionalism for which I owe you my heart-felt gratitude.

Lynn Hightower (Nationally and internationally best-selling novelist and Instructor at UCLA Extension): You taught me the craft of writing, and encouraged me to explore my creativity without fear, to tell stories that matter to me. I hope I make you proud!

Meghan Pinson (https://mytwocentsediting.com/), Gina Sorrell (https://www.ginasorell.com/), and Roland Goodbody: Your expert editing of my manuscript at different stages of its evolution enabled me to get it to the final version. I am deeply indebted to you all!

Shalini, Suju, Mike and Tim: I have never stopped valuing your genuine support and encouragement as I shifted directions and embarked on a career of acting and writing.

Ashok and Rohan: I remember a day, a year or so ago, when you both encouraged me to "Go for it!" as I contemplated submitting my manuscript for the Chanticleer

International Book Award. You had listened to a summary of my story only and had not even read my manuscript. I went for it and got a semifinalist award. Keep up your blind faith in your grandmother!

My sincere thanks also to:

J. James Simonson at The Massachusetts Document Retrieval for giving me accurate information about birth and death certificates in Massachusetts.

The Reference Staff at Harvard University Archives for providing me with information about student registration for 1996-1997.

Chris Clarkson, School of Social Science, The University of Queensland, Brisbane, Qld 4072, Australia, for his permission to tack my fictional story to their real story of the excavation of microliths in Jwalapuram, India.

Daniel Berkowitz at AuthorPop for his guidance and patience as I repeatedly changed my choices while he was building my author website.

About the Author

Vee Kumari grew up in the south of India. A lover of books, her favorite authors were Arthur Conan Doyle and Agatha Christie. She would hide to read, to avoid her mother, who might want her to do a chore or two. It was her mother who directed her to use the dictionary to learn the meanings of new words and construct sentences with them. Vee wanted to become an English professor but went to medical school, where she excelled.

Upon coming to the US, Vee earned a doctorate in Anatomy and became a faculty member at the UC Davis Medical Center, where she worked for over thirty-five years, and later at the Keck School of Medicine for five years. Teaching neuroanatomy to medical students became another passion for her. She published many scientific papers and won several teaching awards. During this time, she continued to read contemporary mystery fiction.

When she retired in 2012, she took classes from The Gotham Writers' Workshop and UCLA Writers Program, and had the privilege to have authors Lynn Hightower and Caroline Leavitt as her mentors. *Dharma, A Rekha Rao Mystery*, is her debut fiction that incorporates her observations on the lives of Indian immigrants and Indian Americans in the US.

Vee lives in Burbank near her daughters and their

families. She is also an actor who has appeared in TV shows, including *Criminal Minds* and *Glow*, and produced and was the lead in the short film, *Halwa*, which garnered first prize in HBO's 2019 APAV contest.

She is at work on her next novel about an Indian immigrant family whose American dream is shattered when one of their twin daughters goes missing.